John Forster

The Life of Charles Dickens Vol. 3

John Forster

The Life of Charles Dickens Vol. 3

ISBN/EAN: 9783742830258

Manufactured in Europe, USA, Canada, Australia, Japa

Cover: Foto ©Andreas Hilbeck / pixelio.de

Manufactured and distributed by brebook publishing software
(www.brebook.com)

John Forster

The Life of Charles Dickens Vol. 3

COLLECTION

OF

BRITISH AUTHORS

TAUCHNITZ EDITION.

VOL. 1288.

THE LIFE OF CHARLES DICKENS
BY
JOHN FORSTER.

VOL. 3.

LEIPZIG: BERNHARD TAUCHNITZ.

PARIS: C. REINWALD & Cⁱᵉ, 15, RUE DES SAINTS PÈRES.

COLLECTION

OF

BRITISH AUTHORS

TAUCHNITZ EDITION.

VOL. 1288.

THE LIFE OF CHARLES DICKENS BY J. FORSTER.

VOL. III.

THE LIFE

OF

CHARLES DICKENS.

BY

JOHN FORSTER.

COPYRIGHT EDITION.

VOL. III.

LEIPZIG

BERNHARD TAUCHNITZ

1873.

The Right of Translation is reserved.

TABLE OF CONTENTS.

CHAPTER XXXII. 1845.

Pages 193-217.

LAST MONTHS IN ITALY. ÆT. 33.

CHAPTER XXXIII.   1845-1846.

Pages 218-241.

AGAIN IN ENGLAND.   ÆT. 33-34.

CHAPTER XXXIV. 1846.

Pages 242-266.

A HOME IN SWITZERLAND. ÆT. 34.

CHAPTER XXXV. 1846.

Pages 267-286.

SWISS PEOPLE AND SCENERY. ÆT. 34.

ILLUSTRATIONS.

LIFE OF CHARLES DICKENS.

CHAPTER XXV.

AMERICAN NOTES.

1842.

THE reality did not fall short of the anticipa- LONDON: 1842. Return from America. tion of home. His return was the occasion of unbounded enjoyment; and what he had planned before sailing as the way we should meet, received literal fulfilment. By the sound of his cheery voice I first knew that he was come; and from my house we went together to Maclise, also "without a moment's warning." A Greenwich Page 260 of Vol. II. dinner in which several friends (Talfourd, Milnes, Procter, Maclise, Stanfield, Marryat, Barham, Hood, and Cruikshank among them) took part, and other immediate greetings, followed; but the most special celebration was reserved for autumn, when, by way of challenge to what he had seen while abroad, a home-journey was arranged with Stanfield, Maclise, and myself for his companions, into such of the most striking scenes of a picturesque English

LONDON:
1842.

county as the majority of us might not before have visited: Cornwall being ultimately chosen.

Before our departure he was occupied by his preparation of the *American Notes;* and to the same interval belongs the arrival in London of Mr. Longfellow, who became his guest, and (for both of us I am privileged to add) our attached friend. Longfellow's name was not then the pleasant and familiar word it has since been in England; but he had already written several of his most felicitous pieces, and he possessed all the qualities of delightful companionship, the culture and the charm, which have no higher type or example than the accomplished and genial American. He reminded me, when lately again in England, of two experiences out of many we had enjoyed together this quarter of a century before. One of them was a day at Rochester, when, met by one of those prohibitions which are the wonder of visitors and the shame of Englishmen, we overleapt gates and barriers, and, setting at defiance repeated threats of all the terrors of law coarsely expressed to us by the custodian of the place, explored minutely the castle ruins. The other was a night among those portions of the population which outrage law and defy its terrors all the days of their lives, the tramps and thieves of London; when, under guidance and protection of the most trusted officers of the two great metropolitan prisons afforded to us by Mr. Chesterton and Lieut. Tracey, we went over the worst haunts of the most dangerous classes. Nor will

Longfellow
in England.

At Rochester
Castle.

Among
London
tramps and
thieves.

Page 98 of
Vol. II.

it be unworthy of remark, in proof that attention
is not drawn vainly to such scenes, that, upon
Dickens going over them a dozen years later
when he wrote a paper about them for his *Household Words*, he found important changes effected
whereby these human dens, if not less dangerous,
were become certainly more decent. On the night
of our earlier visit, Maclise, who accompanied us,
was struck with such sickness on entering the first
of the Mint lodging-houses in the borough, that
he had to remain, for the time we were in them,
under guardianship of the police outside. Longfellow returned home by the Great Western from
Bristol on the 21st of October, enjoying as he
passed through Bath the hospitality of Landor;
and at the end of the following week we started
on our Cornish travel.

But what before this had occupied Dickens in
the writing way must now be told. Not long after
his reappearance amongst us, his house being still
in the occupation of Sir John Wilson, he went to
Broadstairs, taking with him the letters from which
I have quoted so largely to help him in preparing
his *American Notes;* and one of his first announce-
ments to me (18th of July) shows not only this
labour in progress, but the story he was under
engagement to begin in November working in his
mind. "The subjects at the beginning of the
"book are of that kind that I can't *dash* at them,
"and now and then they fret me in consequence.
"When I come to Washington, I am all right.
"The solitary prison at Philadelphia is a good

BROAD-
STAIRS:
1812.
"subject, though; I forgot that for the moment.
"Have you seen the Boston chapter yet? . . . I
"have never been in Cornwall either. A mine
"certainly; and a letter for that purpose shall be
"got from Southwood Smith. I have some notion
"of opening the new book in the lantern of a
"lighthouse!" A letter a couple of months later
(16th of Sept.) recurs to that proposed opening
of his story which after all he laid aside; and
shows how rapidly he was getting his *American
Notes* into shape. "At the Isle of Thanet races
"yesterday I saw—oh! who shall say what an
Thanet races. "immense amount of character in the way of
"inconceivable villainy and blackguardism! I
"even got some new wrinkles in the way of show-
"men, conjurors, pea-and-thimblers, and trampers
Fancy for the
opening of
Chuzzlewit. "generally. I think of opening my new book on
"the coast of Cornwall, in some terribly dreary
"iron-bound spot. I hope to have finished the
"American book before the end of next month;
"and we will then together fly down into that
"desolate region." Our friends having Academy
engagements to detain them, we had to delay a
little; and I meanwhile turn back to his letters to
observe his progress with his *Notes*, and other
employments or enjoyments of the interval. They
require no illustration that they will not themselves
supply: but I may remark that the then collected
Poems of Tennyson had become very favourite
reading with him; and that while in America Mr.
A domestic
friend. Mitchell the comedian had given him a small
white shaggy terrier, who bore at first the im-

posing name of Timber Doodle, and became a
great domestic pet and companion.

BROAD-
STAIRS:
1842.

"I have been reading" (7th of August) "Tenny-
"son all this morning on the seashore.   Among
"other trifling effects, the waters have dried up
"as they did of old, and shown me all the mer-
"men and mermaids, at the bottom of the ocean;
"together with millions of queer creatures, half-
"fish and half-fungus, looking down into all man-
"ner of coral caves and seaweed conservatories;
"and staring in with their great dull eyes at every
"open nook and loop-hole.   Who else, too, could
"conjure up such a close to the extraordinary
"and as Landor would say 'most woonderful'
"series of pictures in the 'dream of fair women,'
"as—

"Merman"
and "mer-
maid."

"Squadrons and squares of men in brazen plates,
  "Scaffolds, still sheets of water, divers woes,
 "Ranges of glimmering vaults with iron grates,
   "And hushed seraglios!

Reading Ten-
nyson.

"I am getting on pretty well, but it was so glit-
"tering and sunshiny yesterday that I was forced
"to make holiday."   Four days later: "I have not
"written a word this blessed day.   I got to New
"York yesterday, and think it goes as it should.
". . . Little doggy improves rapidly, and now
"jumps over my stick at the word of command.
"I have changed his name to Snittle Timbery,
"as more sonorous and expressive.   He unites
"with the rest of the family in cordial regards
"and loves.   *Nota Bene.*   The Margate theatre is

Little doggy.

"open every evening, and the Four Patagonians
"(see Goldsmith's *Essays*) are performing thrice
"a week at Ranelagh . . ."

A visit from me was at this time due, to
which these were held out as inducements; and
there followed what it was supposed I could not
resist, a transformation into the broadest farce of
a deep tragedy by a dear friend of ours. "Now
"you really must come. Seeing only is believing,

"very often isn't that, and even Being the thing
"falls a long way short of believing it. Mrs.
"Nickleby herself once asked me, as you know,
"if I really believed there ever was such a woman;
"but there'll be no more belief, either in me or
"my descriptions, after what I have to tell of our
"excellent friend's tragedy, if you don't come and
"have it played again for yourself 'by particular
"'desire.' We saw it last night, and oh! if you
"had but been with us! Young Betty, doing what
"the mind of man without my help never *can*
"conceive, with his legs like padded boot-trees
"wrapped up in faded yellow drawers, was the
"hero. The comic man of the company enveloped
"in a white sheet, with his head tied with red
"tape like a brief and greeted with yells of laugh-
"ter whenever he appeared, was the venerable

"priest. A poor toothless old idiot at whom the
"very gallery roared with contempt when he was
".called a tyrant, was the remorseless and aged
"Creon. And Ismene being arrayed in spangled
"muslin trowsers very loose in the legs and very
"tight in the ankles, such as Fatima would wear

"in *Blue Beard*, was at her appearance immediately
"called upon for a song. After this, can you
"longer . . . !"

Broad-stairs: 1842.

With the opening of September I had renewed
report of his book, and of other matters. "The
"Philadelphia chapter I think very good, but I
"am sorry to say it has not made as much in
"print as I hoped . . . In America they have
"forged a letter with my signature, which they
"coolly declare appeared in the *Chronicle* with
"the copyright circular; and in which I express Page 271 of Vol. II.
"myself in such terms as you may imagine, in
"reference to the dinners and so forth. It has
"been widely distributed all over the States; and
"the felon who invented it is a 'smart man' of Smart man and forged letter.
"course. You are to understand that it is not
"done as a joke, and is scurrilously reviewed.
"Mr. Park Benjamin begins a lucubration upon
"it with these capitals, DICKENS IS A FOOL, AND
"A LIAR. . . . . I have a new protégé, in the A new protégé.
"person of a wretched deaf and dumb boy whom
"I found upon the sands the other day, half dead,
"and have got (for the present) into the union
"infirmary at Minster. A most deplorable case."

On the 14th he told me: "I have pleased
"myself very much to-day in the matter of Nia-
"gara. I have made the description very brief
"(as it should be), but I fancy it is good. I am
"beginning to think over the introductory chapter,
"and it has meanwhile occurred to me that I
"should like, at the beginning of the volumes, to Proposed Dedication.
"put what follows on a blank page. *I dedicate*

"*this Book to those friends of mine in America,*
"*who, loving their country, can bear the truth, when*
"*it is written good humouredly and in a kind spirit.*
"What do you think? Do you see any objection?"

My reply is to be inferred from what he sent
back on the 20th. "I don't quite see my way
"towards an expression in the dedication of any

"feeling in reference to the American reception.
"Of course I have always intended to glance at
"it, gratefully, in the end of the book; and it will
"have its place in the introductory chapter, if we
"decide for that. Would it do to put in, after
"'friends in America,' *who giving me a welcome I*
"*must ever gratefully and proudly remember, left*
"*my judgment free,* and who, loving, &c. If so,
"so be it."

Before the end of the month he wrote: "For
"the last two or three days I have been rather
"slack in point of work; not being in the vein.
"To-day I had not written twenty lines before I
"rushed out (the weather being gorgeous) to

"bathe. And when I have done that, it is all up
"with me in the way of authorship until to-morrow.
"The little dog is in the highest spirits; and jumps,
"as Mr. Kenwigs would say, perpetivally. I have
"had letters by the Britannia from Felton, Pres-
"cott, Mr. Q., and others, all very earnest and
"kind. I think you will like what I have written

"on the poor emigrants and their ways as I liter-
"ally and truly saw them on the boat from Quebec
"to Montreal."

This was a passage, which, besides being in

itself as attractive as any in his writings, gives
such perfect expression to a feeling that underlies
them all, that I subjoin it in a note.*   On board

* "Cant as we may, and as we shall to the end of all C. D. log.
"things, it is very much harder for the poor to be virtuous
"than it is for the rich; and the good that is in them, shines
"the brighter for it.   In many a noble mansion lives a man,
"the best of husbands and of fathers, whose private worth in
"both capacities is justly lauded to the skies.   But bring
"him here, upon this crowded deck.   Strip from his fair
"young wife her silken dress and jewels, unbind her braided
"hair, stamp early wrinkles on her brow, pinch her pale
"cheek with care and much privation, array her faded form
"in coarsely patched attire, let there be nothing but his love
"to set her forth or deck her out, and you shall put it to
"the proof indeed.   So change his station in the world that Patient Poor
"he shall see, in those young things who climb about his and easy-living Rich.
"knee, not records of his wealth and name, but little
"wrestlers with him for his daily bread; so many poachers
"on his scanty meal; so many units to divide his every sum
"of comfort, and farther to reduce its small amount.   In
"lieu of the endearments of childhood in its sweetest aspect,
"heap upon him all its pains and wants, its sicknesses and
"ills, its fretfulness, caprice, and querulous endurance: let its
"prattle be, not of engaging infant fancies, but of cold, and
"thirst, and hunger: and if his fatherly affection outlive all
"this, and he be patient, watchful, tender; careful of his
"children's lives, and mindful always of their joys and
"sorrows; then send him back to parliament, and pulpit,
"and to quarter sessions, and when he hears fine talk of the
"depravity of those who live from hand to mouth, and
"labour hard to do it, let him speak up, as one who knows,
"and tell those holders-forth that they, by parallel with such
"a class, should be high angels in their daily lives, and lay

Broad-
stairs:
1842.
this Canadian steamboat he encountered crowds
of poor emigrants and their children; and such
Rich and Poor
by new trans-
lation.
was their patient kindness and cheerful endurance,
in circumstances where the easy-living rich could
hardly fail to be monsters of impatience and selfishness, that it suggested to him a reflection than
which it was not possible to have written anything
more worthy of observation, or more absolutely
true. Jeremy Taylor has the same philosophy in
his lesson on opportunities, but here it was beau-
tified by the example with all its fine touches.
It made us read Rich and Poor by new translation.

Coming to the
end.
The printers were now hard at work, and in
the last week of September he wrote: "I send you
"proofs as far as Niagara ... I am rather holiday-
"making this week . . . taking principal part in a
"regatta here yesterday, very pretty and gay in-

C. D. loq.
"but humble siege to heaven at last. . . . Which of us shall
"say what he would be, if such realities, with small relief
"or change all through his days, were his! Looking round
"upon these people: far from home, houseless, indigent,
"wandering, weary with travel and hard living: and seeing
"how patiently they nursed and tended their young children:
"how they consulted ever their wants first, then half sup-
"plied their own; what gentle ministers of hope and faith
"the women were; how the men profited by their example;
"and how very, very seldom even a moment's petulance or
"harsh complaint broke out among them: I felt a stronger
"love and honour of my kind come glowing on my heart, and
"wished to God there had been many atheists in the better
"part of human nature there, to read this simple lesson in
"the book of life."

"deed. We think of coming up in time for Broad-
stairs:
1842.
"Macready's opening, when perhaps you will give
"us a chop; and of course you and Mac will dine Drury-lane
"with *us* the next day? I shall leave nothing of opening.
"the book to do after coming home, please God,
"but the two chapters on slavery and the people
"which I could manage easily in a week, if need
"were ... The policeman who supposed the Duke A shrewd
"of Brunswick to be one of the swell mob, ought guess.
"instantly to be made an inspector. The suspicion
"reflects the highest credit (I seriously think) on
"his penetration and judgment."   Three days
later: "For the last two days we have had gales
"blowing from the north-east, and seas rolling on
"us that drown the pier. To-day it is tremendous.
"Such a sea was never known here at this season,
"and it is running in at this moment in waves of
"twelve feet high. You would hardly know the Heavy seas.
"place. But we shall be punctual to your dinner
"hour on Saturday. If the wind should hold in
"the same quarter, we may be obliged to come
"up by land; and in that case I should start the
"caravan at six in the morning. ... What do you
"think of this for my title—*American Notes for
"General Circulation;* and of this motto?

   "In reply to a question from the Bench, the Solicitor for Rejected
"the Bank observed, that this kind of notes circulated the motto for
"most extensively, in those parts of the world where they Notes.
"were stolen and forged. *Old Bailey Report.*"

   The motto was omitted, objection being made
to it; and on the last day of the month I had the

last of his letters during this Broadstairs visit. "Strange as it may appear to you" (25th of September), "the sea is running so high that we have "no choice but to return by land. No steamer "can come out of Ramsgate, and the Margate "boat lay out all night on Wednesday with all "her passengers on board. You may be sure of "us therefore on Saturday at 5, for I have de-"termined to leave here to-morrow, as we could "not otherwise manage it in time; and have en-"gaged an omnibus to bring the whole caravan

"by the overland route. ... We cannot open a "window, or a door; legs are of no use on the "terrace; and the Margate boats can only take "people aboard at Herne Bay!" He brought with him all that remained to be done of his second volume except the last two chapters, including that to. which he has referred as "introductory;" and on the following Wednesday (5th of October) he told me that the first of these was done. "I want you very much to come and "dine to-day that we may repair to Drury-lane "together; and let us say half-past four, or there "is no time to be comfortable. I am going out "to Tottenham this morning, on a cheerless "mission I would willingly have avoided. Hone,

"of the *Every Day Book*, is dying; and sent "Cruikshank yesterday to beg me to go and see "him, as, having read no books but mine of late, "he wanted to see and shake hands with me be-"fore (as George said) 'he went.' There is no "help for it, of course; so to Tottenham I repair,

"this morning. I worked all day, and till mid-
"night; and finished the slavery chapter yester-
"day."

Broad-
stairs:
1842.
Cheerless
visit.

The cheerless visit had its mournful sequel
before the next month closed, when he went with
the same companion to poor Hone's funeral; and
one of his letters written at the time to Mr. Felton
has so vividly recalled to me the tragi-comedy of
an incident of that day, as for long after he used
to describe it, and as I have heard the other
principal actor in it good-naturedly admit to be
perfectly true, that two or three sentences may be
given here. The wonderful neighbourhood in
this life of ours, of serious and humorous things, The mingled
yarn.
constitutes in itself very much of the genius of
Dickens's writing; the laughter close to the pathos,
but never touching it with ridicule; and this small
occurrence may be taken in farther evidence of
its reality.

"We went into a little parlour where the fu- C. D. loq.
"neral party was, and God knows it was miserable
"enough, for the widow and children were crying
"bitterly in one corner, and the other mourners
"(mere people of ceremony, who cared no more
"for the dead man than the hearse did) were
"talking quite coolly and carelessly together in
"another; and the contrast was as painful and
"distressing as anything I ever saw. There was
"an independent clergyman present, with his
"bands on and a bible under his arm, who, as
"soon as we were seated, addressed C thus, in a
"loud emphatic voice. 'Mr. C, have you seen

London:
1842.
———
Scene at a
funeral.

"'a paragraph respecting our departed friend,
"'which has gone the round of the morning
"'papers?' 'Yes, sir,' says C, 'I have:' looking
"very hard at me the while, for he had told me
"with some pride coming down that it was his
"composition. 'Oh!' said the clergyman. 'Then
"'you will agree with me, Mr. C, that it is not
"'only an insult to me, who am the servant of
"'the Almighty, but an insult to the Almighty,
"'whose servant I am.' 'How is that, sir?' says C.
"'It is stated, Mr. C, in that paragraph,' says the
"minister, 'that when Mr. Hone failed in business
"'as a bookseller, he was persuaded by *me* to try
Shop and
pulpit.
"'the pulpit; which is false, incorrect, unchristian,
"'in a manner blasphemous, and in all respects
"'contemptible. Let us pray.' With which, and
"in the same breath, I give you my word, he
"knelt down, as we all did, and began a very
"miserable jumble of an extemporary prayer. I
"was really penetrated with sorrow for the family"
(he exerted himself zealously for them afterwards,
as the kind-hearted C also did), "but when C,
"upon his knees and sobbing for the loss of an
"old friend, whispered me 'that if that wasn't a
"'clergyman, and it wasn't a funeral, he'd have
"'punched his head,' I felt as if nothing but con-
"vulsions could possibly relieve me."

An intro-
ductory
chapter sup-
pressed.
On the 10th of October I heard from him
that the chapter intended to be introductory to
the *Notes* was written, and waiting our conference
whether or not it should be printed. We decided
against it; on his part so reluctantly, that I had

to undertake for its publication when a more fitting time should come. This in my judgment has arrived, and the chapter first sees the light on this page. There is no danger at present, as there would have been when it was written, that its proper self-assertion should be mistaken for an apprehension of hostile judgments which he was anxious to deprecate or avoid. He is out of reach of all that now; and reveals to us here, as one whom fear or censure can touch no more, his honest purpose in the use of satire even where his humorous temptations were strongest. What he says will on other grounds also be read with unusual interest, for it will be found to connect itself impressively not with his first experiences only, but with his second visit to America at the close of his life. He held always the same high opinion of what was best in that country, and always the same contempt for what was worst in it.

"INTRODUCTORY. AND NECESSARY TO BE READ.

"I have placed the foregoing title at the "head of this page, because I challenge and deny " the right of any person to pass judgment on "this book, or to arrive at any reasonable con- "clusion in reference to it, without first being at "the trouble of becoming acquainted with its . "design and purpose.

"It is not statistical. Figures of arithmetic "have already been heaped upon America's de-

LONDON:
1843.

Suppressed
chapter.

"voted head, almost as lavishly as figures of "speech have been piled above Shakespeare's "grave.

"It comprehends no small talk concerning in-"dividuals, and no violation of the social confi-"dences of private life. The very prevalent "practice of kidnapping live ladies and gentle-

Intentions
and plan for
book.

"men, forcing them into cabinets, and labelling "and ticketing them whether they will or no, for "the gratification of the idle and the curious, is "not to my taste. Therefore I have avoided it.

"It has not a grain of any political ingredient "in its whole composition.

Why silent as
to personal
reception.

"Neither does it contain, nor have I intended "that it should contain, any lengthened and minute "account of my personal reception in the United "States: not because I am, or ever was, insensible "to that spontaneous effusion of affection and "generosity of heart, in a most affectionate "and generous-hearted people; but because I "conceive that it would ill become me to flourish "matter necessarily involving so much of my own "praises, in the eyes of my unhappy readers.

"This book is simply what it claims to be— "a record of the impressions I received from day "to day, during my hasty travels in America, and "sometimes (but not always) of the conclusions

Notes
described.

"to which they, and after-reflection on them, have "led me; a description of the country I passed "through; of the institutions I visited; of the "kind of people among whom I journeyed; and of "the manners and customs that came within my

" observation.   Very many works having just the London: 1842.
"same scope and range, have been already pub- Suppressed
"lished, but I think that these two volumes chapter.
"stand in need of no apology on that account.
"The interest of such productions, if they have
" any, lies in the varying impressions made by the
"same novel things on different minds; and not
" in new discoveries or extraordinary adventures.

"I can scarcely be supposed to be ignorant Risks in-curred.
"of the hazard I run in writing of America at all.
"I know perfectly well that there is, in that
"country, a numerous class of well-intentioned
"persons prone to be dissatisfied with all accounts
"of the Republic whose citizens they are, which
" are not couched in terms of exalted and extra-
"vagant praise.   I know perfectly well that there
"is in America, as in most other places laid
"down in maps of the great world, a numerous
" class of persons so tenderly and delicately con-
" stituted, that they cannot bear the truth in any
"form.   And I do not need the gift of prophecy
"to discern afar off, that they who will be aptest Native critics.
"to detect malice, ill-will, and all uncharitable-
"ness in these pages, and to show, beyond any
"doubt, that they are perfectly inconsistent
"with that grateful and enduring recollection
"which I profess to entertain of the welcome I
"found awaiting me beyond the Atlantic—will
"be certain native journalists, veracious and gen-
"tlemanly, who were at great pains to prove to
"me, on all occasions during my stay there, that
"the aforesaid welcome was utterly worthless.

"But, venturing to dissent even from these "high authorities, I formed my own opinion of "its value in the outset, and retain it to this "hour; and in asserting (as I invariably did on "all public occasions) my liberty and freedom of "speech while I was among the Americans, and "in maintaining it at home, I believe that I best "show my sense of the high worth of that wel- "come, and of the honourable singleness of pur- "pose with which it was extended to me. From "first to last I saw, in the friends who crowded "round me in America, old readers, over-grateful "and over-partial perhaps, to whom I had happily "been the means of furnishing pleasure and

"entertainment; not a vulgar herd who would "flatter and cajole a stranger into turning with "closed eyes from all the blemishes of the nation, "and into chaunting its praises with the discrimi- "nation of a street ballad-singer. From first to "last I saw, in those hospitable hands, a home- "made wreath of laurel; and not an iron muzzle "disguised beneath a flower or two.

"Therefore I take —and hold myself not only "justified in taking, but bound to take—the plain "course of saying what I think, and noting what "I saw; and as it is not my custom to exalt "what in my judgment are foibles and abuses at "home, so I have no intention of softening down, "or glozing over, those that I have observed "abroad.

"If this book should fall into the hands of "any sensitive American who cannot bear to be

"told that the working of the institutions of his London 1842.
"country is far from perfect; that in spite of the Suppressed chapter.
"advantage she has over all other nations in the
"elastic freshness and vigour of her youth, she is
"far from being a model for the earth to copy;
"and that even in those pictures of the national
"manners with which he quarrels most, there is
"still (after the lapse of several years, each of
"which may be fairly supposed to have had its
"stride in improvement) much that is just and
"true at this hour; let him lay it down, now, for
"I shall not please him. Of the intelligent, re-
"flecting, and educated among his countrymen, I
"have no fear; for I have ample reason to believe,
"after many delightful conversations not easily
"to be forgotten, that there are very few topics
"(if any) on which their sentiments differ mate-
"rially from mine.

"I may be asked—'If you have been in any
"'respect disappointed in America, and are as-
"'sured beforehand that the expression of your
"'disappointment will give offence to any class,
"'why do you write at all?' My answer is, that Why write the book at all.
"I went there expecting greater things than I found,
"and resolved as far as in me lay to do justice to
"the country, at the expense of any (in my view)
"mistaken or prejudiced statements that might
"have been made to its disparagement. Coming
"home with a corrected and sobered judgment,
"I consider myself no less bound to do justice to
"what, according to my best means of judgment,
"I found to be the truth."

Of the book for whose opening page this matter introductory was written, it will be enough merely to add that it appeared on the 18th of October; that before the close of the year four large editions had been sold; and that in my opinion it thoroughly deserved the estimate formed of it by one connected with America by the strongest social affections, and otherwise in all respects an honourable, high-minded, upright judge. "You have been very tender," wrote Lord Jeffrey, "to our sensitive friends beyond sea, and "my whole heart goes along with every word you "have written. I think that you have perfectly "accomplished all that you profess or undertake "to do, and that the world has never yet seen a "more faithful, graphic, amusing, kind-hearted "narrative."

———

I permit myself so far to anticipate a later page as to print here a brief extract from one of the letters of the last American visit. Without impairing the interest with which the narrative of that time will be read in its proper place, I shall thus indicate the extent to which present impressions were modified by the experience of twenty-six years later. He is writing from Philadelphia on the fourteenth of January, 1868.

"I see *great changes* for the better, socially. "Politically, no. England governed by the Mary-"lebone vestry and the penny papers, and England "as she would be after years of such governing;

"is what I make of *that*.   Socially, the change in
"manners is remarkable.   There is much greater
"politeness and forbearance in all ways. . . On
"the other hand there are still provincial oddities
"wonderfully quizzical; and the newspapers are
"constantly expressing the popular amazement at
"'Mr. Dicken's extraordinary composure.' They
"seem to take it ill that I don't stagger on to the
"platform overpowered by the spectacle before
"me, and the national greatness. They are all so
"accustomed to do public things with a flourish
"of trumpets, that the notion of my coming in to
"read without somebody first flying up and de-
"livering an 'Oration' about me, and flying down
"again and leading me in, is so very unaccount-
"able to them, that sometimes they have no idea
"until I open my lips that it can possibly be
"Charles Dickens."

London 1842.

Experience of America In 1868.

CHAPTER XXVI.

FIRST YEAR OF MARTIN CHUZZLEWIT.

1843.

CORNWALL:
1843.

THE Cornish trip had come off, meanwhile, with such unexpected and continued attraction for us that we were well into the third week of absence before we turned our faces homeward. Railways helped us then not much; but where the roads were inaccessible to post-horses, we walked. Tintagel was visited, and no part of mountain or sea consecrated by the legends of Arthur was left unexplored. We ascended to the cradle of the highest tower of Mount St. Michael, and descended into several mines. Land and sea yielded each its marvels to us; but of all the impressions brought away, of which some afterwards took forms as lasting as they could receive from the most delightful art, I doubt if any were the

A sunset at
Land's-end

source of such deep emotion to us all as a sunset we saw at Land's-end. Stanfield knew the wonders of the Continent, the glories of Ireland were native to Maclise, I was familiar from boyhood with border and Scottish scenery, and Dickens was fresh from Niagara; but there was something in the sinking of the sun behind the Atlantic that autumn afternoon, as we viewed it together from the top of the rock projecting farthest into the sea, which each in his turn declared to have no parallel in memory.

But with the varied and overflowing gladness of those three memorable weeks it would be unworthy now to associate only the saddened recollection of the sole survivor. "Blessed star of "morning!" wrote Dickens to Felton while yet the glow of its enjoyment was upon him. "Such a "trip as we had into Cornwall just after Long-"fellow went away! . . Sometimes we travelled "all night, sometimes all day, sometimes both. . . "Heavens! If you could have seen the necks of "bottles, distracting in their immense varieties of "shape, peering out of the carriage pockets! If "you could have witnessed the deep devotion of "the post-boys, the wild attachment of the hostlers, "the maniac glee of the waiters! If you could "have followed us into the earthy old churches "we visited, and into the strange caverns on the "gloomy sea-shore, and down into the depths of "mines, and up to the tops of giddy heights where "the unspeakably green water was roaring, I don't "know how many hundred feet below! If you "could have seen but one gleam of the bright "fires by which we sat in the big rooms of ancient "inns at night, until long after the small hours "had come and gone . . . I never laughed in my "life as I did on this journey. It would have "done you good to hear me. I was choking and

Cornwall:
1842.
"gasping and bursting the buckle off the back of "my stock, all the way. And Stanfield got into "such apoplectic entanglements that we were often "obliged to beat him on the back with portman-"teaus before we could recover him. Seriously, "I do believe there never was such a trip. And

Sketches by
Maclise and
Stanfield.'
"they made such sketches, those two men, in the "most romantic of our halting-places, that you "would have sworn we had the Spirit of Beauty "with us, as well as the Spirit of Fun."*

The Logan Stone, by Stanfield, was one of them; and it laughingly sketched both the charm of what was seen and the mirth of what was done, for it perched me on the top of the stone. It is historical, however, the ascent having been made; and of this and other examples of steadiness at heights which deterred the rest, as well as of a subject suggested for a painting of which Dickens became the unknown purchaser, Maclise reminded me in some pleasant allusions many years later, which, notwithstanding their tribute to my athletic achievements, the good-natured reader must forgive my printing. They complete the little picture of our trip. Something I had written to him of recent travel among the mountain scenery of the wilder coasts of Donegal had touched the

* Printed in the *Atlantic Monthly* shortly after his death, and since collected, by Mr. James T. Fields of Boston, with several of later date addressed to himself, and much correspondence having reference to other writers, into a pleasing volume entitled *Yesterdays with Authors.*

chord of these old remembrances. "As to your CORNWALL: 1842. "clambering," he replied, "don't I know what Maclise "happened of old? Don't I still see the Logan to J. F. "Stone, and you perched on the giddy top, while "we, rocking it on its pivot, shrank from all that "lay concealed below! Should I ever have blun- "dered on the waterfall of St. Wighton, if you "had not piloted the way? And when we got to "Land's-end, with the green sea far under us "lapping into solitary rocky nooks where the mer- "maids live, who but you only had the courage "to stretch over, to see those diamond jets of "brightness that I swore then, and believe still, "were the flappings of their tails! And don't I "recall you again, sitting on the tip-top stone of "the cradle-turret over the highest battlement of "the castle of St. Michael's Mount, with not a "ledge or coigne of vantage 'twixt you and the "fathomless ocean under you, distant three thou- "sand feet? Last, do I forget you clambering up "the goat-path to King Arthur's castle of Tintagel, "when, in my vain wish to follow, I grovelled and "clung to the soil like a Caliban, and you, in the "manner of a tricksy spirit and stout Ariel, actually "danced up and down before me!"

The waterfall I led him to was among the re- Maclise's "Girl at the Waterfall." cords of the famous holiday, celebrated also by Thackeray in one of his pen-and-ink pleasantries, which were sent by both painters to the next year's Academy; and so eager was Dickens to possess this landscape by Maclise which included the likeness of a member of his family, yet so

anxious that our friend should be spared the sacrifice which he knew would follow an avowal of
his wish, that he bought it under a feigned name
before the Academy opened, and steadily refused
to take back the money which on discovery of
the artifice Maclise pressed upon him.*   Our
friend, who already had munificently given him a
charming drawing of his four eldest children to
accompany him and his wife to America, had his
generous way nevertheless; and, as a voluntary
offering four years later, painted Mrs. Dickens on
a canvas of the same size as the picture of her
husband in 1839.

Portrait of
Mrs. Dickens.

"Behold finally the title of the new book,"
was the first note I had from Dickens (12th of
November) after our return; "don't lose it, for I
"have no copy."   Title and even story had been
undetermined while we travelled, from the linger-
ing wish he still had to begin it among those
Cornish scenes; but this intention had now been
finally abandoned, and the reader lost nothing by
his substitution for the lighthouse or mine in
Cornwall, of the Wiltshire-village forge on the
windy autumn evening which opens the tale of
Martin Chuzzlewit.   Into that name he finally
settled, but only after much deliberation, as a
mention of his changes will show.   Martin was
the prefix to all, but the surname varied from its

Names first
given to
Chuzzlewit.

* This is mentioned in Mr. O. Driscoll's agreeable little
Memoir, but supposed to refer to Maclise's portrait of
Dickens.

first form of Sweezleden, Sweezleback, and Sweezle- LONDON:
1842.
wag, to those of Chuzzletoe, Chuzzleboy, Chub-
blewig, and Chuzzlewig; nor was Chuzzlewit chosen
at last until after more hesitation and discussion.
What he had sent me in his letter as finally adopted,
ran thus: "The Life and Adventures of Martin Title chosen.
"Chuzzlewig, his family, friends, and enemies.
"Comprising all his wills and his ways. With an
"historical record of what he did and what he
"didn't. The whole forming a complete key to
"the house of Chuzzlewig." All which latter portion of the title was of course dropped as the
work became modified, in its progress, by changes
at first not contemplated; but as early as the third
number he sent me the plan of "old Martin's plot
"to degrade and punish Pecksniff," and the difficulties he encountered in departing from other
portions of his scheme were such as to render
him, in his subsequent stories, more bent upon
constructive care at the outset, and adherence as
far as might be to any design he had formed.

The first number, which appeared in January First No. of
Chuzzlewit.
1843, had not been quite finished when he wrote
to me on the 8th of December: "The Chuzzlewit
"copy makes so much more than I supposed,
"that the number is nearly done. Thank God!"
Beginning so hurriedly as at last he did, altering
his course at the opening and seeing little as yet
of the main track of his design, perhaps no story
was ever begun by him with stronger heart or
confidence. Illness kept me to my rooms for
some days, and he was so eager to try the effect

London:
1842.

Sydney
Smith's
opinion.

of Pecksniff and Pinch that he came down with the ink hardly dry on the last slip to read the manuscript to me. Well did Sydney Smith, in writing to say how very much the number had pleased him, foresee the promise there was in those characters. "Pecksniff and his daughters, "and Pinch, are admirable—quite first-rate paint-"ing, such as no one but yourself can execute!" And let me here at once remark that the notion of taking Pecksniff for a type of character was

Origin of the
book.

really the origin of the book; the design being to show, more or less by every person introduced, the number and variety of humours and vices that have their root in selfishness.

Prologue to a
play.

Another piece of his writing that claims mention at the close of 1842 was a prologue contributed to the *Patrician's Daughter*, Mr. Westland Marston's first dramatic effort, which had attracted him by the beauty of its composition less than by the courage with which its subject had been chosen, from the actual life of the time.

"Not light its import, and not poor its mien;
"Yourselves the actors, and your homes the scene."

This was the date, too, of Mr. Browning's tragedy of the *Blot on the 'Scutcheon*, which I took upon myself, after reading it in the manuscript, privately to impart to Dickens; and I was not mistaken in the belief that it would profoundly touch

MS. shown to
him.

him. "Browning's play," he wrote (25th of November), "has thrown me into a perfect passion

LONDON:
1842.

"of sorrow. To say that there is anything in its
"subject save what is lovely, true, deeply affect-
"ing, full of the best emotion, the most earnest
"feeling, and the most true and tender source of
"interest, is to say that there is no light in the
"sun, and no heat in blood. It is full of genius,
"natural and great thoughts, profound and yet
"simple and beautiful in its vigour. I know no- A tragedy by Browning.
"thing that is so affecting, nothing in any book I
"have ever read, as Mildred's recurrence to that
"'I was so young.—I had no mother.' I know
"no love like it, no passion like it, no moulding
"of a splendid thing after its conception, like it.
"And I swear it is a tragedy that MUST be
"played; and must be played, moreover, by
"Macready. There are some things I would have
"changed if I could (they are very slight, mostly
"broken lines); and I assuredly would have the
"old servant *begin his tale upon the scene;* and be
"taken by the throat, or drawn upon, by his
"master, in its commencement. But the tragedy
"I never shall forget, or less vividly remember
"than I do now. And if you tell Browning that
"I have seen it, tell him that I believe from my
"soul there is no man living (and not many dead)
"who could produce such a work.—Macready
"likes the altered prologue very much." ... There Other opinions of books.
will come a more convenient time to speak of
his general literary likings, or special regard for
contemporary books; but I will say now that nothing interested him more than successes won
honestly in his own field, and that in his large

and open nature there was no hiding-place for little jealousies. An instance occurs to me which may be named at once, when, many years after the present date, he called my attention very earnestly to two tales then in course of publica-

tion in *Blackwood's Magazine*, and afterwards col-lected under the title of *Scenes of Clerical Life.* "Do read them," he wrote. "They are the best "things I have seen since I began my course."

Eighteen hundred and forty-three* opened with the most vigorous prosecution of his *Chuzzle-wit* labour. "I hope the number will be very "good," he wrote to me of number two (8th of January). "I have been hammering away, and "at home all day. Ditto yesterday; except for

"two hours in the afternoon, when I ploughed "through snow half a foot deep, round about the

---

* In one of the letters to his American friend Mr. Felton there is a glimpse of Christmas sports which had escaped my memory, and for which a corner may be found here, inas-much as these gambols were characteristic of him at the plea-sant old season, and were frequently renewed in future years.

"The best of it is" (31 Dec. 1842) "that Forster and I have "purchased between us the entire stock-in-trade of a con-"juror, the practice and display whereof is entrusted to "me. . . . In those tricks which require a confederate I am "assisted (by reason of his imperturbable good humour) by "Stanfield, who always does his part exactly the wrong way, "to the unspeakable delight of all beholders. We come out "on a small scale to-night, at Forster's, where we see "the old year out and the new one in." *Atlantic Monthly,* July 1871.

"wilds of Willesden." For the present, however,
I shall glance only briefly from time to time at
his progress with the earlier portions of the story
on which he was thus engaged until the midsummer of 1844. Disappointments arose in connection with it, unexpected and strange, which
had important influence upon him: but I reserve
the mention of these for awhile, that I may speak
of the leading incidents of 1843.

LONDON: 1843.

"I am in a difficulty," he wrote (12th of
February), "and am coming down to you some
"time to-day or to-night. I couldn't write a line
"yesterday; not a word, though I really tried
"hard. In a kind of despair I started off at half-
"past two with my pair of petticoats to Rich-
"mond; and dined there! Oh what a lovely day
"it was in those parts." His pair of petticoats
were Mrs. Dickens and her sister Georgina: the
latter, since his return from America, having become part of his household, of which she remained a member until his death; and he had
just reason to be proud of the steadiness, depth,
and devotion of her friendship. In a note-book
begun by him in January 1855, where, for the
first time in his life, he jotted down hints and
fancies proposed to be made available in future
writings, I find a character sketched of which, if
the whole was not suggested by his sister-in-law,
the most part was applicable to her. "She—
"sacrificed to children, and sufficiently rewarded.
"From a child herself, always 'the children' (of
"somebody else) to engross her. And so it comes

Miss Georgina Hogarth.

C. D.'s MS. note-book.

"to pass that she is never married; never herself "has a child; is always devoted 'to the children' "(of somebody else); and they love her; and she has "always youth dependent on her till her death—and "dies quite happily." Not many days after that holi-

day at Richmond, a slight unstudied outline in pencil was made by Maclise of the three who formed the party there, as we all sat together; and never did a touch so light carry with it more truth of observation. The likenessses of all are excellent; and I here preserve the drawing because nothing ever done of Dickens himself has conveyed more vividly his look and bearing at this yet youthful time. He is in his most pleasing aspect; flattered, if you will; but nothing that is known to me gives a general impression so lifelike and true of the then frank, eager, handsome face.

It was a year of much illness with me, which had ever helpful and active sympathy from him. "Send me word how you are," he wrote, two days later. "But not so much for that I now "write, as to tell you, peremptorily, that I insist "on your wrapping yourself up and coming here "in a hackney-coach, with a big portmanteau, to-

"morrow. It surely is better to be unwell with a "Quick and Cheerful (and Co) in the neighbour-"hood, than in the dreary vastness of Lincoln's-"inn-fields. Here is the snuggest tent-bedstead "in the world, and there you are with the draw-"ing-room for your workshop, the Q and C for "your pal, and 'everythink in a concatenation ac-"'cordingly.' I begin to have hopes of the re-

"generation of mankind after the reception of
"Gregory last night, though I have none of the
"*Chronicle* for not denouncing the villain. Have
"you seen the note touching my *Notes* in the blue
"and yellow?"

The first of these closing allusions was to the
editor of the infamous *Satirist* having been hissed
from the Drury-lane stage, on which he had presented himself in the character of Hamlet; and I
remember with what infinite pleasure I afterwards
heard Chief Justice Tindal in court, charging the
jury in an action brought by this malefactor
against a publican of St. Giles's for having paid
men to take part in the hissing of him, avow the
pride he felt in "living in the same parish with a
"man of that humble station of life of the defen-
"dant's," who was capable of paying money out
of his own pocket to punish what he believed to
be an outrage to decency. The second allusion
was to a statement of the reviewer of the *Ameri-*
can Notes in the *Edinburgh* to the effect, that, if
he had been rightly informed, Dickens had gone
to America as a kind of missionary in the cause
of international copyright; to which a prompt
contradiction had been given in the *Times*. "I
deny it," wrote Dickens, "wholly. He is wrongly
"informed; and reports, without enquiry, a piece
"of information which I could only characterize
"by using one of the shortest and strongest words
"in the language."

The disputes that had arisen out of the American book, I may add, stretched over great part of the year. It will quite suffice, however, to say here that the ground taken by him in his letters written on the spot, and printed in my former volume, which in all the more material statements his book invited public judgment upon and which he was moved to reopen in *Chuzzlewit*, was so kept by him against all comers, that none of the counter-statements or arguments dislodged him from a square inch of it. But the controversy is dead now; and he took occasion, on his later visit to America, to write its epitaph.

Though I did not, to revert to his February letter, obey its cordial bidding by immediately taking up quarters with him, I soon after joined him at a cottage he rented in Finchley; and here, walking and talking in the green lanes as the midsummer months were coming on, his introduction of Mrs. Gamp, and the uses to which he should apply that remarkable personage, first occurred to him. In his preface to the book he speaks of her as a fair representation, at the time it was published, of the hired attendant on the poor in sickness: but he might have added that the rich were no better off, for Mrs. Gamp's original was in reality a person hired by a most distinguished friend of his own, a lady, to take charge of an invalid very dear to her; and the common habit of this nurse in the sick room, among other Gampish peculiarities, was to rub her nose along the top of the tall fender. Whether or not, on that first mention of her, I had any doubts whether such a character could be made LONDON: 1843. a central figure in his story, I do not now remember; but if there were any at the time, they did not outlive the contents of the packet which introduced her to me in the flesh a few weeks after our return. "Tell me," he wrote from Yorkshire, where he had been meanwhile passing pleasant holiday with a friend, "what you think "of Mrs. Gamp? You'll not find it easy to get "through the hundreds of misprints in her con-"versation, but I want your opinion at once. I "think you know already something of mine. I What he will do with her. "mean to make a mark with her." The same letter enclosed me a clever and pointed little parable in verse which he had written for an annual edited by Lady Blessington.*

* "I have heard, as you have, from Lady Blessington, Service for a friend. "for whose behoof I have this morning penned the lines I "send you herewith. But I have only done so to excuse "myself, for I have not the least idea of their suiting her; "and I hope she will send them back to you for the *Ex.*" C. D. to J. F. July 1843.   The lines are quite worth preserving.

A WORD IN SEASON.

They have a superstition in the East, Parable in verse by C. D.
  That Allah, written on a piece of paper,
Is better unction than can come of priest,
  Of rolling incense, and of lighted taper:
Holding, that any scrap which bears that name
  In any characters its front impress'd on,
Shall help the finder thro' the purging flame,
  And give his toasted feet a place to rest on.

LONDON:
1843.
Change of
editorship at
Chronicle.

Page 131 of
Vol. I.

Another allusion in the February letter reminds me of the interest which his old work for the *Chronicle* gave him in everything affecting its credit, and that this was the year when Mr. John Black ceased to be its editor, in circumstances reviving strongly all Dickens's sympathies. "I am deeply grieved" (3rd of May 1843) "about Black. Sorry

Accordingly, they make a mighty fuss
  With every wretched tract and fierce oration,
And hoard the leaves—for they are not, like us
  A highly civilized and thinking nation:
And, always stooping in the miry ways
  To look for matter of this earthly leaven,
They seldom, in their dust-exploring days,
  Have any leisure to look up to Heaven.

So have I known a country on the earth
  Where darkness sat upon the living waters,
And brutal ignorance, and toil, and dearth
  Were the hard portion of its sons and daughters:
And yet, where they who should have oped the door
  Of charity and light, for all men's finding,
Squabbled for words upon the altar-floor,
  And rent The Book, in struggles for the binding.

The gentlest man among those pious Turks
  God's living image ruthlessly defaces;
Their best High-Churchman, with no faith in works,
  Bowstrings the Virtues in the market-places.
The Christian Pariah, whom both sects curse
  (They curse all other men, and curse each other),
Walks thro' the world, not very much the worse,
  Does all the good he can, and loves his brother.

"from my heart's core. If I could find him out, LONDON: 1843. Dinner to John Black. "I would go and comfort him this moment." He did find him out; and he and a certain number of us did also comfort this excellent man after a fashion extremely English, by giving him a Greenwich dinner on the 20th of May; when Dickens had arranged and ordered all to perfection, and the dinner succeeded in its purpose, as in other ways, quite wonderfully. Among the entertainers were Sheil and Thackeray, Fonblanque and Charles Buller, Southwood Smith and William Johnson Fox, Macready and Maclise, as well as myself and Dickens.

There followed another similar celebration, in which one of these entertainers was the guest and which owed hardly less to Dickens's exertions, when, at the Star-and-garter at Richmond in the autumn, we wished Macready good-speed on his way to America. Dickens took the chair at that Macready bound for America. dinner; and with Stanfield, Maclise, and myself, was in the following week to have accompanied the great actor to Liverpool to say good-bye to him on board the Cunard ship, and bring his wife back to London after their leave-taking; when a word from our excellent friend Captain Marryat, startling to all of us except Dickens himself, struck him out of our party. Marryat A doubt of Marryat's as to C. D. thought that Macready might suffer in the States by any public mention of his having been attended on his way by the author of the *American Notes* and *Martin Chuzzlewit*, and our friend at one agreed with him. "Your main and foremost

London:
1843.

"reason," he wrote to me, "for doubting Marryat's "judgment, I can at once destroy. It has oc-"curred to me many times; I have mentioned the "thing to Kate more than once; and I had inten-"ded *not* to go on board, charging Ralley to let "nothing be said of my being in his house. I have "been prevented from giving any expression to "my fears by a misgiving that I should seem to "attach, if I did so, too much importance to my "own doings. But now that I have Marryat at my "back, I have not the least hesitation in saying that "I am certain he is right. I have very great appre-

Apprehended
disservice to
Macready.

"hensions that the *Nickleby* dedication will damage "Macready. Marryat is wrong in supposing it is not "printed in the American editions, for I have myself "seen it in the shop windows of several cities. If I "were to go on board with him, I have not the "least doubt that the fact would be placarded all "over New York, before he had shaved himself "in Boston. And that there are thousands of "men in America who would pick a quarrel "with him on the mere statement of his being "my friend, I have no more doubt than I have "of my existence. You have only doubted Mar-"ryat because it is impossible for *any man* to "know what they are in their own country, who "has not seen them there."

Works of
charity and
mercy.

This letter was written from Broadstairs, whither he had gone in August, after such help as he only could give, and never took such delight as in giving, to a work of practical humanity. Earlier in the year he had presided at a dinner for the

Printers' Pension-fund, which Thomas Hood,
Douglas Jerrold, and myself attended with him;
and upon the terrible summer-evening accident
at sea by which Mr. Elton the actor lost his life,
it was mainly by Dickens's unremitting exertions,
seconded admirably by Mr. Serle and warmly
taken up by Mr. Elton's own profession (the most
generous in the world), that ample provision was
made for the many children. At the close of
August I had news of him from his favourite
watering-place, too characteristic to be omitted.
The day before had been a day of "terrific heat,"
yet this had not deterred him from doing what
he was too often suddenly prone to do in the
midst of his hardest work. "I performed an in-
"sane match against time of eighteen miles by
"the milestones in four hours and a half, under a
"burning sun the whole way. I could get" (he
is writing next morning) "no sleep at night, and
"really began to be afraid I was going to have a
"fever. You may judge in what kind of author-
"ship-training I am to-day. I could as soon eat
"the cliff as write about anything." A few days
later, however, all was well again; and another
sketch from himself, to his American friend, will
show his sea-side life in ordinary. "In a bay-
"window in a one-pair sits, from nine o'clock to
"one, a gentleman with rather long hair and no
"neckcloth, who writes and grins as if he thought
"he were very funny indeed. At one he disap-
"pears, presently emerges from a bathing-machine,
"and may be seen, a kind of salmon-coloured

MARCUS-
TER I
1843.

C. D. loq.

Opening
of the
Athenæum.

"porpoise, splashing about in the ocean. After
"that he may be viewed in another bay-window
"on the ground floor, eating a strong lunch; and
"after that, walking a dozen miles or so, or lying
"on his back in the sand reading a book. Nobody
"bothers him unless they know he is disposed to
"be talked to; and I am told he is very com-
"fortable indeed. He's as brown as a berry, and
"they *do* say is a small fortune to the innkeeper
"who sells beer and cold punch. But this is
"mere rumour. Sometimes he goes up to London
"(eighty miles or so away), and then I'm told
"there is a sound in Lincoln's-inn-fields at night,
"as of men laughing, together with a clinking of
"knives and forks arld wine-glasses." *

He returned to town "for good" on Monday
the 2nd of October, and from the Wednesday to
the Friday of that week was at Manchester,
presiding at the opening of its great Athenæum,
when Mr. Cobden and Mr. Disraeli also "assisted."
Here he spoke mainly on a matter always nearest
his heart, the education of the very poor. He
protested against the danger of calling a little
learning dangerous; declared his preference for
the very least of the little over none at all; proposed to substitute for the old a new doggerel,

> Though house and lands be never got,
> Learning can give what they can *not;*

told his listeners of the real and paramount

* C. D. to Professor Felton (1st Sept. 1843), in *Atlantic
Monthly* for July 1871.

danger we had lately taken Longfellow to see in LONDON: 1843. Speech on education of the poor. the nightly refuges of London, "thousands of im-
"mortal creatures condemned without alternative
"or choice to tread, not what our great poet calls
"the primrose path to the everlasting bonfire, but
"one of jagged flints and stones laid down by
"brutal ignorance;" and contrasted this with the
unspeakable consolation and blessings that a little
knowledge had shed on men of the lowest estate
and most hopeless means, "watching the stars
"with Ferguson the shepherd's boy, walking the
"streets with Crabbe, a poor barber here in Lan-
"cashire with Arkwright, a tallow-chandler's son
"with Franklin, shoe-making with Bloomfield in
"his garret, following the plough with Burns, and,
"high above the noise of loom and hammer,
"whispering courage in the ears of workers I
"could this day name in Sheffield and in Man-
"chester."

The same spirit impelled him to give eager Ragged schools. welcome to the remarkable institution of Ragged
schools, which, begun by a shoemaker of South-
ampton and a chimney-sweep of Windsor and
carried on by a peer of the realm, has had results
of incalculable importance to society. The year
of which I am writing was its first, as this in
which I write is its last; and in the interval, out
of three hundred thousand children to whom it
has given some sort of education, it is computed
also to have given to a third of that number the
means of honest employment.* "I sent Miss

* "After a period of 27 years, from a single school of

LONDON:
1843.
——
C. D.'s In-
terest in
education.

"Coutts," he had written (24th of September), "a
"sledge-hammer account of the Ragged schools;
"and as I saw her name for two hundred pounds
"in the clergy education subscription-list, took
"pains to show her that religious mysteries and
"difficult creeds wouldn't do for such pupils.   I

A great lady's
beneficence.

"told her, too, that it was of immense importance
"they should be *washed*.   She writes back to
"know what the rent of some large airy premises
"would be, and what the expense of erecting a
"regular bathing or purifying place; touching
"which points I am in correspondence with the
"authorities.   I have no doubt she will do what-

Results of
Ragged
schools.

"five small infants, the work has grown into a cluster of
"some 300 schools, an aggregate of nearly 30,000 children,
"and a body of 3000 voluntary teachers, most of them the
"sons and daughters of toil. . . . Of more than 300,000 chil-
"dren which, on the most moderate calculation, we have a
"right to conclude have passed through these schools since
"their commencement, I venture to affirm that more than
"100,000 of both sexes have been placed out in various
"ways, in emigration, in the marine, in trades, and in
"domestic service.   For many consecutive years I have con-
"tributed prizes to thousands of the scholars; and let no one
"omit to call to mind what these children were, whence they
"came, and whither they were going without this merciful
"intervention.   They would have been added to the perilous
"swarm of the wild, the lawless, the wretched, and the
"ignorant, instead of being, as by God's blessing they are,
"decent and comfortable, earning an honest livelihood, and
"adorning the community to which they belong."   *Letter
of Lord Shaftesbury in the Times of the 13th of November*
1871.

"ever I ask her in the matter. She is a most ex- London: 1843.
"cellent creature, I protest to God, and I have a
"most perfect affection and respect for her."

One of the last things he did at the close of Proposed paper on Ragged schools:
the year, in the like spirit, was to offer to describe
the Ragged schools for the *Edinburgh Review.*
"I have told Napier," he wrote to me, "I will give
"a description of them in a paper on education,
"if the *Review* is not afraid to take ground against
"the church catechism and other mere formularies
"and subtleties, in reference to the education of
"the young and ignorant. I fear it is extremely
"improbable it will consent to commit itself so
"far." His fears were well-founded; but the state- Declined by Ed. Rev.
ments then made by him give me opportunity to
add that it was his impatience of differences on
this point with clergymen of the Established
Church that had led him, for the past year or two,
to take sittings in the Little Portland-street Uni-
tarian chapel; for whose officiating minister, Mr. Unitarianism.
Edward Tagart, he had a friendly regard which
continued long after he had ceased to be a
member of his congregation. That he did so
quit it, after two or three years, I can distinctly
state; and of the frequent agitation of his mind
and thoughts in connection with this all-important
theme, there will be other occasions to speak.
But upon essential points he had never any sympathy so strong as with the leading doctrine and
discipline of the Church of England; to these, as Return to Church of England.
time went on, he found himself able to accom-
modate all minor differences; and the unswerving

faith in Christianity itself, apart from sects and
schisms, which had never failed him at any period
of his life, found expression at its close in the
language of his will.   Twelve months before his
death, these words were written.   "I direct that
"my name be inscribed in plain English letters
"on my tomb . . . I conjure my friends on no
"account to make me the subject of any monu-
"ment, memorial, or testimonial whatever.   I rest
"my claim to the remembrance of my country on
"my published works, and to the remembrance
"of my friends upon their experience of me in
"addition thereto.   I commit my soul to the
"mercy of God, through our Lord and Saviour
"Jesus Christ; and I exhort my dear children
"humbly to try to guide themselves by the teach-
"ing of the New Testament in its broad spirit,
"and to put no faith in any man's narrow con-
"struction of its letter here or there."

Active as he had been in the now ending
year, and great as were its varieties of employment; his genius in its highest mood, his energy
unwearied in good work, and his capacity for
enjoyment without limit; he was able to signalize
its closing months by an achievement supremely
fortunate, which but for disappointments the year
had also brought might never have been thought
of.   He had not begun until a week after his
return from Manchester, where the fancy first occurred to him, and before the end of November
he had finished, his memorable *Christmas Carol.*
It was the work of such odd moments of leisure

as were left him out of the time taken up by two numbers of his *Chuzzlewit;* and though begun with but the special design of adding something to the *Chuzzlewit* balance, I can testify to the accuracy of his own account of what befell him in its composition, with what a strange mastery it seized him for itself, how he wept over it, and laughed, and wept again, and excited himself to an extraordinary degree, and how he walked thinking of it fifteen and twenty miles about the black streets of London, many and many a night after all sober folks had gone to bed. And when it was done, as he told our friend Mr. Felton in America, he let himself loose like a madman. "Forster is out again," he added, by way of illus- trating our practical comments on his celebration of the jovial old season, "and if he don't go in "again after the manner in which we have been "keeping Christmas, he must be very strong in- "deed. Such dinings, such dancings, such con- "jurings, such blind-man's-buffings, such theatre- "goings, such kissings-out of old years and kiss- "ings-in of new ones, never took place in these "parts before."

Yet had it been to him, this closing year, a time also of much anxiety and strange disap- pointments of which I am now to speak; and be- fore, with that view, we go back for a while to its earlier months, one step into the new year may be taken for what marked it with interest and importance to him. Eighteen hundred and forty-four was but fifteen days old when a third

LONDON:
1843.

son (his fifth child, which received the name of
its godfather Francis Jeffrey) was born; and here
is an answer sent by him, two days later, to an
invitation from Maclise, Stanfield, and myself to
dine with us at Richmond. "DEVONSHIRE LODGE,
"*Seventeenth of January*, 1844. FELLOW COUN-
"TRYMEN! The appeal with which you have
"honoured me, awakens within my breast emo-
"tions that are more easily to be imagined than
"described. Heaven bless you. I shall indeed
"be proud, my friends, to respond to such a re-
"quisition. I had withdrawn from Public Life—I
"fondly thought for ever—to pass the evening of
"my days in hydropathical pursuits, and the con-
"templation of virtue.   For which latter pur-
"pose, I had bought a looking-glass.—But, my
"friends, private feeling must ever yield to a stern
"sense of public duty.   The Man is lost in the
"Invited Guest, and I comply.   Nurses, wet and
"dry; apothecaries; mothers-in-law; babbies; with
"all the sweet (and chaste) delights of private
"life; these, my countrymen, are hard to leave.
"But you have called me forth, and I will come.
"Fellow countrymen, your friend and faithful
"servant, CHARLES DICKENS."

Amusing
letter.

CHAPTER XXVII.

CHUZZLEWIT DISAPPOINTMENTS AND CHRISTMAS CAROL.

1843-1844.

CHUZZLEWIT had fallen short of all the expectations formed of it in regard to sale. By much the most masterly of his writings hitherto, the public had rallied to it in far less numbers than to any of its predecessors. The primary cause of this, there is little doubt, had been the change to weekly issues in the form of publication of his last two stories; for into everything in this world mere habit enters more largely than we are apt to suppose. Nor had the temporary withdrawal to America been favourable to an immediate resumption by his readers of their old and intimate relations. This also is to be added, that the excitement by which a popular reputation is kept up to the highest selling mark, will always be subject to lulls too capricious for explanation. But whatever the causes, here was the undeniable fact of a grave depreciation of sale in his writings, unaccompanied by any falling off either in themselves or in the writer's reputa-

London: 1843.

Sale of Chuzzlewit:

Less than that of former books.

LONDON:
1843.
tion. It was very temporary; but it was present, and to be dealt with accordingly. The forty and fifty thousand purchasers of *Pickwick* and *Nickleby*, the sixty and seventy thousand of the early numbers of the enterprize in which the *Old Curiosity Shop* and *Barnaby Rudge* appeared, had fallen to little over twenty thousand. They rose somewhat on Martin's ominous announcement, at the end of the fourth number, that he'd *go to America;* but though it was believed that this resolve, which Dickens adopted as suddenly as his hero, might increase the number of his readers, that reason influenced him less than the challenge to make good his *Notes* which every mail had been bringing him from unsparing assailants beyond the

Effect of American episode.
Atlantic. The substantial effect of the American episode upon the sale was yet by no means great. A couple of thousand additional purchasers were added, but the highest number at any time reached before the story closed was twenty-three thousand. Its sale, since, has ranked next after *Pickwick* and *Copperfield*.

Publishers and authors.
We were now, however, to have a truth brought home to us which few that have had real or varied experience in such matters can have failed to be impressed by—that publishers are bitter bad judges of an author, and are seldom safe persons to consult in regard to the fate or fortunes

Pages 101-3 of Vol. II.
that may probably await him. Describing the agreement for this book in September 1841, I spoke of a provision against the improbable event of its profits proving inadequate to certain neces-

sary repayments. In this unlikely case, which LONDON:
1843. was to be ascertained by the proceeds of the first five numbers, the publishers were to have power to appropriate fifty pounds a month out of *Unlucky clause in Chuzzlewit agreement.* the two hundred pounds payable for authorship in the expenses of each number; but though this had been introduced with my knowledge, I knew also too much of the antecedent relations of the parties to regard it as other than a mere form to satisfy the attorneys in the case. The fifth number, which landed Martin and Mark in America, and the sixth, which described their first experiences, *Critical time for the story.* were published; and on the eve of the seventh, in which Mrs. Gamp was to make her first appearance, I heard with infinite pain that from Mr. Hall, the younger partner of the firm which had enriched itself by *Pickwick* and *Nickleby*, and a very kind well-disposed man, there had dropped an inconsiderate hint to the writer of those books *Premature fears.* that it might be desirable to put the clause in force. It had escaped him without his thinking of all that it involved; certainly the senior partner, whatever amount of as thoughtless sanction he had at the moment given to it, always much regretted it, and made endeavours to exhibit his regret; but the mischief was done, and for the time was irreparable.

"I am so irritated," Dickens wrote to me on *Resentment.* the 28th of June, "so rubbed in the tenderest "part of my eyelids with bay-salt, by what I told "you yesterday, that a wrong kind of fire is burn- "ing in my head, and I don't think I *can* write,

LONDON:
1843.

Resolve to
have other
publishers.

"Nevertheless, I am trying. In case I should "succeed, and should not come down to you this "morning, shall you be at the club or elsewhere "after dinner? I am bent on paying the money. "And before going into the matter with anybody "I should like you to propound from me the one "preliminary question to Bradbury and Evans. "It is more than a year and a half since Clowes "wrote to urge me to give him a hearing, in case "I should ever think of altering my plans. A "printer is better than a bookseller, and it is quite "as much the interest of one (if not more) to join "me. But whoever it is, or whatever, I am bent "upon paying Chapman and Hall *down*. And "when I have done that, Mr. Hall shall have a "piece of my mind."

Pages 151, 201
of Vol. I. and
27 of Vol. II.

What he meant by the proposed repayment will be understood by what formerly was said of his arrangements with these gentlemen on the re-purchase of his early copyrights. Feeling no surprise at this announcement, I yet prevailed with him to suspend proceedings until his return from Broadstairs in October; and what then I had to

A proposal to
his printers.

say led to memorable resolves. The communication he had desired me to make to his printers had taken them too much by surprise to enable them to form a clear judgment respecting it; and they replied by suggestions which were in effect a confession of that want of confidence in themselves. They enlarged upon the great results that would follow a re-issue of his writings in a cheap form; they strongly urged such an undertaking; and they offered to invest to any desired amount in the establishment of a magazine or other periodical to be edited by him. The possible dangers, in short, incident to their assuming the position of publishers as well as printers of new works from his pen, seemed at first to be so much greater than on closer examination they were found to be, that at the outset they shrank from encountering them. And hence the remarkable letter I shall now quote (1st of November, 1843).

"Don't be startled by the novelty and extent "of my project. Both startled *me* at .first; but I "am well assured of its wisdom and necessity. I "am afraid of a magazine—just now. I don't "think the time a good one, or the chances "favourable. I am afraid of putting myself be-"fore the town as writing tooth and nail for "bread, headlong, after the close of a book taking "so much out of one as *Chuzzlewit.* I am afraid "I could not do it, with justice to myself. I know "that whatever we may say at first, a new maga-"zine, or a new anything, would require so much "propping, that I should be *forced* (as in the *Clock*) "to put myself into it, in my old shape. I am "afraid of Bradbury and Evans's desire to force "on the cheap issue of my books, or any of them, "prematurely. I am sure if it took place yet "awhile, it would damage me and damage the "property, *enormously.* It is very natural in them "to want it; but, since they do want it, I have "no faith in their regarding me in any other re-

LONDON:
1843.

"spect than they would regard any other man in
"a speculation. I see that this is really your
"opinion as well; and I don't see what I gain, in
"such a case, by leaving Chapman and Hall. If
"I had made money, I should unquestionably
"fade away from the public eye for a year, and
"enlarge my stock of description and observation

Desire to
travel again.'
"by seeing countries new to me; which it is most
"necessary to me that I should see, and which
"with an increasing family I can scarcely hope to
"see at all, unless I see them now. Already for
"some time I have had this hope and intention
"before me; and though not having made money
"yet, I find or fancy that I can put myself in the
"position to accomplish it. And this is the course
"I have before me. At the close of *Chuzzlewit*
"(by which time the debt will have been mate-

Page 27 of
Vol. II.
"rially reduced) I purpose drawing from Chap-
"man and Hall my share of the subscription—
"bills, or money, will do equally well. I design
"to tell them that it is not likely I shall do any-
"thing for a year; that, in the meantime, I make
"no arrangement whatever with any one; and our
"business matters rest *in statu quo*. The same to
"Bradbury and Evans. I shall let the house if I

A plan for
seeing foreign
cities.
"can; if not, leave it to be let. I shall take all
"the family, and two servants—three at most—to
"some place which I know beforehand to be
"CHEAP and in a delightful climate, in Normandy
"or Brittany, to which I shall go over, first, and
"where I shall rent some house for six or eight
"months. During that time, I shall walk through

"Switzerland, cross the Alps, travel through France LONDON: 1843.
"and Italy; take Kate perhaps to Rome and
"Venice, but not elsewhere; and in short see
"everything that is to be seen. I shall write my
"descriptions to you from time to time, exactly as
"I did in America; and you will be able to judge
"whether or not a new and attractive book may
"not be made on such ground. At the same Other books in his mind.
"time I shall be able to turn over the story I
"have in my mind, and which I have a strong
"notion might be published with great advantage,
"*first in Paris*—but that's another matter to be
"talked over. And of course I have not yet
"settled, either, whether any book about the travel,
"or this, should be the first. 'All very well,'
"you say, 'if you had money enough.' Well, but
"if I can see my way to what would be neces- Ways and means.
"sary without binding myself in any form to any-
"thing; without paying interest, or giving any
"security but one of my Eagle five thousand
"pounds; you would give up that objection. And Self-de- pendence.
"I stand committed to no bookseller, printer,
"money-lender, banker, or patron whatever; and
"decidedly strengthen my position with my readers,
"instead of weakening it, drop by drop, as I
"otherwise must. Is it not so? and is not the
"way before me, plainly this? I infer that in
"reality you do yourself think, that what I first
"thought of is *not* the way? I have told you my
"scheme very baldly, as I said I would. I see its
"great points, against many prepossessions the
"other way—as, leaving England, home, friends,

London:
1842.

"everything I am fond of—but it seems to me,
"at a critical time, *the* step to set me right. A
"blessing on Mr. Mariotti my Italian master, and
"his pupil!—If you have any breath left, tell
"Topping how you are."

Objections to
the scheme.
I had certainly not much after reading this
letter, written amid all the distractions of his work,
with both the *Carol* and *Chuzzlewit* in hand; but
such insufficient breath as was left to me I spent
against the project, and in favour of far more
consideration than he had given to it, before anything should be settled. "I expected you," he
wrote next day (the 2nd of November), "to be
"startled.   If I was startled myself, when I first
"got this project of foreign travel into my head,
"MONTHS AGO, 'how much more must you
"be, on whom it comes fresh: numbering only
"hours! Still, I am very resolute upon it—very.
"I am convinced that my expenses abroad would
"not be more than half of my expenses here; the
"influence of change and nature upon me, enor-

Ills own
opinion of
Chuzzlewit.
"mous. You know, as well as I, that I think *Chuz-*
"*zlewit* in a hundred points immeasurably the
"best of my stories. That I feel my power now,

Confidence in
himself.
"more than I ever did. That I have a greater
"confidence in myself than I ever had. That I
"*know*, if I have health, I could sustain my place
"in the minds of thinking men, though fifty writers
"started up to-morrow. But how many readers
"do *not* think! How many take it upon trust
"from knaves and idiots, that one writes too fast,
"or runs a thing to death! How coldly did this

"very book go on for months, until it forced itself
"up in people's opinion, without forcing itself up
"in sale! If I wrote for forty thousand Forsters, or
"for forty thousand people who know I write be-
"cause I can't help it, I should have no need to
"leave the scene. But this very book warns me
"that if I *can* leave it for a time, I had better
"do so, and must do so. Apart from that again,
"I feel that longer rest after this story would do
"me good. You say two or three months, because
"you have been used to see me for eight years
"never leaving off. But it is not rest enough. It
"is impossible to go on working the brain to that
"extent for ever. The very spirit of the thing, in
"doing it, leaves a horrible despondency behind,
"when it is done; which must be prejudicial to
"the mind, so soon renewed, and so seldom let
"alone. What would poor Scott have given to
"have gone abroad, of his own free will, a young
"man, instead of creeping there, a driveller, in
"his miserable decay! I said myself in my note to
"you—anticipating what you put to me—that it
"was a question *what* I should come out with,
"first. The travel-book, if to be done at all, would
"cost me very little trouble; and surely would go
"very far to pay charges, whenever published.
"We have spoken of the baby, and of leaving it
"here with Catherine's mother. Moving the chil-
"dren into France could not, in any ordinary
"course of things, do them anything but good.
"And the question is, what it would do to that
"by which they live: not what it would do to

London:
1843.

A suggestion
of his printers.
"them.—I had forgotten that point in the B. and "E. negociation; but they certainly suggested instant publication of the reprints, or at all events "of some of them; by which of course I know, "and as you point out, I could provide of myself "what is wanted. I take that as putting the thing "distinctly as a matter of trade, and feeling it so.

Not acceptable.
"And, as a matter of trade with them or anybody "else, as a matter of trade between me and the "public, should I not be better off a year hence, "with the reputation of having seen so much in "the meantime? The reason which induces you "to look upon this scheme with dislike—separation "for so long a time—surely has equal weight with

Bent on his
own plan.
"me. I see very little pleasure in it, beyond the "natural desire to have been in those great scenes; "I anticipate no enjoyment at the time. I have "come to look upon it as a matter of policy and "duty. I have a thousand other reasons, but shall "very soon myself be with you."

There were difficulties, still to be strongly urged, against taking any present step to a final resolve; and he gave way a little. But the pressure was soon renewed. "I have been," he wrote (10th of November), "all day in *Chuzzlewit* ago-"nies—conceiving only. I hope to bring forth "to-morrow. Will you come here at six? I want "to say a word or two about the cover of the

Preparation
of *Carol*.
"*Carol* and the advertising, and to consult you "on a nice point in the tale. It will come won-"derfully I think. Mac will call here soon after, "and we can then all three go to Bulwer's to-

"gether. And do, my dear fellow, do for God's
"sake turn over about Chapman and Hall, and
"look upon my project as *a settled thing*. If you
"object to see them, I must write to them." My
reluctance as to the question affecting his old
publishers was connected with the little story,
which, amid all his perturbations and troubles
and "*Chuzzlewit* agonies," he was steadily carrying to its close; and which remains a splendid
proof of how thoroughly he was borne out in the
assertion just before made, of the sense of his
power felt by him, and his confidence that it had
never been greater than when his readers were
thus falling off from him. He had entrusted the
Carol for publication on his own account, under
the usual terms of commission, to the firm he had
been so long associated with; and at such a
moment to tell them, short of absolute necessity,
his intention to quit them altogether, I thought
a needless putting in peril of the little book's
chances. He yielded to this argument; but the
issue, as will be found, was less fortunate than I
hoped.

Let disappointments or annoyances, however,
beset him as they might, once heartily in his work
and all was forgotten. His temperament of course
coloured everything, cheerful or sad, and his
present outlook was disturbed by imaginary fears;
but it was very certain that his labours and successes thus far had enriched others more than
himself, and while he knew that his mode of living had been scrupulously governed by what he

London:
1843.
believed to be his means, the first suspicion that these might be inadequate made a change necessary to so upright a nature. It was the turning-point of his career; and the issue, though not immediately, ultimately justified him. Much of

Not restless-
ness merely.
his present restlessness I was too ready myself to ascribe to that love of change in him which was always arising from his passionate desire to vary and extend his observation; but even as to this the result showed him right in believing that he should obtain decided intellectual advantage from the mere effects of such farther travel. Here indeed he spoke from experience, for already he had returned from America with wider views than when he started, and with a larger maturity of

Solid grounds
for course
taken.
mind. The money difficulties on which he dwelt were also, it is now to be admitted, unquestionable. Beyond his own domestic expenses necessarily increasing, there were many, never-satisfied, constantly-recurring claims from family quarters, not the more easily avoidable because unreasonable and unjust; and it was after describing to me one such with great bitterness, a few days following the letter last quoted, that he thus replied on the following day (19th of November)

Work and its
interruptions.
to the comment I had made upon it. "I was "most horribly put out for a little while; for I "had got up early to go at it, and was full of "interest in what I had to do. But having eased "my mind by that note to you, and taken a turn "or two up and down the room, I went at it again, "and soon got so interested that I blazed away

"till 9 last night; only stopping ten minutes for
"dinner! I suppose I wrote eight printed pages of
"*Chuzzlewit* yesterday. The consequence is that
"I *could* finish to-day, but am taking it easy, and
"making myself laugh very much." The very next
day, unhappily, there came to himself a repetition of precisely similar trouble in exaggerated
form, and to me a fresh reminder of what was
gradually settling into a fixed resolve. "I am
"quite serious and sober when I say, that I have
"very grave thoughts of keeping my whole men-
"agerie in Italy, three years."

Of the book which awoke such varied feelings
and was the occasion of such vicissitudes of
fortune, some notice is now due; and this, following still as yet my former rule, will be not so
much critical as biographical. He had left for
Italy before the completed tale was published,
and its reception for a time was exactly what his
just-quoted letter prefigures. It had forced itself
up in public opinion without forcing itself up in
sale. It was felt generally to be an advance
upon his previous stories, and his own opinion
is not to be questioned that it was in a hundred
points immeasurably the best of them thus far;
less upon the surface, and going deeper into
springs of character. Nor would it be difficult
to say, in a single word, where the excellence
lay that gave it this superiority. It had brought
his highest faculty into play: over and above

As to Martin Chuzzlewit.

Superiority to former books.

other qualities it had given scope to his imagination; and it first expressed the distinction in this
respect between his earlier and his later books.
Apart wholly from this, too, his letters will have
confirmed a remark already made upon the degree to which his mental power had been altogether deepened and enlarged by the effect of
his visit to America.

In construction and conduct of story *Martin
Chuzzlewit* is defective, character and description
constituting the chief part of its strength. But
what it lost as a story by the American episode
it gained in the other direction; young Martin,
by happy use of a bitter experience, casting off
his slough of selfishness in the poisonous swamp
of Eden. Dickens often confessed, however, the
difficulty it had been to him to have to deal
with this gap in the main course of his narrative;

and I will give an instance from a letter he wrote
to me when engaged upon the number in which
Jonas brings his wife to her miserable home. "I
"write in haste" (28th of July 1843), "for I have
"been at work all day; and, it being against the
"grain with me to go back to America when my
"interest is strong in the other parts of the tale,
"have got on but slowly. I have a great notion
"to work out with Sydney's favourite,* and long

---

* Chuffey. Sydney Smith had written to Dickens on the
appearance of his fourth number (early in April): "Chuffey
"is admirable . . . . I never read a finer piece of writing: it
"is deeply pathetic and affecting."

"to be at him again." But obstructions of this kind with Dickens measured only and always the degree of readiness and resource with which he rose to meet them, and never had his handling of character been so masterly as in *Chuzzlewit*. The persons delineated in former books had been Handling of more agreeable, but never so interpenetrated with character. meanings brought out with a grasp so large, easy, and firm. As well in this as in the passionate vividness of its descriptions, the imaginative power makes itself felt. The windy autumn Descriptions. night, with the mad desperation of the hunted leaves and the roaring mirth of the blazing village forge; the market-day at Salisbury; the winter walk, and the coach journey to London by night; the ship voyage over the Atlantic; the stormy midnight travel before the murder, the stealthy enterprise and cowardly return of the murderer; these are all instances of first-rate description, original in the design, imaginative in all the de- Imaginative tail, and very complete in the execution. But the insight. higher power to which I direct attention is even better discerned in the persons and dialogue. With nothing absent or abated in its sharp impressions of reality, there are more of the subtle requisites which satisfy reflection and thought. We have in this book for the most part, not only observation but the outcome of it, the knowledge as well as the fact. While we witness as vividly the life immediately passing, we are more conscious of the permanent life above and beyond it. Nothing nearly so effective therefore had yet been achieved by him. He had scrutinised as truly and satirised as keenly; but had never shown the imaginative insight with which he now sent his humour and his art into the core of the vices of the time.

Sending me the second chapter of his eighth number on the 15th of August, he gave me the latest tidings from America. "I gather from a "letter I have had this morning that Martin has "made them all stark staring raving mad across "the water. I wish you would consider this. "Don't you think the time has come when I "ought to state that such public entertainments "as I received in the States were either accepted "before I went out, or in the first week after my "arrival there; and that as soon as I began to "have any acquaintance with the country, I set "my face against any public recognition whatever "but that which was forced upon me to the de- "struction of my peace and comfort—and made "no secret of my real sentiments." We did not agree as to this, and the notion was abandoned; though his correspondent had not overstated the violence of the outbreak in the States when those chapters exploded upon them. But though an angry they are a good humoured and a very placable people; and, as time moved on a little, the laughter on that side of the Atlantic became quite as great as our amusement on this side, at the astonishing fun and comicality of these scenes. With a little reflection the Americans had doubtless begun to find out that the ad-

News from
America.

Page 163 of
Vol. II.

American
anger short-
lived.

Its consola-
tions.

vantage was not all with us, nor the laughter
wholly against them.

London:
1843-4.

They had no Pecksniff at any rate. Bred in
a more poisonous swamp than their Eden, of
greatly older standing and much harder to be
drained, Pecksniff was all our own. The confession is not encouraging to national pride, but
this character is so far English, that though our
countrymen as a rule are by no means Pecksniffs, the ruling weakness is to countenance and
encourage the race. When people call the
character exaggerated, and protest that the lines
are too broad to deceive any one, they only refuse, naturally enough, to sanction in a book
what half their lives is passed in tolerating if not
in worshipping. Dickens, illustrating his never-
failing experience of being obliged to subdue in
his books what he knew to be real for fear it
should be deemed impossible, had already made
the remark in his preface to *Nickleby*, that the
world, which is so very credulous in what professes to be true, is most incredulous in what
professes to be imaginary. They agree to
be deceived in a reality, and reward themselves by refusing to be deceived in a fiction.
That a great many people who might have sat
for Pecksniff, should condemn him for a grotesque
impossibility, as Dickens averred to be the case,
was no more than might be expected. A greater
danger he has exposed more usefully in showing
the greater numbers, who, desiring secretly to
be thought better than they are, support eagerly

A worse
swamp than
Eden.

Difficulties
that attend
reality.

Critical com-
promises.

pretensions that keep their own in countenance, and, without being Pecksniffs, render Pecksniffs possible. All impostures would have something too suspicious or forbidding in their look if we were not prepared to meet them half way.

There is one thing favourable to us however, even in this view, which a French critic has lately suggested. Informing us that there are no
Pecksniffs to be found in France, Mr. Taine explains this by the fact that his countrymen have ceased to affect virtue, and pretend only to vice; that a charlatan setting up morality would have no sort of following; that religion and the domestic virtues have gone so utterly to rags as not to be worth putting on for a deceitful garment; and that, no principles being left to parade, the only chance for the French modern Tartuffe is to confess and exaggerate weaknesses. We
seem to have something of an advantage here. We require at least that the respectable homage of vice to virtue should not be omitted. "Charity, "my dear," says our English Tartuffe, upon being bluntly called what he really is, "when I take my "chamber-candlestick to-night, remind me to be "more than usually particular in praying for Mr. "Anthony Chuzzlewit, who has done me an in-"justice." No amount of self-indulgence weakens or lowers his pious and reflective tone. "Those "are her daughters," he remarks, making maudlin overtures to Mrs. Todgers in memory of his deceased wife. "Mercy and Charity, Charity and

"Mercy, not unholy names I hope. She was London:
1843-4.
"beautiful. She had a small property." When
his condition has fallen into something so much
worse than maudlin that his friends have to put
him to bed, they have not had time to descend
the staircase when he is seen to be "fluttering"
on the top landing, desiring to collect their sentiments on the nature of human life. "Let us be Homage of
vice to virtue.
"moral. Let us contemplate existence." He turns
his old pupil out of doors in the attitude of
blessing him, and when he has discharged that
social duty retires to shed his personal tribute of
a few tears in the back garden. No conceivable
position, action, or utterance finds him without
the vice in which his being is entirely steeped
and saturated. Of such consummate consistency
is its practice with him, that in his own house
with his daughters he continues it to keep his
hand in; and from the mere habit of keeping up
appearances, even to himself, falls into the trap
of Jonas. Thackeray used to say that there was A favourite
scene of
Thackeray's.
nothing finer in rascaldom than this ruin of Pecksniff by his son-in-law at the very moment when
the oily hypocrite believes himself to be achieving
his masterpiece of dissembling over the more
vulgar avowed ruffian. "'Jonas!' cried Mr. Peck-
"sniff much affected, 'I am not a diplomatical
"'character; my heart is in my hand. By far the
"'greater part of the inconsiderable savings I
"'have accumulated in the course of—I hope—
"'a not dishonourable or useless career, is al-
"'ready given, devised, or bequeathed (correct

"'me, my dear Jonas, if I am technically wrong),
"'with expressions of confidence which I will not
"'repeat; and in securities which it is unneces-
"'sary to mention; to a person whom I cannot,
"'whom I will not, whom I need not, name.'
"Here he gave the hand of his son-in-law a
"fervent squeeze, as if he would have added,
"'God bless you: be very careful of it when you
"'get it!'"

Certainly Dickens thus far had done nothing
of which, as in this novel, the details were filled in
with such minute and incomparable skill; where
the wealth of comic circumstance was lavished in
such overflowing abundance on single types of
character; or where generally, as throughout the
story, the intensity of his observation of individual humours and vices had taken so many va-

rieties of imaginative form. Everything in *Chuzzlewit* indeed had grown under treatment, as will
be commonly the case in the handling of a man of
genius, who never knows where any given conception may lead him, out of the wealth of resource
in development and incident which it has itself
created. "As to the way," he wrote to me of its
two most prominent figures, as soon as all their
capabilities were revealed to him, "As to the way
"in which these characters have opened out, that

"is, to me, one of the most surprising processes
"of the mind in this sort of invention. Given
"what one knows, what one does not know springs
"up; and I am as absolutely certain of its being
"true, as I am of the law of gravitation—if such

"a thing be possible, more so." The remark dis-LONDON:
1843-4.
plays exactly what in all his important characters
was the very process of creation with him.

Nor was it in the treatment only of his present fiction, but also in its subject or design, that
he had gone higher than in preceding efforts.
Broadly what he aimed at, he would have expressed on the title-page if I had not dissuaded
him, by printing there as its motto a verse *
altered from that prologue of his own composition to which I have formerly referred: "Your Intended
motto for the
story.
"homes the scene. Yourselves, the actors, here!"
Debtors' prisons, parish Bumbledoms, Yorkshire
schools, were vile enough, but something much
more pestiferous was now the aim of his satire;
and he had not before so decisively shown vigour,
daring, or discernment of what lay within reach
of his art, as in taking such a person as Pecksniff for the central figure in a tale of existing life.
Setting him up as the glass through which to
view the groups around him, we are not the less Grand purpose of its
satire.
moved to a hearty detestation of the social vices
they exhibit, and pre-eminently of selfishness in
all its forms, because we see more plainly than
ever that there is but one vice which is quite ir-
remediable. The elder Chuzzlewits are bad enough,
but they bring their self-inflicted punishments;
the Jonases and Tigg Montagues are execrable,
but the law has its halter and its penal servitude;
the Moulds and Gamps have plague-bearing breaths,
from which sanitary wisdom may clear us; but
from the sleek, smiling, crawling abomination of

LONDON:
1843-4.
The vices be-
yond reach of
law.
a Pecksniff, there is no help but self-help. Every
man's hand should be against him, for his is
against every man; and, as Mr. Taine very wisely
warns us, the virtues have most need to be careful that they do not make themselves panders to
his vice. It is an amiable weakness to put the
best face on the worst things, but there is none
more dangerous. There is nothing so common
as the mistake of Tom Pinch, and nothing so rare
as his excuses.

The art with which that delightful character is
placed at Mr. Pecksniff's elbow at the beginning of
the story, and the help he gives to set fairly afloat
the falsehood he innocently believes, contribute
to an excellent management of this part of the
design; and the same prodigal wealth of invention
and circumstance which gives its higher imaginative stamp to the book, appears as vividly in its
lesser as in its leading figures. There are wonderful touches of this suggestive kind in the household
of Mould the undertaker; and in the vivid picture
presented to us by one of Mrs. Gamp's recollections,
we are transported to the youthful games of his
children. "The sweet creeturs! playing at berryins
"down in the shop, and follerin' the order-book
"to its long home in the iron safe!" The American scenes themselves are not more full of life
and fun and freshness, and do not contribute more
to the general hilarity, than the cockney group
at Todgers's; which is itself a little world of the
qualities and humours that make up the interest
of human life, whether it be high or low, vulgar

or fine, filled in with a master's hand.   Here, in
a mere byestroke as, it were, are the very finest
things of the earlier books superadded to the new
and higher achievement that distinguished the
later productions.   No part indeed of the execution of this remarkable novel is inferior.   Young
Bailey and Sweedlepipes are in the front rank of his
humorous creations; and poor Mrs. Todgers, worn
but not depraved by the cares of gravy and soli-
citudes of her establishment, with calculation shining out of one eye but affection and goodhearted-
ness still beaming in the other, is in her way
quite as perfect a picture as even the portentous
Mrs. Gamp with her grim grotesqueness, her
filthy habits and foul enjoyments, her thick and
damp but most amazing utterances, her moist
clammy functions, her pattens, her bonnet, her
bundle, and her umbrella.   But such prodigious
claims must have a special mention.

This world-famous personage has passed into
and become one with the language, which her
own parts of speech have certainly not exalted or
refined.   To none even of Dickens's characters
has there been such a run of popularity; and she
will remain among the everlasting triumphs of
fiction, a superb masterpiece of English humour.
What Mr. Mould says of her in his enthusiasm,
that she's the sort of woman one would bury for
nothing, and do it neatly too, every one feels to
be an appropriate tribute; and this, by a most
happy inspiration, is exactly what the genius to
whom she owes her existence did, when he called

her into life; to the foul original she was taken from. That which enduringly stamped upon his page its most mirth-moving figure, had stamped out of English life for ever one of its disgraces. The mortal Mrs. Gamp was handsomely put into her grave, and only the immortal Mrs. Gamp survived. Age will not wither this one, nor custom stale her variety. In the latter point she has an advantage over even Mr. Pecksniff. She has a friend, an alter ego, whose kind of service to her is expressed by her first utterance in the story; and with this, which introduces her, we may leave her most fitly. "'Mrs. Harris,' I says, "at the very "last case as ever I acted in, which it was but a "young person, 'Mrs. Harris,' I says, 'leave the "'bottle on the chimley-piece, and don't ask me "'to take none, but let me put my lips to it when "'I am so dispoged.' 'Mrs. Gamp,' she says in "answer, 'if ever there was a sober creetur to be "'got at eighteen pence a day for working people, "'and three and six for gentlefolks—night watch- "'ing,' said Mrs. Gamp with emphasis, 'being a "'extra charge—you are that inwallable person.' "'Mrs. Harris,' I says to her, 'don't name the "'charge, for if I could afford to lay all my "'fellow-creeturs out for nothink, I would gladly "'do it, sich is the love I bears 'em.'" To this there is nothing to be added, except that in the person of that astonishing friend every phase of fun and comedy in the character is repeated, under fresh conditions of increased appreciation and enjoyment. By the exuberance of comic in-

Fiction and reality.

Mrs. Harris.

Uses of Mrs. Gamp's friend.

London:
1843-4.

vention which gives his distinction to Mr. Pecksniff,
Mrs. Gamp profits quite as much; the same wealth
of laughable incident which surrounds that worthy
man is upon her heaped to overflowing; but over
and above this, by the additional invention of
Mrs. Harris, it is all reproduced, acted over with
renewed spirit, and doubled and quadrupled in
her favour. This on the whole is the happiest
stroke of humorous art in all the writings of
Dickens.

But this is a chapter of disappointments, and
I have now to state, that as *Martin Chuzzlewit's*
success was to seem to him at first only distant
and problematical so even the prodigious immediate success of the *Christmas Carol* itself was
not to be an unmitigated pleasure. Never had
little book an outset so full of brilliancy of
promise. Published but a few days before Christmas, it was hailed on every side with enthusiastic
greeting. The first edition of six thousand copies
was sold the first day, and on the third of January
1844 he wrote to me that "two thousand of the
"three printed for second and third editions are
"already taken by the trade." But a very few
weeks were to pass before the darker side of the
picture came. "Such a night as I have passed!"
he wrote to me on Saturday morning the 10th of
February. "I really believed I should never get
"up again, until I had passed through all the
"horrors of a fever. I found the *Carol* accounts
"awaiting me, and they were the cause of it. The

Publication
of Christmas
Carol.

Sale and
accounts.

"first six thousand copies show a profit of £230!
"And the last four will yield as much more. I
"had set my heart and soul upon a Thousand,
"clear. What a wonderful thing it is, that such
"a great success should occasion me such in-
"tolerable anxiety and disappointment! My year's
"bills, unpaid, are so terrific, that all the energy
"and determination I can possibly exert will be
"required to clear me before I go abroad; which,
"if next June come and find me alive, I shall do.
"Good Heaven, if I had only taken heart a year
"ago! Do come soon, as I am very anxious to
"talk with you. We can send round to Mac after
"you arrive, and tell him to join us at Hampstead
"or elsewhere. I was so utterly knocked down
"last night, that I came up to the contemplation
"of all these things quite bold this morning. If

"I can let the house for this season, I will be off
"to some seaside place as soon as a tenant offers.
"I am not afraid, if I reduce my expenses; but if
"I do not, I shall be ruined past all mortal hope
"of redemption."

The ultimate result was that his publishers
were changed, and the immediate result that his
departure for Italy became a settled thing; but a
word may be said on these *Carol* accounts before mention is made of his new publishing arrangements.* Want of judgment had been shown

---

* It may interest the reader, and be something of a
curiosity of literature, if I give the expenses of the first edition
of 6000, and of the 7000 more which constituted the five

in not adjusting the expenses of production with
a more equable regard to the selling price, but

following editions, with the profit of the remaining 2000
which completed the sale of fifteen thousand:

CHRISTMAS CAROL.   Publishers'
accounts:

1st Edition, 6000 No.

1843.		£	s.	d.
Dec.	Printing	74	2	9
	Paper	89	2	0
	Drawings and Engravings . . .	49	18	0
	Two Steel Plates	1	4	0
	Printing Plates	15	17	6
	Paper for do.	7	12	0
	Colouring Plates	120	0	0
	Binding	180	0	0
	Incidents and Advertising . .	168	7	8
	Commission	99	4	6
		£805	8	5

2nd to the 7th Edition, making 7000 Copies.

1844.		£	s.	d.
Jan.	Printing	58	18	0
	Paper	103	19	0
	Printing Plates	17	10	0
	Paper	8	17	4
	Colouring Plates	140	0	0
	Binding	199	18	2
	Incidents and Advertising . . .	83	5	8
	Commission	107	18	10
		£720	7	0

Two thousand more, represented by the last item in the On sale of
subjoined balance, were sold before the close of the year, 15,000 copies.
leaving a remainder of 70 copies.

1843.			£	s.	d.
Dec. Balance of a/c to Mr. Dickens's credit			186	16	7
1844.					
Jan. to April.	Do.	Do.	349	12	0
May to Dec.	Do.	Do.	189	11	5
Amount of Profit on the Work			£726	0	0

even as it was, before the close of the year, he
had received £726 from a sale of fifteen thousand
copies; and the difference between this and the
amount realised by the same proportion of the
sale of the successor to the *Carol*, undoubtedly
justified him in the discontent now expressed.
Of that second tale, as well as of the third and
fourth, more than double the numbers of the
Carol were at once sold, and of course there was
no complaint of any want of success: but the
truth really was, as to all the Christmas stories
issued in this form, that the price charged, while
too large for the public addressed by them, was
too little to remunerate their outlay; and when in
later years he put forth similar fancies for Christmas, charging for them fewer pence than the
shillings required for these, he counted his
purchasers, with fairly corresponding gains to
himself, not by tens but by hundreds of thousands.*

It was necessary now that negotiations should
be resumed with his printers, but before any step
was taken Messrs. Chapman and Hall were informed of his intention not to open fresh publishing relations with them after *Chuzzlewit* should
have closed.   Then followed deliberations and
discussions, many and grave, which settled themselves at last into the form of an agreement with

---

* In November 1865 he wrote to me that the sale of his
Christmas fancy for that year (*Doctor Marigold's Prescriptions*)
had gone up, in the first week, to 250,000.

Messrs. Bradbury and Evans executed on the first London, 1844.
of June 1844; by which, upon advance made to Agreement
him of £2800, he assigned to them a fourth share with Brad-
bury and
in whatever he might write during the next ensuing Evans.
eight years, to which the agreement was to be
strictly limited. There were the usual protecting
clauses, but no interest was to be paid, and no
obligations were imposed as to what works should
be written, if any, or the form of them; the only
farther stipulation having reference to the event Proposed
of a periodical being undertaken whereof Dickens periodical.
might be only partially editor or author, in which
case his proprietorship of copyright and profits
was to be two thirds instead of three fourths.
There was an understanding, at the time this
agreement was signed, that a successor to the
Carol would be ready for the Christmas of 1844;
but no other promise was asked or made in Books.
regard to any other book, nor had he himself
decided what form to give to his experiences of
Italy, if he should even finally determine to
publish them at all.

Between this agreement and his journey six
weeks elapsed, and there were one or two characteristic incidents before his departure: but mention must first be interposed of the success quite As to the
without alloy that also attended the little book, Carol.
and carried off in excitement and delight every
trace of doubt or misgiving.

"Blessings on your kind heart!" wrote Jeffrey
to the author of the *Carol*. "You should be happy
"yourself, for you may be sure you have done

London:
1841.
Jeffrey and
Thackeray.
"more good by this little publication, fostered
"more kindly feelings, and prompted more positive
"acts of beneficence, than can be traced to all
"the pulpits and confessionals in Christendom
"since Christmas 1842." "Who can listen," ex-
claimed Thackeray, "to objections regarding such
"a book as this? It seems to me a national benefit,
"and to every man or woman who reads it a
"personal kindness." Such praise expressed what
men of genius felt and said; but the small volume
had other tributes, less usual and not less genuine.
There poured upon its author daily, all through
Letters from
strangers.
that Christmas time, letters from complete strangers
to him which I remember reading with a wonder
of pleasure; not literary at all, but of the simplest
domestic kind; of which the general burden was
to tell him, amid many confidences about their
homes, how the *Carol* had come to be read aloud
there, and was to be kept upon a little shelf by
itself, and was to do them all no end of good.
Anything more to be said of it will not add much
to this.

Message of
the little
book.
There was indeed nobody that had not some
interest in the message of the *Christmas Carol*.
It told the selfish man to rid himself of selfishness; the just man to make himself generous; and
the good-natured man to enlarge the sphere of
his good nature. Its cheery voice of faith and
hope, ringing from one end of the island to the
other, carried pleasant warning alike to all, that
if the duties of Christmas were wanting no good
could come of its outward observances; that it

must shine upon the cold hearth and warm it, London: 1844.
and into the sorrowful heart and comfort it; that
it must be kindness, benevolence, charity, mercy,
and forbearance, or its plum pudding would turn
to bile, and its roast beef be indigestible.* Nor
could any man have said it with the same appro-
priateness as Dickens. What was marked in him C. D. iden-
to the last was manifest now. He had identified tified with Christmas.
himself with Christmas fancies. Its life and spirits,
its humour in riotous abundance, of right belonged
to him. Its imaginations as well as kindly thoughts,
were his; and its privilege to light up with some
sort of comfort the squalidest places, he had made
his own. Christmas Day was not more social or
welcome: New Year's Day not more new: Twelfth

---

* A characteristic letter of this date, which will explain
itself, has been kindly sent to me by the gentleman it was
written to, Mr. James Verry Staples, of Bristol:—"Third of
"April, 1844. I have been very much gratified by the receipt
"of your interesting letter, and I assure you that it would
"have given me heartfelt satisfaction to have been in your
"place when you read my little *Carol* to the Poor in your
"neighbourhood. I have great faith in the poor; to the best
"of my ability I always endeavour to present them in a
"favourable light to the rich; and I shall never cease, I
"hope, until I die, to advocate their being made as happy
"and as wise as the circumstances of their condition, in its
"utmost improvement, will admit of their becoming. I
"mention this to assure you of two things. Firstly, that I
"try to deserve their attention; and secondly, that any such
"marks of their approval and confidence as you relate to
"me are most acceptable to my feelings, and go at once to
"my heart."

Night not more full of characters. The duty of diffusing enjoyment had never been taught by a more abundant, mirthful, thoughtful, ever-seasonable writer.

Something also is to be said of the spirit of the book, and of the others that followed it, which will not anticipate special allusions to be made hereafter. No one was more intensely fond than Dickens of old nursery tales, and he had a secret delight in feeling that he was here only giving them a higher form. The social and manly virtues he desired to teach, were to him not less the charm of the ghost, the goblin, and the fairy fancies of his childhood; however rudely set forth in those earlier days. What now were to be conquered were the more formidable dragons and giants which had their places at our own hearths, and the weapons to be used were of a finer than the "ice-brook's temper." With brave and strong restraints, what is evil in ourselves was to be subdued; with warm and gentle sympathies, what is bad or unreclaimed in others was to be redeemed;

the Beauty was to embrace the Beast, as in the divinest of all those fables; the star was to rise out of the ashes, as in our much-loved Cinderella; and we were to play the Valentine with our wilder brothers, and bring them back with brotherly care to civilization and happiness. Nor is it to be doubted, I think, that, in that largest sense of benefit, great public and private service was done; positive, earnest, practical good; by the extraordinary popularity, and nearly universal accept-

Loxpon:
1811.

Something
better than
literature.

ance, which attended these little holiday volumes. They carried to countless firesides, with new enjoyment of the season, better apprehension of its claims and obligations; they mingled grave with glad thoughts, much to the advantage of both; what seemed almost too remote to meddle with they brought within reach of the charities, and what was near they touched with a dearer tenderness; they comforted the generous, rebuked the sordid, cured folly by kindly ridicule and comic humour, and, saying to their readers *Thus you have done, but it were better Thus*, may for some have realised the philosopher's famous experience, and by a single fortunate thought revised the whole manner of a life. Criticism here is a second-rate thing, and the reader may be spared such discoveries as it might have made in regard to the *Christmas Carol*.

CHAPTER XXVIII.

YEAR OF DEPARTURE FOR ITALY.

1844.

London: 1844.

AND now, before accompanying Dickens on his Italian travel, one or two parting incidents will receive illustration from his letters. A thoughtful little poem written during the past summer for Lady Blessington has been quoted on a previous page: and it may remind me to say here what warmth of regard he had for her, and for Gore-house. all the inmates of Gore-house; how uninterruptedly joyous and pleasurable were his associations with them; and what valued help they now gave in his preparations for Italy. The poem, as we have seen, was written during a visit made in Yorkshire friends. Yorkshire to the house of Mr. Smithson, already named as the partner of his early companion, Mr. Mitton; and this visit he repeated in sadder circumstances during the present year, when (April 1844) he attended Mr. Smithson's funeral. With members or connections of the family of this friend, his intercourse long continued.

In the previous February, on the 26th and 28th respectively, he had taken the chair at two

great meetings, in Liverpool of the Mechanics' LONDON: 1844.
Institution, and in Birmingham of the Polytechnic Liverpool and
Institution, to which reference is made by him in Birmingham Institutes.
a letter of the 21st. I quote the allusion because
it shows thus early the sensitive regard to his position as a man of letters, and his scrupulous consideration for the feelings as well as interest of
the class, which he manifested in many various
and often greatly self-sacrificing ways all through
his life. "Advise me on the following point. And
"as I must write to-night, having already lost a
"post, advise me by bearer. This Liverpool In- A question of
"stitution, which is wealthy and has a high gram- receiving pay-
"mar-school the masters of which receive in
"salaries upwards of £2000 a year (indeed its
"extent horrifies me; I am struggling through its
"papers this morning), writes me yesterday by its
"secretary a business letter about the order of the
"proceedings on Monday; and it begins thus. 'I
"'beg to send you prefixed, with the best respects
"'of our committee, a bank order for twenty pounds
"'in payment of the expenses contingent on your
"'visit to Liverpool.'—And there, sure enough, it
"is. Now my impulse was, *and is*, decidedly to
"return it. Twenty pounds is not of moment to
"me; and any sacrifice of independence is worth
"it twenty times' twenty times told. But haggling Sensitive for
"in my mind is a doubt whether that would be his calling.
"proper, and not boastful (in an inexplicable way);
"and whether as an author, I have a right to put
"myself on a basis which the professors of litera-
"ture in other forms *connected with the Institu-*

"*lion* cannot afford to occupy. Don't you see?
"But of course you do. The case stands thus.
"The Manchester Institution, being in debt,
"appeals to me as it were *in formâ pauperis*, and
"makes no such provision as I have named. The
"Birmingham Institution, just struggling into life
"with great difficulty, applies to me on the same
"grounds. But the Leeds people (thriving) write
"to me, making the expenses a distinct matter of
"business; and the Liverpool, as a point of de-
"licacy, say nothing about it to the last minute,
"and then send the money. Now, what in the
"name of goodness ought I to do?—I am as much
"puzzled with the cheque as Colonel Jack was
"with his gold. If it would have settled the matter
"to put it in the fire yesterday, I should certainly
"have done it. Your opinion is requested. I
"think I shall have grounds for a very good
"speech at Brummagem; but I am not sure about
"Liverpool: having misgivings of over-gentility."
My opinion was clearly for sending the money
back, which accordingly was done.

Both speeches, duly delivered to enthusiastic
listeners at the places named, were good, and
both, with suitable variations, had the same theme:
telling his popular audience in Birmingham that
the principle of their institute, education com-
prehensive and unsectarian, was the only safe one,
for that without danger no society could go on
punishing men for preferring vice to virtue without giving them the means of knowing what virtue
was; and reminding his genteeler audience in

Liverpool, that if happily they had been themselves well taught, so much the more should they
seek to extend the benefit to all, since, whatever
the precedence due to rank, wealth, or intellect,
there was yet a nobility beyond them, expressed
unaffectedly by the poet's verse and in the power
of education to confer.

> Howe'er it be, it seems to me,
>   'Tis only noble to be good:
> True hearts are more than coronets,
>   And simple faith than Norman blood.

He underwent some suffering, which he might
have spared himself, at his return. "I saw the
"*Carol* last night," he wrote to me of a dramatic
performance of the little story at the Adelphi.
"Better than usual, and Wright seems to enjoy
"Bob Cratchit, but *heart-breaking* to me. Oh
"Heaven! if any forecast of *this* was ever in my
"mind! Yet O. Smith was drearily better than I
"expected. It is a great comfort to have that
"kind of meat under done; and his face is quite
"perfect." Of what he suffered from these adapta-
tions of his books, multiplied remorselessly, at
every theatre, I have forborne to speak, but it
was the subject of complaint with him incessantly; and more or less satisfied as he was with
individual performances, such as Mr. Yates's
Quilp or Mantalini and Mrs. Keeley's Smike or
Dot, there was only one, that of Barnaby Rudge
by the Miss Fortescue who became afterwards
Lady Gardner, on which I ever heard him dwell

LONDON:
1841.
His own share
in them.
with a thorough liking. It is true that to the dramatizations of his next and other following Christmas stories he gave help himself; but, even then, all such efforts to assist special representations were mere attempts to render more tolerable what he had no power to prevent, and, with a few rare exceptions, they were never very suc-
Wrongs from piracy.
cessful. Another and graver wrong was the piracy of his writings, every one of which had been reproduced with merely such colourable changes of title, incidents, and names of characters, as were believed to be sufficient to evade the law and adapt them to "penny" purchasers. So shamelessly had this been going on ever since the days of *Pickwick*, in so many outrageous ways* and with all but impunity, that a course repeatedly urged by Talfourd and myself
Proceedings
in Chancery.
was at last taken in the present year with the *Christmas Carol* and the *Chuzzlewit* pirates. Upon a case of such peculiar flagrancy, however, that the vice-chancellor would not even hear Dickens's counsel; and what it cost our dear friend Talfourd to suppress his speech exceeded by very

A pirate's
plea.
* In a letter on the subject of copyright published by Thomas Hood after Dickens's return from America, he described what had passed between himself and one of these pirates who had issued a Master Humphrey's Clock edited by Boz. "Sir," said the man to Hood, "if you had ob-"served the name, it was *Bos*, not *Boz*; s, sir, not z; and, "besides, it would have been no piracy, sir, even with the z, "because *Master Humphrey's Clock*, you see, sir, was not "published as by Boz, but by Charles Dickens!"

much the labour and pains with which he had
prepared it. "'The pirates," wrote Dickens to me,
after leaving the court on the 18th of January,
"are beaten flat. They are bruised, bloody, bat-
"tered, smashed, squelched, and utterly undone.
"Knight Bruce would not hear Talfourd, but in-
"stantly gave judgment. He had interrupted
"Anderdon constantly by asking him to produce
"a passage which was not an expanded or con-
"tracted idea from my book. And at every
"successive passage he cried out, 'That is Mr.
"'Dickens's case. Find another!' He said that
"there was not a shadow of doubt upon the
"matter. That there was no authority which
"would bear a construction in their favour; the
"piracy going beyond all previous instances.
"They might mention it again in a week, he
"said, if they liked, and might have an issue if
"they pleased; but they would probably consider
"it unnecessary after that strong expression of
"his opinion. Of course I will stand by what
"we have agreed as to the only terms of com-
"promise with the printers. I am determined
"that I will have an apology for their affidavits.
"The other men may pay their costs and get out
"of it, but I will stick to my friend the author."
Two days later he wrote: "The farther affidavits
"put in by way of extenuation by the printing
"rascals *are* rather strong, and give one a pretty
"correct idea of what the men must be who hold
"on by the heels of literature. Oh! the agony
"of Talfourd at Knight Bruce's not hearing him!

London:
1844.

Judge and
counsel.

End of
Chancery
suit.

Hangers-on
of literature.

"He had sat up till three in the morning, he
"says, preparing his speech; and would have
"done all kinds of things with the affidavits. It
"certainly was a splendid subject. We have
"heard nothing from the vagabonds yet. I once
"thought of printing the affidavits without a word
"of comment, and sewing them up with *Chuzzle-*
"*wit*. Talfourd is strongly disinclined to com-
"promise with the printers on any terms. In
"which case it would be referred to the master
"to ascertain what profits had been made by the
"piracy, and to order the same to be paid to me.
Wear and tear
of law. "But wear and tear of law is my consideration."
The undertaking to which he had at last to submit was, that upon ample public apology, and
payment of all costs, the offenders should be let
go; but the real result was that, after infinite
vexation and trouble, he had himself to pay all
the costs incurred on his own behalf; and, a
couple of years later, upon repetition of the
wrong he had suffered in so gross a form that
Result of
Chancery
experience. proceedings were again advised by Talfourd and
others, he wrote to me from Switzerland the condition of mind to which his experience had
brought him. "My feeling about the——is the
"feeling common, I suppose, to three fourths of
"the reflecting part of the community in our hap-
"piest of all possible countries; and that is, that
"it is better to suffer a great wrong than to have
"recourse to the much greater wrong of the
Never again
to resort to it. "law. I shall not easily forget the expense, and
"anxiety, and horrible injustice of the *Carol* case,

"wherein, in asserting the plainest right on earth, LONDON: 1844.
"I was really treated as if I were the robber in-
"stead of the robbed. Upon the whole, I certainly
"would much rather NOT proceed. What do you
"think of sending in a grave protest against what Piracy pre-
"has been done in this case, on account of the ferred.
"immense amount of piracy to which I am daily
"exposed, and because I have been already met
"in the court of chancery with the legal doctrine
"that silence under such wrongs barred my
"remedy: to which Talfourd's written opinion
"might be appended as proof that we stopped
"under no discouragement. It is useless to affect
"that I don't know I have a morbid susceptibility A confusion.
"of exasperation, to which the meanness and bad-
"ness of the law in such a matter would be
"stinging in the last degree. And I know of no-
"thing that *could* come, even of a successful ac-
"tion, which would be worth the mental trouble
"and disturbance it would cost."*

---

* The reader may be amused if I add in a note what he
said of the pirates in those earlier days when grave matters
touched him less gravely. On the eve of the first number
of *Nickleby* he had issued a proclamation. "Whereas we Proclamation
"are the only true and lawful Boz. And whereas it hath on the eve of
"been reported to us, who are commencing a new work, that *Nickleby.*
"some dishonest dullards resident in the by-streets and cellars
"of this town impose upon the unwary and credulous, by
"producing cheap and wretched imitations of our delectable
"works. And whereas we derive but small comfort under
"this injury from the knowledge that the dishonest dullards
"aforesaid cannot, by reason of their mental smallness,

London:
1844.
Reliefs to
work.

A few notes of besetting temptations during his busiest days at *Chuzzlewit*, one taken from each of the first four months of the year when he was working at its masterly closing scenes, will amusingly exhibit, side by side, his powers of resistance and capacities of enjoyment. "I had "written you a line" (16th of January), "pleading

"follow near our heels, but are constrained to creep along "by dirty and little-frequented ways, at a most respectful "and humble distance behind. And whereas, in like man- "ner, as some other vermin are not worth the killing for the "sake of their carcases, so these kennel pirates are not worth "the powder and shot of the law, inasmuch as whatever "damages they may commit they are in no condition to pay

Warning to
pirates.

"any. · This is to give notice, that we have at length devised "a mode of execution for them, so summary and terrible, "that if any gang or gangs thereof presume to hoist but one "shred of the colours of the good ship *Nickleby*, we will "hang them on gibbets so lofty and enduring that their re- "mains shall be a monument of our just vengeance to all suc- "ceeding ages; and it shall not lie in the power of any lord "high admiral, on earth, to cause them to be taken down "again." The last paragraph of the proclamation informed the potentates of Paternoster-row, that from the then ensuing

Invitation to
booksellers.

day of the thirtieth of March, until farther notice, "we shall "hold our Levees, as heretofore, on the last evening but one "of every month, between the hours of seven and nine, at "our Board of Trade, number one hundred and eighty-six in "the Strand, London; where we again request the attendance "(in vast crowds) of their accredited agents and ambassadors. "Gentlemen to wear knots upon their shoulders; and patent "cabs to draw up with their doors towards the grand en- "trance, for the convenience of loading."

"Jonas and Mrs. Gamp, but this frosty day tempts LONDON:
1844.
"me sorely. I am distractingly late; but I look
"at the sky, think of Hampstead, and feel hideously
"tempted. Don't come with Mac, and fetch me. The tempted.
"I couldn't resist if you did." In the next (18th
of February), he is not the tempted, but the
tempter. "Stanfield and Mac have come in, and
"we are going to Hampstead to dinner. I leave
"Betsey Prig as you know, so don't you make a
"scruple about leaving Mrs. Harris. We shall The tempter.
"stroll leisurely up, to give you time to join us,
"and dinner will be on the table at Jack Straw's
"at four. . . . In the very improbable (surely im-
"possible?) case of your not coming, we will call
"on you at a quarter before eight, to go to the
"ragged school." The next (5th of March) shows
him in yielding mood, and pitying himself for his
infirmity of compliance. "Sir, I will—he—he—
"he—he—he—he—I will NOT eat with you, either
"at your own house or the club. But the morning
"looks bright, and a walk to Hampstead would
"suit me marvellously. If you should present
"yourself at my gate (bringing the R. A.'s along
"with you) I shall not be sapparized. So no
"more at this writing from Poor MR. DICKENS."
But again the tables are turned, and he is tempter
in the last; written on that Shakespeare day (23rd Shakespeare-
day.
of April) which we kept always as a festival, and
signed in character expressive of his then present
unfitness for any of the practical affairs of life,
including the very pressing business which at the
moment ought to have occupied him, namely,

London:
1844.
attention to the long deferred nuptials of Miss
Charity Pecksniff. "November blasts! Why it's
"the warmest, most genial, most intensely bland,
"delicious, growing, springy, songster-of-the-grovy,
"bursting-forth-of-the-buddy, day as ever was. At
"half-past four I shall expect you. Ever, MODDLE."

A favourite
bit of humour:
Moddle, the sentimental noodle hooked by
Miss Pecksniff who flies on his proposed wedding-
day from the frightful prospect before him, the
reader of course knows; and has perhaps admired
for his last supreme outbreak of common sense.
It was a rather favourite bit of humour with
Dickens; and I find it pleasant to think that he
never saw the description given of it by a trained
and skilful French critic, who has been able to
pass under his review the whole of English literature without any apparent sense or understanding of one of its most important as well as richest
elements. A man without the perception of humour

criticized
without
humour.
taking English prose literature in hand, can of
course set about it only in one way. Accordingly,
in Mr. Taine's decisive judgments of our last great
humourist, which proceed upon a principle of
psychological analysis which it is only fair to say
he applies impartially to everybody, *Pickwick*,

M. Henri
Taine on C. D.
Oliver Twist, and *The Old Curiosity Shop* are not
in any manner even named or alluded to; Mrs.
Gamp is only once mentioned as always talking
of Mrs. Harris; and Mr. Micawber also only once
as using always the same emphatic phrases; the
largest extracts are taken from the two books in
all the Dickens series that are weakest on the

humorous side, *Hard Times* and the *Chimes;* *Nickleby*, with its many laughter-moving figures, is dismissed in a line and a half; Mr. Toots, Captain Cuttle, Susan Nipper, Toodles, and the rest have no place in what is said of *Dombey;* and, to close with what has caused and must excuse my digression, Mr. Augustus Moddle is introduced as a gloomy maniac who makes us laugh and makes us shudder, and as drawn so truly for a madman that though at first sight agreeable, he is in reality horrible!*

Moddle as a maniac.

A month before the letter subscribed by Dickens in the character, so happily unknown

---

* This might seem not very credible if I did not give the passage literally, and I therefore quote it from the careful translation of *Taine's History of English Literature* by Mr. Van Laun, one of the masters of the Edinburgh Academy, where I will venture to hope that other authorities on English Literature are at the same time admitted. "Jonas" (also in *Chuzzlewit*) "is on the verge of madness. There are other "characters quite mad. Dickens has drawn three or four "portraits of madmen, very agreeable at first sight, but so "true that they are in reality horrible. It needed an imagi-"nation like his, irregular, excessive, capable of fixed ideas, "to exhibit the derangements of reason. Two especially "there are, which make us laugh, and which make us shud-"der. Augustus, the gloomy maniac, who is on the point "of marrying Miss Pecksniff; and poor Mr. Dick, half an "idiot, half a monomaniac, who lives with Miss Trotwood ". . . . The play of these shattered reasons is like the creak-"ing of a dislocated door; it makes one sick to hear it." (Vol. ii. p. 346.) The original was published before Dickens's death, but he certainly never saw it.

Taine on English literature.

LONDON:
1844.

to himself, of this gloomy maniac, he had written
to me from amidst his famous chapter in which
the tables are turned on Pecksniff; but here I
quote the letter chiefly for noticeable words at

Macready in
New Orleans.

its close. "I heard from Macready by the Hibernia.
"I have been slaving away regularly, but the weather
"is against rapid progress. I altered the verbal
"error, and substituted for the action you didn't
"like some words expressive of the hurry of the
"scene. Macready sums up slavery in New Orleans
"in the way of a gentle doubting on the subject,
"by a 'but' and a dash. I believe it is in New
"Orleans that the man is lying under sentence of
"death, who, not having the fear of God before
"his eyes, did not deliver up a captive slave to

Slavery in
America.

"the torture? The largest gun in that country has
"not burst yet—*but it will*. Heaven help us, too,
"from explosions nearer home! I declare I never
"go into what is called 'society' that I am not
"aweary of it, despise it, hate it, and reject it.

Society in
England.

"The more I see of its extraordinary conceit, and
"its stupendous ignorance of what is passing out
"of doors, the more certain I am that it is ap-
"proaching the period when, being incapable of
"reforming itself, it will have to submit to be re-
"formed by others off the face of the earth."
Thus we see that the old radical leanings were
again rather strong in him at present, and I may
add that he had found occasional recent vent for

Writing in the
Chronicle.

them by writing in the *Morning Chronicle*.
    Some articles thus contributed by him having
set people talking, the proprietors of the paper

rather eagerly mooted the question what payment he would ask for contributing regularly; and ten guineas an article was named. Very sensibly, however, the editor who had succeeded his old friend Black pointed out to him, that though even that sum would not be refused in the heat of the successful articles just contributed, yet (I quote his own account in a letter of the 7th of March 1844) so much would hardly be paid continuously; and thereupon an understanding was come to, that he would write as a volunteer and leave his payment to be adjusted to the results. "Then "said the editor—and this I particularly want you "to turn over in your mind, at leisure—supposing "me to go abroad, could I contemplate such a "thing as the writing of a letter a week under "any signature I chose, with such scraps of de- "scriptions and impressions as suggested them- "selves to my mind? If so, would I do it for the "*Chronicle?* And if so again, what would I do it "for? He thought for such contributions Easthope "would pay anything. I told him that the idea "had never occurred to me; but that I was afraid "he did not know what the value of such con- "tributions would be. He repeated what he had "said before; and I promised to consider whether "I could reconcile it to myself to write such letters "at all. The pros and cons need to be very care- "fully weighed. I will not tell you to which side "I incline, but if we should disagree, or waver "on the same points, we will call Bradbury and "Evans to the council. I think it more than

"probable that we shall be of exactly the same
"mind, but I want you to be in possession of the
"facts and therefore send you this rigmarole."

The rigmarole is not unimportant; because, though
we did not differ on the wisdom of saying No
to the *Chronicle*, the "council" spoken of was
nevertheless held, and in it lay the germ of
another newspaper enterprise he permitted himself to engage in twelve months later, to which
he would have done more wisely to have also
answered No.

The preparation for departure was now actively
going forward, and especially his enquiries for
two important adjuncts thereto, a courier and a
carriage. As to the latter it occurred to him that
he might perhaps get for little money "some good
"old shabby devil of a coach—one of those vast
"phantoms that hide themselves in a corner of
"the Pantechnicon;" and exactly such a one he
found there; sitting himself inside it, a perfect
Sentimental Traveller, while the managing man
told him its history. "As for comfort—let me
"see—it is about the size of your library; with
"night-lamps and day-lamps and pockets and
"imperials and leathern cellars, and the most
"extraordinary contrivances. Joking apart, it is a
"wonderful machine. And when you see it (if
"you *do* see it) you will roar at it first, and will
"then proclaim it to be 'perfectly brilliant, my
"'dear fellow.'" It was marked sixty pounds; he
got it for five-and-forty; and my own emotions
respecting it he had described by anticipation

quite correctly. In finding a courier he was even more fortunate; and these successes were followed by a third apparently very promising, but in the result less satisfactory. His house was let to not very careful people.

The tenant having offered herself for Devonshire-terrace unexpectedly, during the last week or two of his stay in England he went into temporary quarters in Osnaburgh-terrace; and here a domestic difficulty befell of which the mention may be amusing, when I have disposed of an incident that preceded it too characteristic for omission. The Mendicity Society's officers had caught a notorious begging-letter writer, had identified him as an old offender against Dickens of which proofs were found on his person, and had put matters in train for his proper punishment; when the wretched creature's wife made such appeal before the case was heard at the police-court, that Dickens broke down in his character of prosecutor, and at the last moment, finding what was said of the man's distress at the time to be true, relented. "When the Mendicity "officers themselves told me the man was in dis-"tress, I desired them to suppress what they "knew about him, and slipped out of the bundle "(in the police office) his first letter, which was "the greatest lie of all. For he looked wretched, "and his wife had been waiting about the street "to see me, all the morning. It was an exceed-"ingly bad case however, and the imposition, all "through, very great indeed. Insomuch that I

LONDON: 1844. Courier.

In temporary quarters.

Page 31 of Vol. II.

Begging-letter case.

"could not *say* anything in his favour, even when
"I saw him.   Yet I was not sorry that the crea-
"ture found the loophole for escape.   The of-
"ficers had taken him illegally without any war-
"rant; and really they messed it all through, quite
"facetiously."

He will himself also best relate the small
domestic difficulty into which he fell in his temporary dwelling, upon his unexpectedly discover-
ing it to be unequal to the strain of a dinner
party for which invitations had gone out just
before the sudden "let" of Devonshire-terrace.

The letter is characteristic in other ways, or I
should hardly have gone so far into domesticities
here; and it enables me to add that with the last
on its list of guests, Mr. Chapman the chairman
of Lloyd's, he held much friendly intercourse,
and that few things more absurd or unfounded
have been invented, even of Dickens, than that
he found any part of the original of Mr. Dombey
in the nature, the appearance, or the manners of
this estimable gentleman.   "Advise, advise," he
wrote (9 Osnaburgh-terrace, 28th of May 1844),
"advise with a distracted man.   Investigation
"below stairs renders it, as my father would say,
"'manifest to any person of ordinary intelligence,
"'if the term may be considered allowable,' that
"the Saturday's dinner cannot come off here with
"safety.   It would be a toss-up, and might come
"down heads, but it would put us into an agony
"with that kind of people . . Now, I feel a diffi-
"culty in dropping it altogether, and really fear

"that this might have an indefinably suspicious
"and odd appearance.   Then said I at breakfast
"this morning, I'll send down to the Clarendon.
" Then says Kate, have it at Richmond.   Then I
"say, that might be inconvenient to the people.
"Then she says, how could it be if we dine late
"enough?   Then I am very much offended with-
"out exactly knowing why; and come up here, in
"a state of hopeless mystification . . What do you
"think? Ellis would be quite as dear as anybody
"else; and unless the weather changes, the place
"is objectionable.   I must make up my mind to
"do one thing or other, for we shall meet Lord
"Denman at dinner to-day.   Could it be dropped
"decently?   That, I think very doubtful.   Could
"it be done for a couple of guineas apiece at the
"Clarendon? . . In a matter of more importance
"I could make up my mind.   But in a matter of
"this kind I bother and bewilder myself, and
"come to no conclusion whatever.   Advise! Ad-
"vise! . . List of the Invited.   There's Lord Nor-
"manby.   And there's Lord Denman.   There's
"Easthope, wife, and sister.   There's Sydney Smith.
"There's you and Mac.   There's Babbage.   There's
"a Lady Osborne and her daughter.   There's
"Southwood Smith.   And there's Quin.   And there
"are Thomas Chapman and his wife.   So many
"of these people have never dined with us, that
"the fix is particularly tight.   Advise! Advise!"
My advice was for throwing over the party altogether, but additional help was obtained and the

London:
1844.

Letter-
opening.

"The Even-
"ings of a
"Working-
"man."

Death of John
Overs.

'dinner went off very pleasantly. It was the last time we saw Sydney Smith.

Of one other characteristic occurrence he wrote before he left; and the very legible epigraph round the seal of his letter, "It is particularly "requested that if Sir James Graham should open "this, he will not trouble himself to seal it again," expresses both its date and its writer's opinion of a notorious transaction of the time. "I wish" (28th of June) "you would read this, and give it "me again when we meet at Stanfield's to-day. "Newby has written to me to say that he hopes "to be able to give Overs more money than was "agreed on." The enclosure was the proof-sheet of a preface written by him to a small collection of stories by a poor carpenter dying of consumption, who hoped by their publication, under protection of such a name, to leave behind him some small provision for his ailing wife and little children.* The book was dedicated to the kind

* He wrote from Marseilles (17th Dec. 1844). "When "poor Overs was dying he suddenly asked for a pen and ink "and some paper, and made up a little parcel for me which "it was his last conscious act to direct. She (his wife) told "me this and gave it me. I opened it last night. It was a "copy of his little book in which he had written my name, "'With his devotion.' I thought it simple and affecting of "the poor fellow." From a later letter a few lines may be added. "Mrs. Overs tells me" (Monte Vacchi, 30th March, 1845) "that Miss Coutts has sent her, at different times, "sixteen pounds, has sent a doctor to her children, and has "got one of the girls into the Orphan School. When I

physician, Doctor Elliotson, whose name was for nearly thirty years a synonym with us all for un- wearied, self-sacrificing, beneficent service to every one in need.

The last incident before Dickens's departure was a farewell dinner to him at Greenwich, which took also the form of a celebration for the completion of *Chuzzlewit*, or, as the Ballantynes used to call it in Scott's case, a christening dinner; when Lord Normanby took the chair, and I remember sitting next the great painter Turner, who had come with Stanfield, and had enveloped his throat, that sultry summer day, in a huge red belcher-handkerchief which nothing would induce him to remove. He was not otherwise demon- strative, but enjoyed himself in a quiet silent way, less perhaps at the speeches than at the changing lights on the river. Carlyle did not come; telling me in his reply to the invitation that he truly loved Dickens, having discerned in the inner man of him a real music of the genuine kind, but that he'd rather testify to this in some other form than that of dining out in the dog-days.

"wrote her a word in the poor woman's behalf, she wrote
"me back to the effect that it was a kindness to herself to
"have done so, "for 'what is the use of my means but to
"'try and do some good with them?'"

CHAPTER XXIX.

IDLENESS AT ALBARO: VILLA BAGNERELLO.

1844.

MARSEILLES
1844.

The travel.

New ex-
periences.

THE travelling party arrived at Marseilles on the evening of Sunday the 14th of July. Not being able to get vetturino horses in Paris, they had come on, post; paying for nine horses but bringing only four, and thereby saving a shilling a mile out of what the four would have cost in England. So great thus far, however, had been the cost of travel, that "what with distance, cara-"van, sight-seeing, and everything," two hundred pounds would be nearly swallowed up before they were at their destination. The success otherwise had been complete. The children had not cried in their worst troubles, the carriage had gone lightly over abominable roads, and the courier had proved himself a perfect gem. "Surrounded "by strange and perfectly novel circumstances," Dickens wrote to me from Marseilles, "I feel as "if I had a new head on side by side with my "old one."

To what shrewd and kindly observation the old .one had helped him at every stage of his

journey, his published book of travel tells, and of Marseilles:
1844.
all that there will be nothing here; but a couple
of experiences at his outset, of which he told me
afterwards, have enough character in them to be
worth mention.

Shortly before there had been some public
interest about the captain of a Boulogne steamer
apprehended on a suspicion of having stolen
specie, but reinstated by his owners after a
public apology to him on their behalf; and
Dickens had hardly set foot on the boat that was
to carry them across, when he was attracted by A character:
the look of its captain, and discovered him after
a few minutes' talk to be that very man. "Such
"an honest, simple, good fellow, I never saw,"
said Dickens, as he imitated for me the homely
speech in which his confidences were related.
The Boulogne people, he said, had given him a
piece of plate, "but Lord bless us! it took a deal honesty
under cloud.
"more than that to get him round again in his
"own mind; and for weeks and weeks he was
"uncommon low to be sure. Newgate, you see!
"What a place for a sea-faring man as had held
"up his head afore the best on 'em, and had
"more friends, I mean to say, and I do tell you
"the daylight truth, than any man on this station
"—ah! or any other, I don't care where!"

His first experience in a foreign tongue he
made immediately on landing, when he had gone
to the bank for money, and after delivering with
most laborious distinctness a rather long address French
thrown away.
in French to the clerk behind the counter, was

ALBARO
1844.

disconcerted by that functionary's cool enquiry in
the native-born Lombard-street manner, "How
would you like to take it, sir?" He took it, as
everybody must, in five-franc pieces, and a most
inconvenient coinage he found it; for he required
so much that he had to carry it in a couple of
small sacks, and was always "turning hot about
suddenly" taking it into his head that he had
lost them.

Villa taken
for him.

The evening of Tuesday the 16th of July saw
him in a villa at Albaro, the suburb of Genoa in
which, upon the advice of our Gore-house friends,
he had resolved to pass the summer months before taking up his quarters in the city. His wish
was to have had Lord Byron's house there, but it
had fallen into neglect and become the refuge of
a third-rate wineshop. The matter had then been
left to Angus Fletcher who just now lived near
Genoa, and he had taken at a rent absurdly above
its value* an unpicturesque and uninteresting

Page 73 of
Vol. II.

A house he
might have
had.

* He regretted one chance missed by his eccentric friend,
which he described to me just before he left Italy. "I saw
"last night an old palazzo of the Doria, six miles from here,
"upon the sea, which De la Rue urged Fletcher to take for
"us, when he was bent on that detestable villa Bagnerello;
"which villa the Genoese have hired, time out of mind, for
"one fourth of what I paid, as they told him again and again
"before he made the agreement. This is one of the strangest
"old palaces in Italy, surrounded by beautiful *woods* of great
"trees (an immense rarity here) some miles in extent: and
"has upon the terrace a high tower, formerly a prison for
"offenders against the family, and a defence against the

dwelling, which at once impressed its new tenant ALBARO: 1844.
with its likeness to a pink jail. "It is," he said Account of it.
to me, "the most perfectly lonely, rusty, stagnant
"old staggerer of a domain that you can possibly
"imagine. What would I give if you could only
"look round the courtyard! *I* look down into it,
"whenever I am near that side of the house, for
"the stable is so full of 'vermin and swarmers'
"(pardon the quotation from my inimitable friend)
"that I always expect to see the carriage going
"out bodily, with legions of industrious fleas har-
"nessed to and drawing it off, on their own ac-
"count. We have a couple of Italian work-people Italian and English.
"in our establishment; and to hear one or other
"of them talking away to our servants with the
"utmost violence and volubility in Genoese, and
"our servants answering with great fluency in
"English (very loud: as if the others were only
"deaf, not Italian), is one of the most ridiculous
"things possible. The effect is greatly enhanced Pantomimic talk.
"by the Genoese manner, which is exceedingly
"animated and pantomimic; so that two friends

"pirates. The present Doria lets it as it stands for £40
"English—for the year . . . And the grounds are no ex-
"pense; being proudly maintained by the Doria, who spends
"this rent, when he gets it, in repairing the roof and windows.
"It is a wonderful house; full of the most unaccountable
"pictures and most incredible furniture: every room in it
"like the most quaint and fanciful of Cattermole's pictures;
"and how many rooms I am afraid to say." 2nd of June
1845.

"of the lower class conversing pleasantly in the "street, always seem on the eve of stabbing each "other forthwith. And a stranger is immensely "astonished at their not doing it."

Heat.

The heat tried him less than he expected, excepting always the sirocco, which, near the sea as they were, and right in the course of the wind as it blew against the house, made everything hotter than if there had been no wind. "One feels it "most, on first getting up. Then, it is really so "oppressive that a strong determination is neces-"sary to enable one to go on dressing; one's ten-"dency being to tumble down anywhere and lie "there." It seemed to hit him, he said, behind the knee, and made his legs so shake that he could not walk or stand. He had unfortunately a whole week of this without intermission, soon after his arrival; but then came a storm, with wind from the mountains; and he could bear the ordinary heat very well. What at first had been a home-discomfort, the bare walls, lofty ceilings, icy floors, and lattice blinds, soon became agreeable; there were regular afternoon breezes from the sea; in his courtyard was a well of very pure and very cold water; there were new milk and eggs by the bucketful, and, to protect from the summer insects these and other dainties, there were fresh vine-leaves by the thousand; and he satisfied himself, by the experience of a day or two in the city, that he had done well to come first to its suburb by the sea. What startled and disappointed him most were the frequent cloudy

Sirocco.

Country pleasures.

days.* He opened his third letter (3rd of August) Albaro: 1844. by telling me there was a thick November fog, Cloudy that rain was pouring incessantly, and that he weather. did not remember to have seen in his life, at that time of year, such cloudy weather as he had seen beneath Italian skies.

'"The story goes that it is in autumn and win-"ter, when other countries are dark and foggy, "that the beauty and clearness of this are most "observable. I hope it may prove so; for I have "postponed going round the hills which encircle "the city, or seeing any of the sights, until the "weather is more favourable.** I have never yet

* "We have had a London sky until to-day," he wrote London skies. on the 20th of July, "grey and cloudy as you please : but "I am most disappointed, I think, in the evenings, which "are as commonplace as need be; for there is no twilight, "and as to the stars giving more light here than elsewhere, "that is humbug." The summer of 1844 seems to have been, however, an unusually stormy and wet season. He wrote to me on the 21st of October that they had had, so far, only four really clear days since they came to Italy.

** "My faith on that point is decidedly shaken, which Simond's "reminds me to ask you whether you ever read Simond's *Tour in Italy.* "Tour in Italy. It is a most charming book, and eminently "remarkable for its excellent sense, and determination not to "give in to conventional lies." In a later letter he says: "None of the books are unaffected and true but Simond's, "which charms me more and more by its boldness, and its "frank exhibition of that rare and admirable quality which "enables a man to form opinions for himself without a "miserable and slavish reference to the pretended opinions "of other people. His notices of the leading pictures en-

"seen it so clear, for any long time of the day "together, as on a bright, lark-singing, coast-of- "France-discerning day at Broadstairs; nor have "I ever seen so fine a sunset, *throughout*, as is "very common there. But the scenery is exqui- "site, and at certain periods of the evening and "the morning the blue of the Mediterranean sur- "passes all conception or description. It is the "most intense and wonderful colour, I do believe, "in all nature."

In his second letter from Albaro there was more of this subject; and an outbreak of whim- sical enthusiasm in it, meant especially for Maclise, is followed by some capital description. "I address "you, my friend," he wrote, "with something of "the lofty spirit of an exile, a banished commoner, "a sort of Anglo-Pole. I don't exactly know what "I have done for my country in coming away "from it, but I feel it is something; something "great; something virtuous and heroic. Lofty "emotions rise within me, when I see the sun set "on the blue Mediterranean. I am the limpet on "the rock. My father's name is Turner, and my "boots are green . . . Apropos of blue. In a "certain picture called the Serenade for which "Browning wrote that verse* in Lincoln's-inn-

"chant me. They are so perfectly just and faithful, and so "whimsically shrewd," Rome, 9th of March, 1845.

* I send my heart up to thee, all my heart
    In this my singing!
  For the stars help me, and the sea bears part;
    The very night is clinging

"fields, you, O Mac, painted a sky. If you ever Albaro! 1844.
"have occasion to paint the Mediterranean, let it
"be exactly of that colour. It lies before me now,
"as deeply and intensely blue. But no such
"colour is above me. Nothing like it. In the
"south of France, at Avignon, at Aix, at Marseilles, French and
"I saw deep blue skies; and also in America. Italian skies.
"But the sky above me is familiar to my sight.
"Is it heresy to say that I have seen its twin
"brother shining through the window of Jack
"Straw's—that down in Devonshire-terrace I have
"seen a better sky? I dare say it is; but like a
"great many other heresies, it is true. . . . But
"such green, green, green, as flutters in the vine-
"yard down below the windows, *that* I never saw;
"nor yet such lilac and such purple as float be-
"tween me and the distant hills; nor yet in any-
"thing, picture, book, or vestal boredom, such
"awful, solemn, impenetrable blue, as in that same
"sea. It has such an absorbing, silent, deep, pro- The Medi-
"found effect, that I can't help thinking it sug- terranean.
"gested the idea of Styx. It looks as if a draught
"of it, only so much as you could scoop up on
"the beach in the hollow of your hand, would
"wash out everything else, and make a great blue
"blank of your intellect . . . When the sun sets

> Closer to Venice' streets to leave one space
> Above me, whence thy face
> May light my joyous heart to thee its dwelling-place.
> Written to express Maclise's subject in the Academy ca-
> talogue.

"clearly, then, by Heaven, it is majestic. From
"any one of eleven windows here, or from a ter-
"race overgrown with grapes, you may behold the
"broad sea, villas, houses, mountains, forts, strewn
"with rose leaves. Strewn with them! Steeped in
"them! Dyed, through and through and through.
"For a moment. No more. The sun is im-
"patient and fierce (like everything else in these
"parts), and goes down headlong. Run to fetch
"your hat—and it's night. Wink at the right
"time of black night—and it's morning. Every-
The cicala: "thing is in extremes. There is an insect here
"that chirps all day. There is one outside the
"window now. The chirp is very loud: some-
"thing like a Brobdingnagian grasshopper. The
"creature is born to chirp; to progress in chirping;
"to chirp louder, louder, louder; till it gives one
typical in life   "tremendous chirp and bursts itself. That is its
and death.   "life and death. Everything is 'in a concatena-
"'tion accordingly.' The day gets brighter, brighter,
"brighter, till it's night. The summer gets hotter,
"hotter, hotter, till it explodes. The fruit gets
"riper, riper, riper, till it tumbles down and rots
". . . Ask me a question or two about fresco: will
"you be so good? All the houses are painted in
"fresco, hereabout (the outside walls I mean, the
"fronts, backs, and sides), and all the colour has
"run into damp and green seediness; and the very
"design has straggled away into the component
A warning.   "atoms of the plaster. Beware of fresco! Sometimes
"(but not often) I can make out a Virgin with a
"mildewed glory round her head, holding nothing

"in an undiscernible lap with invisible arms; and Albaro: 1844.
"occasionally the leg or arm of a cherub. But it
"is very melancholy and dim. There are two old Perishing
"fresco-painted vases outside my own gate, one on frescoes.
"either hand, which are so faint that I never saw
"them till last night; and only then, because I
"was looking over the wall after a lizard who had
"come upon me while I was smoking a cigar
"above, and crawled over one of these embellish-
"ments in his retreat . . ."

That letter sketched for me the story of his
travel through France, and I may at once say that
I thus received, from week to week, the "first
sprightly runnings" of every description in his
Pictures from Italy. But my rule as to the Nothing in
American letters must be here observed yet more here.
strictly; and nothing resembling his printed book,
however distantly, can be admitted into these
pages. Even so my difficulty of rejection will
not be less; for as he had not actually decided,
until the very last, to publish his present experiences at all, a larger number of the letters
were left unrifled by him. He had no settled plan
from the first, as in the other case.

His most valued acquaintance at Albaro was French
the French consul-general, a student of our litera- Consul of Genoa.
ture who had written on his books in one of the
French reviews, and who with his English wife
lived in the very next villa, though so oddly shut
away by its vineyard that to get from the one
adjoining house to the other was a mile's journey.*

* "Their house is next to ours on the right, with vine-

Albano:
1844.

Describing, in that August letter, his first call from this new friend thus pleasantly self-recommended, he makes the visit his excuse for breaking off from a facetious description of French inns to introduce to me a sketch, from a pencil outline by Fletcher, of what bore the imposing name of the Villa di Bella vista, but which he called by the homelier one of its proprietor, Bagnerello. "This, my friend, is quite accurate. Allow me to "explain it. You are standing, sir, in our vine-"yard, among the grapes and figs. The Mediter-"ranean is at your back as you look at the house: "of which two sides, out of four, are here depicted. "The lower story (nearly concealed by the vines) "consists of the hall, a wine-cellar, and some store-"rooms. The three windows on the left of the "first floor belong to the sala, lofty and white-"washed, which has two more windows round the "corner. The fourth window *did* belong to the "dining-room, but I have changed one of the "nurseries for better air; and it now appertains "to that branch of the establishment. The fifth "and sixth, or two right-hand windows, sir, admit "the light to the inimitable's (and uxor's) chamber; "to which the first window round the right-hand "corner, which you perceive in shadow, also be-"longs. The next window in shadow, young sir, "is the bower of Miss H. The next, a nursery "window; the same having two more round the

Pencil sketch
by Angus
Fletcher.

Rooms in
villa de-
scribed.

"yard between; but the place is so oddly contrived that one "has to go a full mile round to get to their door."

"corner again. The bowery-looking place stretch-
"which opens out from a French window in the
"drawing-room on the same floor, of which you
"see nothing: and forms one side of the court-
"yard. The upper windows belong to some of
"those uncounted chambers upstairs; the fourth
"one, longer than the rest, being in F.'s bedroom.
"There. is a kitchen or two up there besides, and
"my dressing-room: which you can't see from this
"point of view. The kitchens and other offices
"in use are down below, under that part of the
"house where the roof is longest. On your left,

"off, the Alps stretch off into the far horizon; on "your right, at three or four miles distance, are "mountains crowned with forts. The intervening "space on both sides is dotted with villas, "some green, some red, some yellow, some "blue, some (and ours among the number) pink. "At your back, as I have said, sir, is the ocean; "with the slim Italian tower of the ruined church
"of St. John the Baptist rising up before it, "on the top of a pile of savage rocks. You "go through the court-yard, and out at the "gate, and down a narrow lane to the sea. Note. "The sala goes sheer up to the top of the house; "the ceiling being conical, and the little bed- "rooms built round the spring of its arch. You "will observe that we make no pretension to "architectural magnificence, but that we have "abundance of room. And here I am, beholding "only vines and the sea for days together . . .
"Good Heavens! How I wish you'd come for a "week or two, and taste the white wine at a penny "farthing the pint. It is excellent." . . . Then, after seven days: "I have got my paper and ink-
"stand and figures now (the box from Osnaburgh- "terrace only came last Thursday), and can think "—I have begun to do so every morning—with
"a business-like air, of the Christmas book. My "paper is arranged, and my pens are spread "out, in the usual form. I think you know the "form—Don't you? My books have not passed "the custom-house yet, and I tremble for some "volumes of Voltaire . . . I write in the best bed-

"room. The sun is off the corner window at the
"side of the house by a very little after twelve;
"and I can then throw the blinds open, and look
"up from my paper, at the sea, the mountains,
"the washed-out villas, the vineyards, at the blister-
"ing white hot fort with a sentry on the draw-
"bridge standing in a bit of shadow no broader
"than his own musket, and at the sky, as often
"as I like. It is a very peaceful view, and
"yet a very cheerful one. Quiet as quiet can
"be."

Not yet however had the time for writing Work in abeyance.
come. A sharp attack of illness befell his youngest
little daughter, Kate, and troubled him much.
Then, after beginning the Italian grammar himself, he had to call in the help of a master; and
this learning of the language took up time. But Learning Italian.
he had an aptitude for it, and after a month's
application told me (24th of August) that he
could ask in Italian for whatever he wanted in
any shop or coffee-house, and could read it pretty
well. "I wish you could see me" (16th of September), "without my knowing it, walking about
"alone here. I am now as bold as a lion in the
"streets. The audacity with which one begins to
"speak when there is no help for it, is quite
"astonishing." The blank impossibility at the
outset, however, of getting native meanings con-
veyed to his English servants, he very humor- The English servants.
ously described to me; and said the spell was
first broken by the cook, "being really a clever
"woman, and not entrenching herself in that

Albaro,
1844.

"astonishing pride of ignorance which induces
"the rest to oppose themselves to the receipt of
"any information through any channel, and which
"made A. careless of looking out of window, in
"America, even to see the Falls of Niagara." So
that he soon had to report the gain, to all of
them, from the fact of this enterprising woman
having so primed herself with "the names of all
"sorts of vegetables, meats, soups, fruits, and
"kitchen necessaries," that she was able to order
whatever was needful of the peasantry that were
trotting in and out all day, basketed and bare-
footed. Her example became at once contagi-
ous;* and before the end of the second week of

Domestic
news.

September news reached me that "the servants
"are beginning to pick up scraps of Italian; some

May 1845.

* Not however, happily for them, in another important
particular, for on the eve of their return to England she declared her intention of staying behind and marrying an
Italian. "She will have to go to Florence, I find" (12th of
May 1845), "to be married in Lord Holland's house: and
"even then is only married according to the English law:
"having no legal rights from such a marriage, either in
"France or Italy. The man hasn't a penny. If there were
"an opening for a nice clean restaurant in Genoa—which I
"don't believe there is, for the Genoese have a natural en-
"joyment of dirt, garlic, and oil—it would still be a very
"hazardous venture; as the priests will certainly damage the
"man, if they can, for marrying a Protestant woman. How-
"ever, the utmost I can do is to take care, if such a crisis
"should arrive, that she shall not want the means of getting
"home to England. As my father would observe, she has
"sown and must reap."

"of them go to a weekly conversazione of servants
"at the Governor's every Sunday night, having
"got over their consternation at the frequent in-
"troduction of quadrilles on these occasions; and
"I think they begin to like their foreigneering
"life."

In the tradespeople they dealt with at Albaro
he found amusing points of character. Sharp as
they were after money, their idleness quenched
even that propensity. Order for immediate de-
livery two or three pounds of tea, and the tea-
dealer would be wretched. "Won't it do to-
"morrow!" "I want it now," you would reply;
and he would say, "No, no, there can be no
"hurry!" He remonstrated against the cruelty.
But everywhere there was deference, courtesy,
more than civility. "In a café a little tumbler of
"ice costs something less than three-pence, and
"if you give the waiter in addition what you
"would not offer to an English beggar, say, the
"third of a halfpenny, he is profoundly grateful."
The attentions received from English residents
were unremitting.* In moments of need at the

---

* He had carried with him, I may here mention, letters
of introduction to residents in all parts of Italy, of which I
believe he delivered hardly one. Writing to me a couple of
months before he left the country he congratulated himself
on this fact. "We are living very quietly; and I am now
"more than ever glad that I have kept myself aloof from the
"'receiving' natives always, and delivered scarcely any of
"my letters of introduction. If I had, I should have seen
"nothing and known less. I have observed that the English

Albaro:
1844.

English
residents.

City streets.

Genoa the
Superb.

outset, they bestirred themselves ("large merchants
"and grave men") as if they were the family's
salaried purveyors; and there was in especial one
gentleman named Curry whose untiring kindness
was long remembered.

The light, eager, active figure soon made itself familiar in the streets of Genoa, and he never
went into them without bringing some oddity
away. I soon heard of the strada Nuova and
strada Balbi; of the broadest of the two as nar-
rower than Albany-street, and of the other as less
wide than Drury-lane or Wych-street; but both
filled with palaces of noble architecture and of
such vast dimensions that as many windows as
there are days in the year might be counted in
one of them, and this not covering by any means
the largest plot of ground. I heard too of the
other streets, none with footways, and all varying
in degrees of narrowness, but for the most part
like Field-lane in Holborn, with little breathing-
places like St. Martin's-court; and the widest only
in parts wide enough to enable a carriage and
pair to turn. "Imagine yourself looking down a

"women who have married foreigners are invariably the most
"audacious in the license they assume. Think of one lady
"married to a royal chamberlain (not here) who said at
"dinner to the master of the house at a place where I was
"dining—that she had brought back his *Satirist*, but didn't
"think there was quite so much 'fun' in it as there used to
"be. I looked at the paper afterwards, and found it crammed
"with such vile obscenity as positively made one's hair stand
"on end."

"street of Reform Clubs cramped after this odd "fashion, the lofty roofs almost seeming to meet "in the perspective." In the churches nothing struck him so much as the profusion of trash and tinsel in them that contrasted with their real splendours of embellishment. One only, that of the Cappucini friars, blazed every inch of it with gold, precious stones, and paintings of priceless art; the principal contrast to its radiance being the dirt of its masters, whose bare legs, corded waists, and coarse brown serge never changed by night or day, proclaimed amid their corporate wealth their personal vows of poverty. He found them less pleasant to meet and look at than the country people of their suburb on festa-days, with the Indulgences that gave them the right to make merry stuck in their hats like turnpike-tickets. He did not think the peasant girls in general good-looking, though they carried them-selves daintily and walked remarkably well: but the ugliness of the old women, begotten of hard work and a burning sun, with porters' knots of coarse grey hair grubbed up over wrinkled and cadaverous faces, he thought quite stupendous. He was never in a street a hundred yards long without getting up perfectly the witch part of *Macbeth*.

With the theatres of course he soon became acquainted, and of that of the puppets he wrote to me again and again with humorous rapture. "There are other things," he added, after giving me the account which is published in his book,

Albaro:
1844.
The puppets.
"too solemnly surprising to dwell upon. They
"must be seen. They must be seen. The
"enchanter carrying off the bride is not greater
"than his men brandishing fiery torches and
"dropping their lighted spirits of wine 'at every
"shake. Also the enchanter himself, when, hunted
"down and overcome, he leaps into the roll-
"ing sea, and finds a watery grave. Also the
"second comic man, aged about 55 and like
"George the Third in the face, when he gives
"out the play for the next night. They must all
"be seen. They can't be told about. Quite im-
Italian plays. "possible." The living performers he did not
think so good, a disbelief in Italian actors having
been always a heresy with him, and the deplorable length of dialogue to the small amount of
action in their plays making them sadly tiresome.
The first that he saw at the principal theatre was
a version of Balzac's *Père Goriot.* "The domestic
"Lear I thought at first was going to be very
"clever. But he was too pitiful—perhaps the
"Italian reality would be. He was immensely
"applauded, though." He afterwards saw a version
Dumas' *Kean.* of Dumas' preposterous play of *Kean*, in which
most of the representatives of English actors wore
red hats with steeple crowns, and very loose
blouses with broad belts and buckles round their
waists. "There was a mysterious person called
"the Prince of Var-lees" (Wales), "the youngest
"and slimmest man in the company, whose ba-
"dinage in Kean's dressing-room was irresistible;
"and the dresser wore top-boots, a Greek skull-

"cap, a black velvet jacket, and leather breeches.
"One or two of the actors looked very hard at Italian
"me to see how I was touched by these English English.
"peculiarities—especially when Kean kissed his
"male friends on both cheeks." The arrangements of the house, which he described as larger
than Drury-lane, he thought excellent. Instead
of a ticket for the private box he had taken on
the first tier, he received the usual key for ad-
mission which let him in as if he lived there;
and for the whole set-out, "quite as comfortable
"and private as a box at our opera," paid only
eight and fourpence English. The opera itself Opera.
had not its regular performers until after Christmas, but in the summer there was a good' comic
company, and he saw the *Scaramuccia* and the
Barber of Seville brightly and pleasantly done.
There was also a day theatre, beginning at half Day-theatre.
past four in the afternoon; but beyond the novelty
of looking on at the covered stage as he sat in
the fresh pleasant air, he did not find much amusement in the Goldoni comedy put before him.
There came later a Russian circus, which the unusual rains of that summer prematurely extin-
guished.

The Religious Houses he made early and Religious
many enquiries about, and there was one that houses.
had stirred and baffled his curiosity much before he discovered what it really was. All that
was visible from the street was a great high wall,
apparently quite alone, no thicker than a party
wall, with grated windows, to which iron screens

gave farther protection. At first he supposed there
had been a fire; but by degrees came to know that
on the other side were galleries, one above another,
one above another, and nuns always pacing them
to and fro. Like the wall of a racket-ground outside, it was inside a very large nunnery; and let
the poor sisters walk never so much, neither they
nor the passers-by could see anything of each
other. It was close upon the Acqua Sola, too;
a little park with still young but very pretty trees,
and fresh and cheerful fountains, which the Genoese made their Sunday promenade; and under-
neath which was an archway with great public
tanks, where, at all ordinary times, washerwomen
were washing away, thirty or forty together. At
Albaro they were worse off in this matter: the
clothes there being washed in a pond, beaten
with gourds, and whitened with a preparation of
lime: "so that," he wrote to me (24th of August),
"what between the beating and the burning they
"fall into holes unexpectedly, and my white trow-
"sers, after six weeks' washing, would make very
"good fishing-nets. It is such a serious damage
"that when we get into the Peschiere we mean to
"wash at home."

Exactly a fortnight before this date, he had
hired rooms in the Peschiere from the first of the
following October; and so ended the house-hunting for his winter residence, that had taken him
so often to the city. The Peschiere was the
largest palace in Genoa let on hire, and had the
advantage of standing on a height aloof from the

town, surrounded by its own gardens. The rooms
taken had been occupied by an English colonel,
the remainder of whose term was let to Dickens
for 500 francs a month (£20); and a few days
after (20th of August) he described to me a fellow tenant: "A Spanish duke has taken the room A fellow
"under me in the Peschiere. The duchess was his tenant.
"mistress many years, and bore him (I think) six
"daughters. He always promised her that if she
"gave birth to a son, he would marry her; and
"when at last the boy arrived, he went into her Lucky
"bedroom, saying—'Duchess, I am charmed to arrival.
"'salute you!' And he married her in good
"earnest, and legitimatized (as by the Spanish law
"he could) all the other children." The beauty
of the new abode will justify a little description
when he takes up his quarters there. One or two
incidents may be related, meanwhile, of the closing weeks of his residence at Albaro.

In the middle of August he dined with the Dinner at
French consul-general, and there will now be no French consul's.
impropriety in printing his agreeable sketch of the
dinner. "There was present, among other Ge-
"noese, the Marquis di Negri: a very fat and
"much older Jerdan, with the same thickness of
"speech and size of tongue. He was Byron's
"friend, keeps open house here, writes poetry, im-
"provises, and is a very good old Blunderbore;
"just the sort of instrument to make an artesian
"well with, anywhere. Well, sir, after dinner, the Compliment
"consul proposed my health, with a little French to C. D.
"conceit to the effect that I had come to Italy to

"have personal experience of its lovely climate,
"and that there was this similarity between the
"Italian sun and its visitor, that the sun shone
"into the darkest places and made them bright
"and happy with its benignant influence, and that
"my books had done the like with the breasts of

"men, and so forth. Upon which Blunderbore
"gives his bright-buttoned blue coat a great rap
"on the breast, turns up his fishy eye, stretches
"out his arm like the living statue defying the
"lightning at Astley's, and delivers four impromptu
"verses in my honour, at which everybody is en-
"chanted, and I more than anybody—perhaps
"with the best reason, for I didn't understand a
"word of them. The consul then takes from his
"breast a roll of paper, and says, 'I shall read
"'them!' Blunderbore then says, 'Don't!' But the
"consul does, and Blunderbore beats time to the
"music of the verse with his knuckles on the
"table; and perpetually ducks forward to look
"round the cap of a lady sitting between himself
"and me, to see what I think of them. I exhibit
"lively emotion. The verses are in French—short
"line—on the taking of Tangiers by the Prince de

"Joinville; and are received with great applause;
"especially by a nobleman present who is reported
"to be unable to read and write. They end in
"my mind (rapidly translating them into prose)
"thus,—

"The cannon of France   "Of the wondering sea,
"Shake the foundation   "The artillery on the shore

"Is put to silence,
"Honour to Joinville
"And the Brave!
"The Great Intelligence
"Is borne
"Upon the wings of Fame
"To Paris.
"Her national citizens
"Exchange caresses
"In the streets!
"The temples are crowded
"With religious patriots;
"Rendering thanks
"To Heaven.

"The King
"And all the Royal Family
"Are bathed
"In tears.
"They call upon the name
"Of Joinville!
"France also
"Weeps, and echoes it.
"Joinville is crowned
"With Immortality;
"And Peace and Joinville,
"And the Glory of France,
"Diffuse themselves
"Conjointly.

"If you can figure to yourself the choice absurdity
"of receiving anything into one's mind in this
"way, you can imagine the labour I underwent
"in my attempts to keep the lower part of my
"face square, and to lift up one eye gently, as
"with admiring attention. But I am bound to add
"that this is really pretty literal; for I read them
"afterwards."

This, too, was the year of other uncomfortable glories of France in the last three years of her Orleans dynasty; among them the Tahiti business, as politicians may remember; and so hot became rumours of war with England at the opening of September that Dickens had serious thoughts of at once striking his tent. One of his letters was filled with the conflicting doubts in which they lived for nigh a fortnight, every day's arrival contradicting the arrival of the day before: so that, as he told me, you met a man in the street to-day, who told you there would certainly be war in a week; and you met the same man in the street to-morrow, and he swore he always knew there would be nothing but peace; and you met him again the day after, and he said it all depended *now* on something perfectly new and unheard of before, which somebody else said had just come to the knowledge of some consul in some dispatch which said something about some telegraph which had been at work somewhere, signalizing some prodigious intelligence. However, it all passed harmlessly away, leaving him undisturbed opportunity to avail himself of a pleasure that arose out of the consul-general's dinner party, and to be present at a great reception given shortly after by the good "old Blunderbore" just mentioned, on the occasion of his daughter's birthday.

The Marquis had a splendid house, but Dickens found the grounds so carved into grottoes and fanciful walks as to remind him of nothing so much as our old White-conduit-house, except that he would have been well pleased, on the present occasion, to have discovered a waiter crying, "Give your orders, gents!" it being not easy to him at any time to keep up, the whole night through, on ices and variegated lamps merely. But the scene for awhile was amusing

enough, and not rendered less so by the delight of the Marquis himself, "who was constantly div-"ing out into dark corners and then among the

"lattice-work and flower pots, rubbing his hands ALBÁRO:
"and going round and round with explosive 1844.
"chuckles in his huge satisfaction with the enter-
"tainment." With horror it occurred to Dickens,
however, that four more hours of this kind of
entertainment would be too much; that the Genoa
gates closed at twelve; and that as the carriage
had not been ordered till the dancing was expected to be over and the gates to reopen, he
must make a sudden bolt if he would himself get
back to Albaro. "I had barely time," he told Flight of the
me, "to reach the gate before midnight; and guest.
"was running as hard as I could go, downhill,
"over uneven ground, along a new street called
"the strada Sevra, when I came to a pole fastened
"straight across the street, nearly breast high,
"without any light or watchman—quite in the
"Italian style. I went over it, headlong, with A tumble.
"such force that I rolled myself completely white
"in the dust; but although I tore my clothes to
"shreds, I hardly scratched myself except in one
"place on the knee. I had no time to think of
"it then, for I was up directly and off again to
"save the gate: but when I got outside the wall,
"and saw the state I was in, I wondered I had
"not broken my neck. I 'took it easy' after
"this, and walked home, by lonely ways enough,
"without meeting a single soul. But there is
"nothing to be feared, I believe, from midnight Midnight
"walks in this part of Italy. In other places you walks.
"incur the danger of being stabbed by mistake;
"whereas the people here are quiet and good

"tempered, and very rarely commit any outrage."

Such adventures, nevertheless, are seldom without consequences, and there followed in this case a short but sharp attack of illness. It came on with the old "unspeakable and agonizing pain "in the side," for which Bob Fagin had prepared and applied the hot bottles in the old warehouse time; and it yielded quickly to powerful remedies. But for a few days he had to content himself with the minor sights of Albaro. He sat daily in the shade of the ruined chapel on the seashore. He looked in at the festa in the small country church, consisting mainly of a tenor singer, a seraphine, and four priests sitting gaping in a row on one side of the altar "in flowered "satin dresses and little cloth caps, looking ex-"actly like the band at a wild-beast-caravan." He was interested in the wine-making, and in seeing the country tenants preparing their annual presents for their landlords, of baskets of grapes and other fruit prettily dressed with flowers. The season of the grapes, too, brought out after dusk strong parties of rats to eat them as they ripened, and so many shooting parties of peasants to get rid of these despoilers, that as he first listened to the uproar of the firing and the echoes he half fancied it a siege of Albaro. The flies mustered strong, too, and the mosquitos;* so that

* What his poor little dog suffered should not be omitted from the troubles of the master who was so fond of him. "Timber has had every hair upon his body cut off because

at night he had to lie covered up with gauze, like cold meat in a safe.

Of course all news from England, and espe- cially visits paid him by English friends who might be travelling in Italy, were a great delight. This was the year when O'Connell was released from prison by the judgment of the Lords on appeal. "I have no faith in O'Connell taking "the great position he might upon this: being "beleaguered by vanity always. Denman delights "me. I am glad to think I have always liked "him so well. I am sure that whenever he makes "a mistake, it *is* a mistake; and that no man "lives who has a grander and nobler scorn of "every mean and dastard action. I would to "Heaven it were decorous to pay him some public "tribute of respect . . . . O'Connell's speeches are "the old thing: fretty, boastful, frothy, waspish "at the voices in the crowd, and all that: but "with no true greatness. . . What a relief to turn "to that noble letter of Carlyle's" (in which a

---

"of the fleas, and he looks like the ghost of a drowned dog "come out of a pond after a week or so. It is very awful "to see him slide into a room. He knows the change upon "him, and is always turning round and round to look for "himself. I think he'll die of grief." Three weeks later: "Timber's hair is growing again, so that you can dimly per- "ceive him to be a dog. The fleas only keep three of his "legs off the ground now, and he sometimes moves of his "own accord towards some place where they don't want "to go." His improvement was slow, but after this con- tinuous.

Albaro:
1844. timely testimony had been borne to the truthful-
ness and honour of Mazzini), "which I think
"above all praise. My love to him." Among his
Ante, p. 59. English visitors were Mr. Tagart's family, on their
way from a scientific congress at Milan; and
Lord Robert-
son. Peter (now become Lord) Robertson from Rome,
of whose talk he wrote very pleasantly. The sons
of Burns had been entertained during the summer
in Edinburgh at what was called a Burns Festival,
of which, through Jerrold who was present, I had
sent him no very favourable account; and this
was now confirmed by Robertson, whose letters
had given him an "awful" narrative of Wilson's
Burns
festival. speech, and of the whole business. "There was
"one man who spoke a quarter of an hour or so,
"to the toast of the navy; and could say nothing
"more than 'the—British—navy—always appre-
"'ciates—' which remarkable sentiment he re-
"peated over and over again for that space of
"time; and then sat down. Robertson told me
"also that Wilson's allusion to, or I should rather
"say expatiation upon, the 'vices' of Burns, ex-
"cited but one sentiment of indignation and dis-
"gust: and added, very sensibly, 'By God!—I
"'want to know *what Burns did!* I never heard
Professor
Wilson's
speech. "'of his doing anything that need be strange or
"'unaccountable to the Professor's mind. I think
"'he must have mistaken the name, and fancied
"'it a dinner to the sons of *Burke*'—meaning of
"course the murderer. In short he fully con-
"firmed Jerrold in all respects." The same letter
told me, too, something of his reading. Jerrold's

Story of a Feather he had derived much enjoyment from. "Gauntwolf's sickness and the career
"of that snuffbox, masterly.* I have been deep
"in Voyages and Travels, and in De Foe. Ten-
"nyson I have also been reading, again and
"again. What a great creature he is! . . . What
"about the *Goldsmith?* Apropos, I am all eager-
"ness to write a story about the length of that
"most delightful of all stories, the *Vicar of Wake-
"field.*"

In the second week of September he went to
meet his brother Frederick at Marseilles, and
bring him back over the Cornice road to pass a
fortnight's holiday at Genoa; and his description
of the first inn upon the Alps they slept in is too
good to be lost. "We lay last night," he wrote
(9th of September) "at the first halting-place on
"this journey, in an inn which is not entitled, as
"it ought to be, The house of call for fleas and
"vermin in general, but is entitled the grand hotel
"of the Post! I hardly know what to compare
"it to. It seemed something like a house in
"Somers-town originally built for a wine-vaults
"and never finished, but grown very old. There
"was nothing to eat in it and nothing to drink.
"They had lost the teapot; and when they found

---

* A characteristic message for Jerrold came in a later
letter (12th of May, 1845): "I wish you would suggest to
"Jerrold for me as a Caudle subject (if he pursue that idea),
" 'Mr. Caudle has incidentally remarked that the housemaid
" 'is good-looking.' "

ALBARO
1844.

"it, they couldn't make out what had become of
"the lid, which, turning up at last and being
"fixed on to the teapot, couldn't be got off again for
"the pouring in of more water. Fleas of elephan-
"tine dimensions were gambolling boldly in the
"dirty beds; and the mosquitoes!—But here let
"me draw a curtain (as I would have done if
"there had been any). We had scarcely any
"sleep, and rose up with hands and arms hardly
"human."

In four days they were at Albaro, and the
morning after their arrival Dickens underwent
the terrible shock of seeing his brother very
nearly drowned in the bay. He swam out into
too strong a current,* and was only narrowly
saved by the accident of a fishing-boat preparing
to leave the harbour at the time. "It was a world
"of horror and anguish," Dickens wrote to me,
"crowded into four or five minutes of dreadful
"agitation; and, to complete the terror of it,
"Georgy, Charlotte," (the nurse), "and the chil-
"dren were on a rock in full view of it all, cry-
"ing, as you may suppose, like mad creatures."
His own bathing was from the rock, and, as he
had already told me, of the most primitive kind.
He went in whenever he pleased, broke his head

His brother in
danger.

Sea-bathing.

A monk
drowned.

* Of the dangers of the bay he had before written to me
(10th of August). "A monk was drowned here on Saturday
"evening. He was bathing with two other monks, who
"bolted when he cried out that he was sinking—in con-
"sequence, I suppose, of his certainty of going to Heaven."

against sharp stones if he went in with that end
foremost, floundered about till he was all over
bruises, and then climbed and staggered out
again. "Everybody wears a dress. Mine ex-
"tremely theatrical: Masaniello to the life: shall
"be preserved for your inspection in Devonshire-
"terrace." I will add another personal touch,
also Masaniello-like, which marks the beginning
of a change which, though confined for the present to his foreign residence and removed when
he came to England, was resumed somewhat
later, and in a few more years wholly altered
the aspect of his face. "The moustaches are
"glorious, glorious. I have cut them shorter,
"and trimmed them a little at the ends to improve
"the shape. They are charming, charming. With-
"out them, life would be a blank."

Albaro
1844.

A change
beginning.

CHAPTER XXX.

WORK IN GENOA: PALAZZO PESCHIERE.

1844.

Genoa:
1844.

In the last week of September they moved from Albaro into Genoa, amid a violent storm of wind and wet, "great guns blowing," the lightning incessant, and the rain driving down in a dense thick cloud. But the worst of the storm was over when they reached the Peschiere. As they passed into it along the stately old terraces, flanked on either side with antique sculptured figures, all the seven fountains were playing in its gardens, and the sun was shining brightly on its groves of camellias and orange-trees.

Palace of the Fishponds.

It was a wonderful place, and I soon became familiar with the several rooms that were to form their home for the rest of their stay in Italy. In the centre was the grand sala, fifty feet high, of an area larger than "the dining-room of the "Academy," and painted, walls and ceiling, with frescoes three hundred years old, "as fresh as if "the colours had been laid on yesterday." On the same floor as this great hall were a drawing-room, and a dining-room,* both covered also

* "Into which we might put your large room—I wish

with frescoes still bright enough to make them
thoroughly cheerful, and both so nicely proportioned as to give to their bigness all the effect of

snugness.* Out of these opened three other

"we could!—away in one corner, and dine without know-
"ing it."

* "Very vast you will say, and very dreary; but it is not
"so really. The paintings are so fresh, and the proportions
"so agreeable to the eye, that the effect is not only cheerful
"but snug. . . . We are a little incommoded by applica-
"tions from strangers to go over the interior. The paintings

chambers that were turned into sleeping-rooms and nurseries. Adjoining the sala, right and left, were the two best bed-rooms; "in size and shape "like those at Windsor-castle but greatly higher;" both having altars, a range of three windows with stone balconies, floors tesselated in patterns of black and white stone, and walls painted every inch: on the left, nymphs pursued by

satyrs "as large as life and as wicked;" on the right, "Phaeton larger than life, with horses big-"ger than Meux and Co.'s, tumbling headlong "down into the best bed." The right-hand one he occupied with his wife, and of the left took possession as a study; writing behind a big screen he had lugged into it, and placed by one of the windows, from which he could see over the city, as he wrote, as far as the lighthouse in its

harbour. Distant little over a mile as the crow flew, flashing five times in four minutes, and on dark nights, as if by magic, illuminating brightly the whole palace-front every time it shone, this lighthouse was one of the wonders of Genoa.

When it had all become more familiar to

"were designed by Michael Angelo, and have a great re-"putation . . . Certain of these frescoes were reported of-"ficially to the Fine Art Commissioners by Wilson as the "best in Italy . . . I allowed a party of priests to be shown "the great hall yesterday . . . It is in perfect repair, and the "door almost shut—which is quite a miraculous circum-"stance. I wish you could see it, my dear F. Gracious "Heavens! if you could only *come back* with me, wouldn't I "soon flash on your astonished sight." (6th of October.)

him, he was fond of dilating on its beauties; and
even the dreary sound of the chaunting from
neighbouring mass-performances, as it floated in
at all the open windows, which at first was a sad
trouble, came to have its charm for him. I remember a vivid account he gave me of a great
festa on the hill behind the house, when the
people alternately danced under tents in the open
air and rushed to say a prayer or two in an adjoining church bright with red and gold and blue
and silver; so many minutes of dancing, and of
praying, in regular turns of each. But the view
over into Genoa, on clear bright days, was a never
failing enjoyment. The whole city then, without
an atom of smoke, and with every possible variety
of tower and steeple pointing up into the sky, lay
stretched out below his windows. To the right
and left were lofty hills, with every indentation
in their rugged sides sharply discernible; and on
one side of the harbour stretched away into the
dim bright distance the whole of the Cornice, its
first highest range of mountains hoary with snow.
Sitting down one Spring day to write to me, he
thus spoke of the sea and of the garden. "Beyond
"the town is the wide expanse of the Medi-
"terranean, as blue, at this moment, as the most
"pure and vivid prussian blue on Mac's palette
"when it is newly set; and on the horizon there
"is a red flush, seen nowhere as it is here. Im-
"mediately below the windows are the gardens of
"the house, with gold fish swimming and diving
"in the fountains; and below them, at the foot of

Dancing and
praying.

Distant
scenery.

Peschiero
garden.

"a steep slope, the public garden and drive, where
"the walks are marked out by hedges of pink
"roses, which blush and shine through the green
"trees and vines, close up to the balconies of
"these windows. No custom can impair, and no
"description enhance, the beauty of the scene."

Trying to
write.
All these and other glories and beauties, however, did not come to him at once. They counted
for little indeed when he first set himself seriously
to write. "Never did I stagger so upon a threshold
"before. I seem as if I had plucked myself out
"of my proper soil when I left Devonshire-terrace;
"and could take root no more until I return to
"it. . . . Did I tell you how many fountains we
"have here? No matter. If they played nectar,
"they wouldn't please me half so well as the West
"Middlesex water-works at Devonshire-terrace."

Difficulties in
the way.
The subject for his new Christmas story he had
chosen, but he had not found a title for it, or the
machinery to work it with; when, at the moment
of what seemed to be his greatest trouble, both
reliefs came. Sitting down one morning resolute
for work, though against the grain, his hand being
out and everything inviting to idleness, such a
peal of chimes arose from the city as he found
to be "maddening." All Genoa lay beneath him,
and up from it, with some sudden set of the wind,
A peal of
chimes.
came in one fell sound the clang and clash of all
its steeples, pouring into his ears, again and
again, in a tuneless, grating, discordant, jerking,
hideous vibration that made his ideas "spin round
"and round till they lost themselves in a whirl of

"vexation and giddiness, and dropped down dead."
He had never before so suffered, nor did he again;
but this was his description to me next day, and
his excuse for having failed in a promise to send
me his title. Only two days later, however, came
a letter in which not a syllable was written but
"We have heard THE CHIMES at midnight, Master A little found.
"Shallow!" and I knew he had discovered what
he wanted.

Other difficulties were still to be got over.
He craved for the London streets. He so missed
his long night-walks before beginning anything
that he seemed, as he said, dumbfounded without them. "I can't help thinking of the boy in
"the school-class whose button was cut off by Walter
"Scott and his friends. Put me down on Water- Craving for
"loo-bridge at eight o'clock in the evening, with streets by night.
"leave to roam about as long as I like, and I
"would come home, as you know, panting to go
"on. I am sadly strange as it is, and can't settle.
"You will have lots of hasty notes from me while
"I am at work: but you know your man; and
"whatever strikes me, I shall let off upon you as
"if I were in Devonshire-terrace. It's a great
"thing to have my title, and see my way how to
"work the bells. Let them clash upon me now
"from all the churches and convents in Genoa, I
"see nothing but the old London belfry I have set
"them in. In my mind's eye, Horatio. I like more Design for his
"and more my notion of making, in this little book, book.
"a great blow for the poor. Something powerful, I
"think I can do, but I want to be tender too, and

"cheerful; as like the *Carol* in that respect as
"may be, and as unlike it as such a thing can be.
"The duration of the action will resemble it a
"little, but I trust to the novelty of the machinery
"to carry that off; and if my design be anything
"at all, it has a grip upon the very throat of the
"time." (8th of October.)

Thus bent upon his work, for which he never
had been in more earnest mood, he was disturbed
by hearing that he must attend the levee of the
Governor who had unexpectedly arrived in the
city, and who would take it as an affront, his eccentric friend Fletcher told him, if that courtesy
were not immediately paid. "It was the morning
"on which I was going to begin, so I wrote round
"to our consul," — praying, of course, that excuse
should be made for him. Don't bother yourself,
replied that sensible functionary, for all the con-
suls and governors alive; but shut yourself up by
all means. "So," continues Dickens, telling me
the tale, "he went next morning in great state and
"full costume, to present two English gentlemen.
"'Where's the great poet?' said the Governor. 'I
"'want to see the great poet.' 'The great poet,
"'your excellency,' said the consul, 'is at work,
"'writing a book, and begged me to make his
"'excuses.' 'Excuses!' said the Governor, 'I
"'wouldn't interfere with such an occupation for
"'all the world. Pray tell him that my house is
"'open to the honour of his presence when it is
"'perfectly convenient for him; but not otherwise.
"'And let no gentleman,' said the Governor, a

"'surweyin' of his suite with a majestic eye, 'call
"'upon Signor Dickens till he is understood to be
"'disengaged.' And he sent somebody with his
"own cards next day. Now I *do* seriously call
"this, real politeness and pleasant consideration
"—not positively American, but still gentlemanly
"and polished. The same spirit pervades the in-
"ferior departments; and I have not been required
"to observe the usual police regulations, or to put
"myself to the slightest trouble about anything."
(18th of October.)

Genoa:
1844.
Governor's
message to
him.

The picture I am now to give of him at work
should be prefaced by a word or two that may
throw light on the design he was working at. It
was a large theme for so small an instrument; and
the disproportion was not more characteristic of
the man, than the throes of suffering and passion
to be presently undergone by him for results that
many men would smile at. He was bent, as he
says, on striking a blow for the poor. They had
always been his clients, they had never been forgotten in any of his books, but here nothing else
was to be remembered. He had become, in short,
terribly earnest in the matter. Several months
before he left England I had noticed in him the
habit of more gravely regarding many things before passed lightly enough; the hopelessness of
any true solution of either political or social pro-
blems by the ordinary Downing-street methods
had been startlingly impressed on him in Carlyle's
writings; and in the parliamentary talk of that day

Subject he is
working at.

How
originated.

he had come to have as little faith for the putting down of any serious evil, as in a then notorious city Alderman's gabble for the putting down of suicide. The latter had stirred his indignation to its depths just before he came to Italy, and his increased opportunities of solitary reflection since had strengthened and extended it. When he came therefore to think of his new story for Christmas time, he resolved to make it a plea for the poor. He did not want it to resemble his *Carol*, but the same kind of moral was in his mind. He was to try and convert Society, as he had converted Scrooge, by showing that its happiness rested on the same foundations as those of the individual, which are mercy and charity not less than justice. Whether right or wrong in these assumptions, need not be questioned here, where facts are merely stated to render intelligible what will follow; he had not made politics at any time a study, and they were always an instinct with him rather than a science; but the instinct was wholesome and sound, and to set class against class never ceased to be as odious to him as he thought it righteous at all times to help each to a kindlier knowledge of the other. And so, here in Italy, amid the grand surroundings of this Palazzo Peschiere, the hero of his imagination was to be a sorry old drudge of a London ticket-porter, who in his anxiety not to distrust or think hardly of the rich, has fallen into the opposite extreme of distrusting the poor. From such distrust it is the

A plea for the poor.

C. D.'s politics.

Choice of a hero.

Page 209-10 of Vol. I.

object of the story to reclaim him; and, to the Genoa: 1844.
writer of it, the tale became itself of less moment
than what he thus intended it to enforce. Far
beyond mere vanity in authorship went the passionate zeal with which he began, and the exulta-
tion with which he finished, this task. When we
met at its close, he was fresh from Venice, which
had impressed him as "the wonder" and "the
"new sensation" of the world: but well do I re- Master-passion.
member how high above it all arose the hope
that filled his mind. "Ah!" he said to me, "when
"I saw those places, how I thought that to leave
"one's hand' upon the time, lastingly upon the
"time, with one tender touch for the mass of toil-
"ing people that nothing could obliterate, would
"be to lift oneself above the dust of all the Doges
"in their graves, and stand upon a giant's staircase
"that Sampson couldn't overthrow!" In varying
forms this ambition was in all his life.

Another incident of these days will exhibit Religious sentiment.
aspirations of a more solemn import that were
not less part of his nature. It was depth of sentiment rather than clearness of faith which kept
safe the belief on which they rested against all
doubt or question of its sacredness, but every year
seemed to strengthen it in him. This was told me Ante, pp. 59-60.
in his second letter after reaching the Peschiere;
the first having sent me some such commissions
in regard to his wife's family as his kindly care
for all connected with him frequently led to.
"Let me tell you," he wrote (30th of September),
"of a curious dream I had, last Monday night;

"and of the fragments of reality I can collect,
"which helped to make it up. I have had a
"return of rheumatism in my back, and knotted
"round my waist like a girdle of pain; and had
"laid awake nearly all that night under the in-
"fliction, when I fell asleep and dreamed this

"dream. Observe that throughout I was as real,
"animated, and full of passion as Macready (God
"bless him!) in the last scene of *Macbeth*. In an
"indistinct place, which was quite sublime in its
"indistinctness, I was visited by a Spirit. I could
"not make out the face, nor do I recollect that I
"desired to do so. It wore a blue drapery, as
"the Madonna might in a picture by Raphael;
"and bore no resemblance to any one I have
"known except in stature. I think (but I am not
"sure) that I recognized the voice. Anyway, I

"knew it was poor Mary's spirit. I was not at all
"afraid, but in a great delight, so that I wept very
"much, and stretching out my arms to it called it
"'Dear.' At this, I thought it recoiled; and I felt
"immediately, that not being of my gross nature,
"I ought not to have addressed it so familiarly.
"'Forgive me!' I said. 'We poor living creatures
"'are only able to express ourselves by looks and
"'words. I have used the word most natural to
"'*our* affections; and you know my heart.' It
"was so full of compassion and sorrow for me—
"which I knew spiritually, for, as I have said, 'I
"didn't perceive its emotions by its face—that it

"cut me to the heart; and I said, sobbing, 'Oh!
"'give me some token that you have really visited

" 'me!' 'Form a wish,' it said. I thought, reason-
"ing with myself: 'If I form a selfish wish, it will
" 'vanish.' So I hastily discarded such hopes and
"anxieties of my own as came into my mind, and
"said, 'Mrs. Hogarth is surrounded with great dis-
" 'tresses'—observe, I never thought of saying
" 'your mother' as to a mortal creature—'will you
" 'extricate her?' 'Yes.' 'And her extrication is
" 'to be a certainty to me, that this has really
" 'happened?' 'Yes.' 'But answer me one other
" 'question!' I said, in an agony of entreaty lest it
"should leave me. 'What is the True religion?'
"As it paused a moment without replying, I said
"—Good God in such an agony of haste, lest it
"should go away!—'You think, as I do, that the
" 'Form of religion does not so greatly matter, if
" 'we try to do good? or,' I said, observing that
"it still hesitated, and was moved with the greatest
"compassion for me, 'perhaps the Roman Catholic
" 'is the best? perhaps it makes one think of God
" 'oftener, and believe in him more steadily?'
" 'For you,' said the Spirit, full of such heavenly
"tenderness for me, that I felt as if my heart
"would break; 'for you, it is the best!' Then I
"awoke, with the tears running down my face,
"and myself in exactly the condition of the dream.
"It was just dawn. I called up Kate, and repeated
"it three or four times over, that I might not un-
"consciously make it plainer or stronger after-
"wards. It was exactly this. Free from all hurry,
"nonsense, or confusion, whatever. Now, the
"strings I can gather up, leading to this, were

"three. The first you know, from the main sub-
"ject of my last letter. The second was, that
"there is a great altar in our bed-room, at which
"some family who once inhabited this palace had
"mass performed in old time: and I had observed
"within myself, before going to bed, that there
"was a mark in the wall, above the sanctuary,
"where a religious picture used to be; and I had
"wondered within myself what the subject might
"have been, *and what the face was like.* Thirdly,
"I had been listening to the convent bells (which
"ring at intervals in the night), and so had thought,
"no doubt, of Roman Catholic services. And yet,
"for all this, put the case of that wish being ful-
"filled by any agency in which I had no hand;
"and I wonder whether I should regard it as a
"dream, or an actual Vision!" It was perhaps
natural that he should omit, from his own considerations awakened by the dream, the very first
that would have risen in any mind to which his
was intimately known—that it strengthens other
evidences, of which there are many in his life, of
his not having escaped those trying regions of
reflection which most men of thought and all men
of genius have at some time to pass through. In
such disturbing fancies during the next year or
two, I may add that the book which helped him
most was the *Life of Arnold.* "I respect and
"reverence his memory," he wrote to me in the
middle of October, in reply to my mention of
what had most attracted myself in it, "beyond
"all expression. I must have that book. Every

"sentence that you quote from it is the text-book GENOA:
1844.
"of my faith."

He kept his promise that I should hear from
him while writing, and I had frequent letters
when he was fairly in his work. "With my steam *Hard at work.*
"very much up, I find it a great trial to be so
"far off from you, and consequently to have no
"one (always excepting Kate and Georgy) to
"whom to expatiate on my day's work. And ,I
"want a crowded street to plunge into at night.
"And I want to be 'on the spot' as it were. But
"apart from such things, the life I lead is favour-
"able to work." In his next letter: "I am in re-
"gular, ferocious excitement with the *Chimes;* get
"up at seven; have a cold bath before breakfast;
"and blaze away, wrathful and red-hot, until
"three o'clock or so: when I usually knock off
"(unless it rains) for the day .. I am fierce to
"finish in a spirit bearing some affinity to those
"of truth and mercy, and to shame the cruel
"and the canting. I have not forgotten my
"catechism. 'Yes verily, and with God's help,
"'so I will!'"

Within a week he had completed his first *First part*
part, or quarter. "I send you to-day" (18th of *finished.*
October), "by mail, the first and longest of the
"four divisions. This is great for the first week,
"which is usually up-hill. I have kept a copy in
"shorthand in case of accidents. I hope to send
"you a parcel every Monday until the whole is
"done. I do not wish to influence you, but it
"has a great hold upon me, and has affected me,

"in the doing, in divers strong ways, deeply,
"forcibly. To give you better means of judg-
"ment I will sketch for you the general idea, but
"pray don't read it until you have read this first
"part of the MS." I print it here. It is a good
illustration of his method in all his writing. His
idea is in it so thoroughly, [that, by comparison
with the tale as printed, we see the strength of
its mastery over his first design. Thus always,
whether his tale was to be written in one or in
twenty numbers, his fancies controlled him. He
never, in any of his books, accomplished what he
had wholly preconceived, often as he attempted
it. Few men of genius ever did. Once at the
sacred heat that opens regions beyond ordinary
vision, imagination has its own laws; and where
characters are so real as to be treated as
existences, their creator himself cannot help them
having their own wills and ways. Fern the farm-
labourer is not here, nor yet his niece the little
Lilian (at first called Jessie) who is to give to the
tale its most tragical scene; and there are intima-
tions of poetic fancy at the close of my sketch
which the published story fell short of. Altogether
the comparison is worth observing.

    "The general notion is this. That what hap-
"pens to poor Trotty in the first part, and what
"will happen to him in the second (when he
"takes the letter to a punctual and a great man
"of business, who is balancing his books and
"making up his accounts, and complacently ex-
"patiating on the necessity of clearing off every

"liability and obligation, and turning over a new
"leaf and starting fresh with the new year), so
"dispirits him, who can't do this, that he comes
"to the conclusion that his class and order have
"no business with a new year, and really are
"'intruding.' And though he will pluck up for
"an hour or so, at the christening (I think) of a
"neighbour's child, that evening: still, when he
"goes home, Mr. Filer's precepts will come into
"his mind, and he will say to himself, 'we are a
"'long way past the proper average of children,
"'and it has no business to be born:' and will
"be wretched again. And going home, and sitting
"there alone, he will take that newspaper out of
"his pocket, and reading of the crimes and of-
"fences of the poor, especially of those whom
"Alderman Cute is going to put down, will be
"quite confirmed in his misgiving that they are
"bad; irredeemably bad. In this state of mind,
"he will fancy that the Chimes are calling to
"him; and saying to himself 'God help me. Let
"'me go up to 'em. I feel as if I were going to
"'die in despair—of a broken heart; 'let me die
"'among the bells that have been a comfort to
"'me!'—will grope his way up into the tower;
"and fall down in a kind of swoon among them.
"Then the third quarter, or in other words the
"beginning of the second half of the book, will
"open with the Goblin part of the thing: the
"bells ringing, and innumerable spirits (the sound
"or vibration of them) flitting and tearing in and
"out of the church-steeple, and bearing all sorts

"of missions and commissions and reminders and
"reproaches, and comfortable recollections and
"what not, to all sorts of people and places.
"Some bearing scourges; and others flowers, and
"birds, and music; and others pleasant faces in
"mirrors, and others ugly ones: the bells haunt-
"ing people in the night (especially the last of
"the old year) according to their deeds. And
"the bells themselves, who have a goblin likeness
"to humanity in the midst of their proper shapes,
"and who shine in a light of their own, will say
"(the Great Bell being the chief spokesman)
"Who is he that being of the poor doubts the
"right of poor men to the inheritance which
"Time reserves for them, and echoes an 'unmean-
"ing cry against his fellows? Toby, all aghast,
"will tell him it is he, and why it is.   Then the
"spirits of the bells will bear him through the air
"to various scenes, charged with this trust: That
"they show him how the poor and wretched, at
"the worst—yes, even in the crimes that alder-
"men put down, and he has thought so horrible
"—have some deformed and hunch-backed good-
"ness clinging to them; and how they have their
"right and share in Time.   Following out the
"history of Meg the Bells will show her, that
"marriage broken off and all friends dead, with
"an infant child; reduced so low, and made so
"miserable, as to be brought at last to wander
"out at night.   And in Toby's sight, her father's,
"she will resolve to drown herself and the child
"together.   But before she goes down to the

"water, Toby will see how she covers it with a
"part of her own wretched dress, and adjusts its
"rags so as to make it pretty in its sleep, and
"hangs over it, and smooths its little limbs, and
"loves it with the dearest love that God ever
"gave to mortal creatures; and when she runs
"down to the water, Toby will cry 'Oh spare
"'her! Chimes, have mercy on her! Stop her!'—
"and the bells will say, 'Why stop her? She is
"'bad at heart—let the bad die.' And Toby on
"his knees will beg and pray for mercy: and in
"the end the bells will stop her, by their voices,
"just in time. Toby will see, too, what great
"things the punctual man has left undone on the
"close of the old year, and what accounts he has
"left unsettled: punctual as he is. And he will
"see a great many things about Richard, once so
"near being his son-in-law, and about a great
"many people. And the moral of it all will be,
"that he has his portion in the new year no less
"than any other man, and that the poor require
"a deal of beating out of shape before their
"human shape is gone; that even in their frantic
"wickedness there may be good in their hearts
"triumphantly asserting itself, though all the
"aldermen alive say 'No,' as he has learnt from
"the agony of his own child; and that the truth
"is Trustfulness in them, not doubt, nor putting
"down, nor filing them away. And when at last
"a great sea rises, and this sea of Time comes
"sweeping down, bearing the alderman and such
"mudworms of the earth away to nothing, dash-

GENOA.
1811.

First outline
of the Chime..

"ing them to fragments in its fury—Toby will
"climb a rock and hear the bells (now faded
"from his sight) pealing out upon the waters.
"And as he hears them, and looks round for
"help, he will wake up and find himself with the
"newspaper lying at his foot; and Meg sitting
"opposite to him at the table, making up the
"ribbons for her wedding to-morrow; and the
"window open, that the sound of the bells ring-
"ing the old year out and the new year in may
"enter. They will just have broken out, joyfully;
"and Richard will dash in to kiss Meg before
"Toby, and have the first kiss of the new year
"(he'll get it too); and the neighbours will crowd
"round with good wishes; and a band will strike

"up gaily (Toby knows a Drum in private); and
"the altered circumstances, and the ringing of
"the bells, and the jolly musick, will so transport
"the old fellow that he will lead off a country
"dance forthwith in an entirely new step, con-
"sisting of his old familiar trot. Then quoth the
"inimitable—Was it a dream of Toby's after all?
"Or is Toby but a dream? and Meg a dream?
"and all a dream! In reference to which, and
"the realities of which dreams are born, the in-
"imitable will be wiser than he can be now,
"writing for dear life, with the post just going,
"and the brave C booted . . . Ah how I hate
"myself, my dear fellow, for this lame and halt-
"ing outline of the Vision I have in my mind.
"But it must go to you . . . You will say what is
"best for the frontispiece" . .

With the second part or quarter, after a
week's interval, came announcement of the en- Liking for
largement of his plan, by which he hoped better the subject.
to carry out the scheme of the story, and to get,
for its following part, an effect for his heroine
that would increase the tragic interest. "I am
"still in stout heart with the tale. I think it well-
"timed and a good thought; and as you know I
"wouldn't say so to anybody else, I don't mind
"saying freely thus much. It has great possession
"of me every moment in the day; and drags me
"where it will. . . . If you only could have read
"it all at once!—But you never would have done
"that, anyway, for I never should have been able
"to keep it to myself; so that's nonsense. I hope
"you'll like it. I would give a hundred pounds
"(and think it cheap) to see you read it. . . . .
"Never mind."

That was the first hint of an intention of Third part
which I was soon to hear more; but meanwhile, after finished.
eight more days, the third part came, with the
scene from which he expected so much, and with
a mention of what the writing of it had cost him.
"This book (whether in the Hajji Baba sense or
"not I can't say, but certainly in the literal one)
"has made my face white in a foreign land. My What the
"cheeks, which were beginning to fill out, have writing of it cost him.
"sunk again; my eyes have grown immensely
"large; my hair is very lank; and the head
"inside the hair is hot and giddy. Read the
"scene at the end of the third part, twice. I
"wouldn't write it twice, for something. . . You

Genoa:
1841.

"will see that I have substituted the name of
"Lilian for Jessie. It is prettier in sound, and
"suits my music better. I mention this, lest you
"should wonder who and what I mean by that
"name. To-morrow I shall begin afresh (starting
"the next part with a broad grin, and ending it
"with the very soul of jollity and happiness); and
"I hope to finish by next Monday at latest. Per-
"haps on Saturday. I hope you will like the
"little book. Since I conceived at the beginning
"of the second part, what must happen in the
"third, I have undergone as much sorrow and
"agitation as if the thing were real; and have
"wakened up with it at night. I was obliged to
"lock myself in when I finished it yesterday, for
"my face was swollen for the time to twice its
"proper size, and was hugely ridiculous." . . .
His letter ended abruptly. "I am going for a
"long walk, to clear my head. I feel that I am
"very shakey from work, and throw down my
"pen for the day. There! (That's where it fell.)"
A huge blot represented it, and, as Hamlet says,
the rest was silence.

Two days later, answering a letter from me
that had reached in the interval, he gave spright-
lier account of himself, and described a happy
change in the weather. Up to this time, he protested, they had not had more than four or five
clear days. All the time he had been writing
they had been wild and stormy. "Wind, hail,
"rain, thunder and lightning. To-day," just before he sent me his last manuscript, "has been

Realities of
fictitious
sorrow.

Wild
weather.

"November slack-baked, the sirocco having come
"back; and to-night it blows great guns with a Mountain
"raging storm." "Weather worse," he wrote after rain.
three Mondays, "than any November English
"weather I have ever beheld, or any weather I
"have had experience of anywhere. So horrible
"to-day that all power has been rained and
"gloomed out of me. Yesterday, in pure de-
"termination to get the better of it, I walked
"twelve miles in mountain rain. You never saw
"it rain. Scotland and America are nothing to
"it." But now all this was over. "The weather A change.
"changed on Saturday night, and has been glori-
"ous ever since. I am afraid to say more in its
"favour, lest it should change again." It did not.
I think there were no more complainings. I heard
now of autumn days with the mountain wind
lovely, enjoyable, exquisite past expression. I
heard of mountain walks behind the Peschiere,
most beautiful and fresh, among which, and along
the beds of dry rivers and torrents, he could
"pelt away," in any dress, without encountering a
soul but the contadini. I heard of his starting
off one day after finishing work, "fifteen miles to Fifteen miles'
"dinner—oh my stars! at such an inn!!!" On walk to dinner.
another day, of a party to dinner at their pleasant
little banker's at Quinto six miles off, to which,
while the ladies drove, he was able, "to walk in
"the sun of the middle of the day and to walk
"home again at night." On another, of an expedition up the mountain on mules. And on
another of a memorable tavern-dinner with their

Genoa:
1844.

Banquet at
the Whistle.

Startling
news.

Coming to
London.

merchant friend Mr. Curry, in which there were such successions of surprising dishes of genuine native cookery that they took two hours in the serving, but of the component parts of not one of which was he able to form the remotest conception: the site of the tavern being on the city wall, its name in Italian sounding very romantic and meaning "the Whistle," and its bill of fare kept for an experiment to which, before another month should be over, he dared and challenged my cookery in Lincoln's-inn.

A visit from him to London was to be expected almost immediately! That all remonstrance would be idle, under the restless excitement his work had awakened, I well knew. It was not merely the wish he had, natural enough, to see the last proofs and the woodcuts before the day of publication, which he could not otherwise do; but it was the stronger and more eager wish, before that final launch, to have a vivider sense than letters could give him of the effect of what he had been doing. "If I come, I shall put up at Cuttris's" (then the Piazza-hotel in Covent-garden) "that I may be close to you. Don't say "to anybody, except our immediate friends, that "I am coming. Then I shall not be bothered. If "I should preserve my present fierce writing "humour, in any pass I may run to Venice, "Bologna, and Florence, before I turn my face "towards Lincoln's-inn-fields; and come to England by Milan and Turin. But this of course "depends in a great measure on your reply." My

reply, dwelling on the fatigue and cost, had the
reception I foresaw. "Notwithstanding what you
"say, I am still in the same mind about coming
"to London. Not because the proofs concern me
"at all (I should be an ass as well as a thankless
"vagabond if they did), but because of that un- "Unspeak-
"able restless
"speakable restless something which would render "something."
"it almost as impossible for me to remain here
"and not see the thing complete, as it would be
"for a full balloon, left to itself, not to go up. I
"do not intend coming from *here*, but by way of
"Milan and Turin (previously going to Venice),
"and so, across the wildest pass of the Alps that
"may be open, to Strasburg... As you dislike
"the Young England gentleman I shall knock
"him out, and replace him by a man (I can dash
"him in at your rooms in an hour) who recog-
"nizes no virtue in anything but the good old
"times, and talks of them, parrot-like, whatever
"the matter is. A real good old city tory, in a
"blue coat and bright buttons and a white cravat,
"and with a tendency of blood to the head. File
"away at Filer, as you please; but bear in mind
"that the *Westminster Review* considered Scrooge's
"presentation of the turkey to Bob Cratchit as
"grossly incompatible with political economy. I
"don't care at all for the skittle-playing." These
were among things I had objected to.

But the close of his letter revealed more than
its opening of the reason, not at once so frankly
confessed, for the long winter-journey he was
about to make; and if it be thought that, in

GENOA:
1844.

Eager to try
effect of the
story.

Plans a
reading at
my rooms.

The tale
finished.

printing the passage, I take a liberty with my
friend, it will be found that equal liberty is taken
with myself, whom it goodnaturedly caricatures;
so that the reader can enjoy his laugh at either
or both. "Shall I confess to you, I particularly
"want Carlyle above all to see it before the rest
"of the world, when it is done; and I should like
"to inflict the little story on him and on dear old
"gallant Macready with my own lips, and to have
"Stanny and the other Mac sitting by. Now, if
"you was a real gent, you'd get up a little circle
"for me, one wet evening, when I come to town:
"and would say, 'My boy (SIR, will you have the
"'goodness to leave those books alone and to go
"'downstairs—WHAT the Devil are you doing!
"'And mind, sir, I can see nobody—do you
"'hear? Nobody. I am particularly engaged with
"'a gentleman from Asia)—My boy, would you
"'give us that little Christmas book (a little Christ-
"'mas book of Dickens's, Macready, which I'm anx-
"'ious you should hear); and don't slur it, now, or be
"'too fast, Dickens, please!'—I say, if you was a real
"gent, something to this effect might happen. I
"shall be under sailing orders the moment I have
"finished. And I shall produce myself (please
"God) in London on the very day you name.
"For one week: to the hour."

The wish was complied with, of course; and
that night in Lincoln's-inn-fields led to rather
memorable issues. His next letter told me the
little tale was done. "Third of November, 1844.
"Half-past two, afternoon. Thank God! I have

"finished the *Chimes*. This moment I take up
"my pen again to-day, to say only that much;
"and to add that I have had what women call
"'a real good cry!'" Very genuine all this, it is
hardly necessary to say. The little book thus
completed was not one of his greater successes,
and it raised him up some objectors; but there
was that in it which more than repaid the suffering its writing cost him, and the enmity its
opinions provoked; and in his own heart it had
a cherished corner to the last. The intensity of
it seemed always best to represent to himself
what he hoped to be longest remembered for;
and exactly what he felt as to this, his friend
Jeffrey warmly expressed. "All the tribe of selfish-
"ness, and cowardice and cant, will hate you in
"their hearts, and cavil when they can; will ac-
"cuse you of wicked exaggeration, and excite-
"ment to discontent, and what they pleasantly
"call disaffection! But never mind. The good
"and the brave are with you, and the truth
"also."

He resumed his letter on the fourth of November. "Here is the brave courier measuring
"bits of maps with a carving-fork, and going up
"mountains on a tea-spoon. He and I start on
"Wednesday for Parma, Modena, Bologna, Venice,
"Verona, Brescia, and Milan. Milan being within
"a reasonable journey from here, Kate and Georgy
"will come to meet me when I arrive there on
"my way towards England; and will bring me all
"letters from you. I shall be there on the 18th

". . . . . Now, you know my punctiwality. Frost, "ice, flooded rivers, steamers, horses, passports, "and custom-houses may damage it. But my "design is, to walk into Cuttris's coffee-room on "Sunday the 1st of December, in good time for "dinner. I shall look for you at the farther table

"by the fire—where we generally go. . . . . But "the party for the night following? I know you "have consented to the party. Let me see. Don't "have any one, this particular night, to dinner, "but let it be a summons for the special purpose "at half-past 6. Carlyle, indispensable, and I should "like his wife of all things: *her* judgment would "be invaluable. You will ask Mac, and why not "his sister? Stanny and Jerrold I should particu- "larly wish; Edwin Landseer; Blanchard; perhaps "Harness; and what say you to Fonblanque and "Fox? I leave it to you. You know the effect I "want to try . . . . Think the *Chimes* a letter, my "dear fellow, and forgive this. I will not fail to "write to you on my travels. Most probably from "Venice. And when I meet you (in sound health "I hope) oh Heaven! what a week we will have."

CHAPTER XXXI.

ITALIAN TRAVEL.

1844.

So it all fell out accordingly. He parted from FERRARA :
1844.
his disconsolate wife, as he told me in his first
letter from Ferrara, on Wednesday the 6th of
November: left her shut up in her palace like a .
baron's lady in the time of the crusades; and had
his first real experience of the wonders of Italy.
He saw Parma, Modena, Bologna, Ferrara, Venice, Cities and
Verona, and Mantua. As to all which the impres- people.
sions conveyed to me in his letters have been more
or less given in his published *Pictures*. They are
charmingly expressed. There is a sketch of a
cicerone at Bologna which will remain in his
books among their many delightful examples of
his unerring and loving perception for every gentle,
heavenly, and tender soul, under whatever conventional disguise it wanders here on earth,
whether as poorhouse orphan or lawyer's clerk,
architect's pupil at Salisbury or cheerful little
guide to graves at Bologna; and there is another
memorable description in his Rembrandt sketch,
in form of a dream, of the silent, unearthly, watery

:

wonders of Venice. This last, though not written until after his London visit, had been prefigured so vividly in what he wrote at once from the spot, that those passages from his letter* may be read still with a quite undiminished interest. "I must "not," he said, "anticipate myself. But, my dear "fellow, nothing in the world that ever you have "heard of Venice, is equal to the magnificent and "stupendous reality. The wildest visions of the "Arabian Nights are nothing to the piazza of

---

* "I began this letter, my dear friend" (he wrote it from Venice on Tuesday night the 12th of November), "with the "intention of describing my travels as I went on. But I "have seen so much, and travelled so hard (seldom dining, "and being almost always up by candle light), that I must "reserve my crayons for the greater leisure of the Peschiere "after we have met, and I have again returned to it. As "soon as I have fixed a place in my mind, I bolt—at such "strange seasons and at such unexpected angles, that the "brave C stares again. But in this way, and by insisting on "having everything shewn to me whether or no, and against "all precedents and orders of proceeding, I get on wonder-"fully." Two days before he had written to me from Fer-rara, after the very pretty description of the vineyards be-tween Piacenza and Parma which will be found in the *Pic-tures from Italy* (pp. 203-4): "If you want an antidote to "this, I may observe that I got up, this moment, to fasten "the window; and the street looked as like some byeway in "Whitechapel—or—I look again—like Wych Street, down "by the little barber's shop on the same side of the way as "Holywell Street—or—I look again—as like Holywell "Street itself—as ever street was like to street, or ever will "be, in this world."

"Saint Mark, and the first impression of the inside
"of the church. The gorgeous and wonderful
"reality of Venice is beyond the fancy of the wildest
"dreamer. Opium couldn't build such a place,
"and enchantment couldn't shadow it forth in a
"vision. All that I have heard of it, read of it
"in truth or fiction, fancied of it, is left thousands
"of miles behind. You know that I am liable to
"disappointment in such things from over-expecta-
"tion, but Venice is above, beyond, out of all
"reach of coming near, the imagination of a man.
"It has never been rated high enough. It is a
"thing you would shed tears to see. When I
"came *on board* here last night (after a five miles'
"row in a gondola; which somehow or other, I
"wasn't at all prepared for); when, from seeing
"the city lying, one light, upon the distant water,
"like a ship, I came plashing through the silent
"and deserted streets; I felt as if the houses were
"reality—the water, fever-madness. But when, in
"the bright, cold, bracing day, I stood upon the
"piazza this morning, by Heaven the glory of the
"place was insupportable! And diving down from
"that into its wickedness and gloom—its awful
"prisons, deep below the water; its judgment
"chambers, secret doors, deadly nooks, where the
"torches you carry with you blink as if they
"couldn't bear the air in which the frightful scenes
"were acted; and coming out again into the radiant,
"unsubstantial Magic of the town; and diving
"in again, into vast churches, and old tombs—
"a new sensation, a new memory, a new mind

"came upon me. Venice is a bit of my brain
"from this time. My dear Forster, if you could
"share my transports (as you would if you were
"here) what would I not give! I feel cruel not to
"have brought Kate and Georgy; positively cruel
"and base. Canaletti and Stanny, miraculous in
"their truth. Turner, very noble. But the reality
"itself, beyond all pen or pencil. I never saw
"the thing before that I should be afraid to de-
"scribe. But to tell what Venice is, I feel to be
"an impossibility. And here I sit alone, writing
"it: with nothing to urge me on, or goad me to
"that estimate, which, speaking of it to anyone I
"loved, and being spoken to in return, would lead
"me to form. In the sober solitude of a famous
"inn; with the great bell of Saint Mark ringing
"twelve at my elbow; with three arched windows
"in my room (two stories high) looking down
"the grand canal and away, beyond, to where the
"sun went down to-night in a blaze; and thinking
"over again those silent speaking faces of Titian
"and Tintoretto; I swear (uncooled by any
"humbug I have seen) that Venice is *the* wonder
"and the new sensation of the world! If you could
"be set down in it, never having heard of it, it
"would still be so. With your foot upon its
"stones, its pictures before you, and its history in
"your mind, it is something past all writing of or
"speaking of—almost past all thinking of. You
"couldn't talk to me in this room, nor I to you,
"without shaking hands and saying 'Good God
"'my dear fellow, have we lived to see this!'"

Lodi:
1844.
17th Novem-
ber.

Five days later, Sunday the 17th, he was at
Lodi, from which he wrote to me that he had
been, like Leigh Hunt's pig, up "all manner of
"streets" since he left his palazzo; that with one
exception he had not on any night given up
more than five hours to rest; that all the days
except two had been bad ("the last two foggy as
"Blackfriars-bridge on Lord Mayor's day"); and
that the cold had been dismal. But what cheerful, keen, observant eyes he carried everywhere;
and, in the midst of new and unaccustomed
scenes, and of objects and remains of art for
which no previous study had prepared him, with
what a delicate play of imagination and fancy
the minuteness and accuracy of his ordinary
vision was exalted and refined; I think strikingly Refining influences.
shown by the few unstudied passages I am preserving from these friendly letters. He saw everything for himself; and from mistakes in judging
for himself which not all the learning and study
in the world will. save ordinary men, the intuition
of genius almost always saved him. Hence there
is hardly anything uttered by him, of this much-
trodden and wearisomely-visited, but eternally
beautiful and interesting country, that will not be
found worth listening to.

"I am already brim-full of cant about pictures, About
paintings.
"and shall be happy to enlighten you on the
"subject of the different schools, at any length
"you please. It seems to me that the preposter-
"ous exaggeration in which our countrymen de-
"light in reference to this Italy, hardly extends to

"the really good things.* Perhaps it is in its

* Four months later, after he had seen the galleries at
Rome and the other great cities, he sent me a remark which
has since had eloquent reinforcement from critics of undeniable authority. "The most famous of the oil paintings
"in the Vatican you know through the medium of the finest
"line-engravings in the world; and as to some of them I
"much doubt, if you had seen them with me, whether you
"might not think you had lost little in having only known
"them hitherto in that translation. Where the drawing is
"poor and meagre, or alloyed by time,—it is so, and it must
"be, often; though no doubt it is a heresy to hint at such a
"thing—the engraving presents the forms and the idea to
"you, in a simple majesty which such defects impair. Where
"this is not the case, and all is stately and harmonious, still
"it is somehow in the very grain and nature of a delicate
"engraving to suggest to you (I think) the utmost delicacy,
"finish, and refinement, as belonging to the original. There-
"fore, though the Picture in this latter case will greatly
"charm and interest you, it does not take you by surprise.
"You are quite prepared beforehand for the fullest excellence
"of which it is capable." In the same letter he wrote of
what remained always a delight in his memory, the charm of
the more private collections. He found magnificent portraits
and paintings in the private palaces, where he thought them
seen to greater advantage than in galleries; because in numbers not so large as to distract attention or confuse the eye.
"There are portraits innumerable by Titian, Rubens, Rem-
"brandt and Vandyke; heads by Guido, and Domenichino,
"and Carlo Dolci; subjects by Raphael, and Correggio, and
"Murillo, and Paul Veronese, and Salvator; which it would
"be difficult indeed to praise too highly, or to praise enough.
"It is a happiness to me to think that they cannot be felt, as
"they should be felt, by the profound connoisseurs who fall

"nature, that there it should fall short. I have   Lond:
"never seen any praise of Titian's great picture   Titian's
"of the Transfiguration of the Virgin at Venice, Transfigu-
"which soared half as high as the beautiful and ration.
"amazing reality. It is perfection. Tintoretto's
"picture too, of the Assembly of the Blest, at
"Venice also, with all the lines in it (it is of im-
"mense size and the figures are countless) tend- Works of
"ing majestically and dutifully to Almighty God Tintoretto.
"in the centre, is grand and noble in the extreme.
"There are some wonderful portraits there, be-
"sides; and some confused, and hurried, and
"slaughterous battle pieces, in which the surpris-
"ing art that presents the generals to your eye,
"so that it is almost impossible you can miss
"them in a crowd though they are in the thick
"of it, is very pleasant to dwell upon. I have
"seen some delightful pictures; and some (at

"into fits upon the longest notice and the most unreasonable Art wholly
"terms. Such tenderness and grace, such noble elevation, satisfactory.
"purity, aud beauty, so shine upon me from some well- '
"remembered spots in the walls of these galleries, as to re-
"lieve my tortured memory from legions of whining friars
"and waxy holy families. I forgive, from the bottom of my
"soul, whole orchestras of earthy angels, and whole groves
"of St. Sebastians stuck as full of arrows according to pat-
"tern as a lying-in pincushion is stuck with pins. And I
"am in no humour to quarrel even with that priestly infatua-
"tion, or priestly doggedness of purpose, which persists in
"reducing every mystery of our religion to some literal de-
"velopment in paint and canvas, equally repugnant to the
"reason and the sentiment of any thinking man."

"Verona and Mantua) really too absurd and ridi-
"culous even to laugh at. Hampton-court is a
"fool to 'em—and oh there are some rum 'uns
"there, my friend. Some werry rum 'uns. . . .
"Two things are clear to me already. One is,

"that the rules of art are much too slavishly fol-
"lowed; making it a pain to you, when you go
"into galleries day after day, to be so very pre-
"cisely sure where this figure will be turning
"round, and that figure will be lying down, and
"that other will have a great lot of drapery
"twined about him, and so forth. This becomes
"a perfect nightmare. The second is, that these
"great men, who were of necessity very much in
"the hands of the monks and priests, painted
"monks and priests a vast deal too often. I con-
"stantly see, in pictures of tremendous power,
"heads quite below the story and the painter;

"and I invariably observe that those heads are of
"the convent stamp, and have their counterparts,
"exactly, in the convent inmates of this hour. I
"see the portraits of monks I know at Genoa, in
"all the lame parts of strong paintings: so I have
"settled with myself that in such cases the lame-
"ness was not with the painter, but with the
"vanity and ignorance of his employers, who
"*would* be apostles on canvas at all events."*

In the same letter he described the Inns. "It
"is a great thing—quite a matter of course—with

---

* The last two lines he has printed in the *Pictures*,
p. 249, "certain of " being inserted before "his employers."

"English travellers, to decry the Italian inns. Of Lonn: 1846.
"course you have no comforts that you are used
"to in England; and travelling alone, you dine
"in your bedroom always. Which is opposed to
"our habits. But they are immeasurably better
"than you would suppose. The attendants are
"very quick; very punctual; and so obliging, if
"you speak to them politely, that you would be
"a beast not to look cheerful, and take every-
"thing pleasantly. I am writing this in a room Place of entertain-
"like a room on the two-pair front of an un- ment.
"finished house in Eaton-square: the very walls
"make me feel as if I were a bricklayer distin-
"guished by Mr. Cubitt with the favour of having
"it to take care of. The windows won't open,
"and the doors won't shut; and these latter (a Windows and
"cat could get in, between them and the floor) doors:
"have a windy command of a colonnade which
"is open to the night, so that my slippers posi-
"tively blow off my feet, and make little circuits
"in the room—like leaves. There is a very ashy
"wood-fire, burning on an immense hearth which
"has no fender (there is no such thing in Italy);
"and it only knows two extremes—an agony of
"heat when wood is put on, and an agony of wood fires.
"cold when it has been on two minutes. There
"is also an uncomfortable stain in the wall, where
"the fifth door (not being strictly indispensable)
"was walled up a year or two ago, and never
"painted over. But the bed is clean; and I have
"had an excellent dinner; and without being ob-
"sequious or servile, which is not at all the char-

"acteristic of the people in the North of Italy,
"the waiters are so amiably disposed to invent
"little attentions which they suppose to be Eng-
"lish, and are so lighthearted and goodnatured,
"that it is a pleasure to have to do with them.
"But so it is with all the people. Vetturino-
"travelling involves a stoppage of two hours in
"the middle of the day, to bait the horses. At
"that time I always walk on. If there are many
"turns in the road, I necessarily have to ask my
"way, very often: and the men are such gentle-
"men, and the women such ladies, that it is quite
"an interchange of courtesies."

Of the help his courier continued to be to
him I had whimsical instances in almost every
letter, but he appears too often in the published
book to require such celebration here. He is
however an essential figure to two little scenes
sketched for me at Lodi, and I may preface them
by saying that Louis Roche, a native of Avignon,
justified to the close his master's high opinion.

He was again engaged for nearly a year in Switzerland, and soon after, poor fellow, though with a
jovial robustness of look and breadth of chest
that promised unusual length of days, was killed
by heart-disease. "The brave C continues to be
"a prodigy. He puts out my clothes at every inn
"as if I were going to stay there twelve months;
"calls me to the instant every morning; lights the
"fire before I get up; gets hold of roast fowls and
"produces them in coaches at a distance from
"all other help, in hungry moments; and is in-

"valuable to me. He is such a good fellow, too, Lodi, 1844.
"that little rewards don't spoil him. I always give Master and
"him, after I have dined, a tumbler of Sauterne servant.
"or Hermitage or whatever I may have; sometimes
"(as yesterday) when we have come to a public-
"house at about eleven o'clock, very cold, having
"started before day-break and had nothing, I make
"him take his breakfast with me; and this renders
"him only more anxious than ever, by redoubling
"attentions, to show me that he thinks he has got
"a good master ... I didn't tell you that the day
"before I left Genoa, we had a dinner-party— Dinner at the
"our English consul and his wife; the banker; Peschiere.
"Sir George Crawford and his wife; the De la
"Rues; Mr. Curry; and some others, fourteen in
"all. At about nine in the morning, two men in
"immense paper caps enquired at the door for
"the brave C, who presently introduced them in
"triumph as the Governor's cooks, his private
"friends, who had come to dress the dinner!
"Jane wouldn't stand this, however; so we were
"obliged to decline. Then there came, at half- Resources of
"hourly intervals, six gentlemen having the appear- a courier.
"ance of English clergymen; other private friends
"who had come to wait... We accepted *their*
"services; and you never saw anything so nicely
"and quietly done. He had asked, as a special
"distinction, to be allowed the supreme control
"of the dessert; and he had ices made like fruit,
"had pieces of crockery turned upside down so
"as to look like other pieces of crockery non-
"existent in this part of Europe, and carried a

"case of tooth-picks in his pocket. Then his "delight was, to get behind Kate at one end of "the table, to look at me at the other, and to say "to Georgy in a low voice whenever he handed "her anything, 'What does master think of datter "'rangement? Is he contént?'..... If you could "see what these fellows of couriers are when their "families are not upon the move, you would feel "what a prize he is. I can't make out whether "he was ever a smuggler, but nothing will induce

"him to give the custom-house-officers anything: "in consequence of which that portmanteau of "mine has been unnecessarily opened twenty times. "Two of them will come to the coach-door, at the "gate of a town. . 'Is there anything contraband "in this carriage, signore?'—'No, no. There's "'nothing here. I am an Englishman, and this is "'my servant.' 'La buona mano signore?' 'Roche,' "'(in English) 'give him something, and get rid "'of him.' He sits unmoved. 'La buona mano "'signore' 'Go along with you!' says the brave C. "'Signore, I am a custom-house-officer!' 'Well, "'then, more shame for you!'—he always makes

"the same answer. And then he turns to me and "says in English: while the custom-house-officer's " face is a portrait of anguish framed in the coach- "window, from his intense desire to know what is "being told to his disparagement: 'Datter chip,' "shaking his fist at him, 'is greatest tief—and "'you know it you rascal—as never did en-razh "'me so, that I cannot bear myself!'   I suppose "chip to mean chap, but it may include the "custom-house-officer's father and have some "reference to the old block, for anything I dis- "tinctly know."

He closed his Lodi letter next day at Milan, whither his wife and her sister had made an eighty miles journey from Genoa, to pass a couple of days with him in Prospero's old Dukedom before he left for London. "We shall go our several "ways on Thursday morning, and I am still bent "on appearing at Cuttris's on Sunday the first, as "if I had walked thither from Devonshire-terrace. "In the meantime I shall not write to you again... "to enhance the pleasure (if anything *can* enhance "the pleasure) of our meeting...I am opening my "arms so wide!" One more letter I had nevertheless; written at Strasburg on Monday night the 25th; to tell me I might look for him one day earlier, so rapid had been his progress. He had been in bed only once, at Friburg for two or three hours, since he left Milan; and he had sledged through the snow on the top of the Simplon in the midst of prodigious cold. "I am "sitting here *in* a wood-fire, and drinking brandy "and water scalding hot, with a faint idea of "coming warm in time. My face is at present "tingling.with the frost and wind, as I suppose "the cymbals may, when that turbaned turk at- "tached to the life guards' band has been newly "clashing at them in St. James's-park. I am in "hopes it may be the preliminary agony of re- "turning animation."

There was certainly no want of animation

when we met. I have but to write the words to
bring back the eager face and figure, as they
flashed upon me so suddenly this wintry Saturday
night that almost before I could be conscious of
his presence I felt the grasp of his hand. It is
almost all I find it possible to remember of the
brief, bright, meeting. Hardly did he seem to
have come when he was gone. But all that the
visit proposed he accomplished. He saw his little
book in its final form for publication; and, to a
select few brought together on Monday the 2nd
of December at my house, had the opportunity

of reading it aloud. An occasion rather memorable, in which was the germ of those readings to
larger audiences by which, as much as by his
books, the world knew him in his later life; but
of which no detail beyond the fact remains in my
memory, and all are now dead who were present
at it excepting only Mr. Carlyle and myself.

Among those however who have thus passed away
was one, our excellent Maclise, who, anticipating
the advice of Captain Cuttle, had "made a note
"of" it in pencil, which I am able here to re-
produce. It will tell the reader all he can wish
to know. He will see of whom the party con-
sisted; and may be assured (with allowance for a
touch of caricature to which I may claim to be
considered myself as the chief victim), that in the
grave attention of Carlyle, the eager interest of
Stanfield and Maclise, the keen look of poor

Laman Blanchard, Fox's rapt solemnity, Jerrold's
skyward gaze, and the tears of Harness and Dyce,

the characteristic points of the scene are sufficiently rendered. All other recollection of it is
passed and gone; but that at least its principal
actor was made glad and grateful, sufficient farther
testimony survives. Such was the report made of
it, that once more, on the pressing intercession of
our friend Thomas Ingoldsby (Mr. Barham), there
was a second reading to which the presence and
enjoyment of Fonblanque gave new zest;* and
when I expressed to Dickens, after he left us, my
grief that he had had so tempestuous a journey
for such brief enjoyment, he replied that the visit
had been one happiness and delight to him. "I
"would not recall an inch of the way to or from
"you, if it had been twenty times as long and
"twenty thousand times as wintry. It was worth
"any travel—anything! With the soil of the road
"in the very grain of my cheeks, I swear I wouldn't
"have missed that week, that first night of our
"meeting, that one evening of the reading at your
"rooms, aye, and the second reading too, for any
"easily stated or conceived consideration."

He wrote from Paris, at which he had stopped
on his way back to see Macready, whom an engagement to act there with Mr. Mitchell's English
company had prevented from joining us in Lin-

* I find the evening mentioned in the diary which Mr.
Barham's son quotes in his Memoir. "December 5, 1844.
"Dined at Forster's with Charles Dickens, Stanfield, Maclise,
"and Albany Fonblanque. Dickens read with remarkable
"effect his Christmas story, the *Chimes*, from the proofs..."
(ii. 191.)

coln's-inn-fields. There had been no such frost
and snow since 1829, and he gave dismal report
of the city. With Macready he had gone two
nights before to the Odéon to see Alexandre
Dumas' *Christine* played by Madame St. George,
"once Napoleon's mistress; now of an immense
"size, from dropsy I suppose; and with little weak
"legs which she can't stand upon. Her age, withal,
"somewhere about 80 or 90. I never in my life
"beheld such a sight. Every stage-conventionality
"she ever picked up (and she has them all) has
"got the dropsy too, and is swollen and bloated
"hideously. The other actors never looked at
"one another, but delivered all their dialogues to
"the pit, in a manner so egregiously unnatural
"and preposterous that I couldn't make up my
"mind whether to take it as a joke or an outrage."
And then came allusion to a project we had

started on the night of the reading, that a private
play should be got up by us on his return from
Italy. "You and I, sir, will reform this altogether."
He had but to wait another night, however, when
he saw it all reformed at the Italian opera where
Grisi was singing in *Il Pirato*, and "the passion
"and fire of a scene between her, Mario, and
"Fornasari, was as good and great as it is possible

"for anything operatic to be. They drew on one
"another, the two men—not like stage-players,
"but like Macready himself: and she, rushing in
"between them; now clinging to this one, now to
"that, now making a sheath for their naked swords
"with her arms, now tearing her hair in distraction

"as they broke away from her and plunged again
"at each other; was prodigious." This was the
theatre at which Macready was immediately to act,
and where Dickens saw him next day rehearse the
scene before the doge and council in *Othello*,
"not as usual facing the float but arranged on
"one side," with an effect that seemed to him to
heighten the reality of the scene.

He left Paris on the night of the 13th with
the malle poste, which did not reach Marseilles
till fifteen hours behind its time, after three days
and three nights travelling over horrible roads.
Then, in a confusion between the two rival
packets for Genoa, he unwillingly detained one
of them more than an hour from sailing; and
only managed at last to get to her just as she
was moving out of harbour. As he went up the
side, he saw a strange sensation among the angry
travellers whom he had detained so long; heard a
voice exclaim "I am blarmed if it ain't DICKENS!"
and stood in the centre of a group of *Five
Americans!* But the pleasantest part of the story
is that they were, one and all, glad to see him;
that their chief man, or leader, who had met him
in New York, at once introduced them all round
with the remark, "Personally our countrymen, and
"you, can fix it friendly sir, I do expectuate;"
and that, through the stormy passage to Genoa
which followed, they were excellent friends. For
the greater part of the time, it is true, Dickens
had to keep to his cabin; but he contrived to get
enjoyment out of them nevertheless. The member

On Board
for Genoa:
1844.
of the party who had the travelling dictionary
wouldn't part with it, though he was dead sick in
the cabin next to my friend's; and every now and
then Dickens was conscious of his fellow-travellers
coming down to him, crying out in varied tones
of anxious bewilderment, "I say, what's French
"for a pillow?" "Is there any Italian phrase for
"a lump of sugar? Just look, will you?" "What
"the devil does echo mean? The garsong says
"echo to everything!" They were excessively
curious to know, too, the population of every
little town on the Cornice, and all its statistics;
"perhaps the very last subjects within the capacity
"of the human intellect," remarks Dickens, "that
"would ever present themselves to an Italian
"steward's mind. He was a very willing fellow, our
"steward; and, having some vague idea that they
"would like a large number, said at hazard fifty
"thousand, ninety thousand, four hundred thou-
"sand, when they asked about the population of
"a place not larger than Lincoln's-inn-fields. And
"when they said *Non Possible!* (which was the
"leader's invariable reply), he doubled or trebled
"the amount; to meet what he supposed to be
"their views, and make it quite satisfactory."

Information
for travellers.

CHAPTER XXXII.

LAST MONTHS IN ITALY.

1846.

ON the 22nd of December he had resumed his ordinary Genoa life; and of a letter from Jeffrey, to whom he had dedicated his little book, he wrote as "most energetic and enthusiastic. "Filer sticks in his throat rather, but all the rest "is quivering in his heart. He is very much struck "by the management of Lilian's story, and cannot "help speaking of that; writing of it all indeed "with the freshness and ardour of youth, and not "like a man whose blue and yellow has turned "grey." Some of its words have been already given. "Miss Coutts has sent Charley, with the "best of letters to me, a Twelfth Cake weighing "ninety pounds, magnificently decorated; and only "think of the characters, Fairburn's Twelfth Night "characters, being detained at the custom-house "for Jesuitical surveillance! But these fellows "are—— Well! never mind. Perhaps you have "seen the history of the Dutch minister at Turin, "and of the spiriting away of his daughter by the "Jesuits? It is all true; though, like the history

Genoa: 1844. Jeffrey on the Chimes.

Birthday gift.

Suspicious characters.

"of our friend's servant,* almost incredible. But "their devilry is such that I am assured by our "consul that if, while we are in the south, we were "to let our children go out with servants on whom "we could not implicitly rely, these holy men "would trot even their small feet into churches "with a view to their ultimate conversion! It is "tremendous even to see them in the streets, or "slinking about this garden." Of his purpose to start for the south of Italy in the middle of January, taking his wife with him, his letter the following week told me; dwelling on all he had missed, in that first Italian Christmas, of our old enjoyments of the season in England; and closing its pleasant talk with a postscript at midnight. "First "of January, 1845. Many many many happy re- "turns of the day! A life of happy years! The "Baby is dressed in thunder, lightning, rain, and "wind. His birth is most portentous here."

It was of ill-omen to me, one of its earliest incidents being my only brother's death; but Dickens had a friend's true helpfulness in sorrow, and a portion of what he then wrote to me I

* In a previous letter he had told me that history. "Apropos of servants, I must tell you of a child-bearing "handmaiden of some friends of ours, a thorough out and "outer, who, by way of expiating her sins, caused herself, "the other day, to be received into the bosom of the in- "fallible church. She had two marchionesses for her spon- "sors; and she is heralded in the Genoa newspapers as Miss "B—, an English lady, who has repented of her errors and "saved her soul alive."

permit myself to preserve in a note * for what it Genoa: 1844.
relates of his own sad experiences and solemn Travel south-
beliefs and hopes. The journey southward began ward.
on the 20th January, and five days later I had a
letter written from La Scala, at a little inn, "sup-
"ported on low brick arches like a British hay-
"stack," the bed in their room "like a mangle,"
the ceiling without lath or plaster, nothing to
speak of available for comfort or decency, and
nothing particular to eat or drink. "But for all
"this I have become attached to the country and
"I don't care who knows it." They had left Pisa
that morning and Carrara the day before: at the Carrara and
latter place an ovation awaiting him, the result Pisa.
of the zeal of our eccentric friend Fletcher, who
happened to be staying there with an English

---

* "I feel the distance between us now, indeed. I would
"to Heaven, my dearest friend, that I could remind you in
"a manner more lively and affectionate than this dull sheet
"of paper can put on, that you have a Brother left. One
"bound to you by ties as strong as ever Nature forged. By Comfort in
"ties never to be broken, weakened, changed in any way— sorrow.
"but to be knotted tighter up, if that be possible, until the
"same end comes to them as has come to these. That end
"but the bright beginning of a happier union, I believe;
"and have never more strongly and religiously believed (and
"oh! Forster, with what a sore heart I have thanked God
"for it) than when that shadow has fallen on my own hearth,
"and made it cold and dark as suddenly as in the home of
"that poor girl you tell me of . . . When you write to me
"again, the pain of this will have passed. No consolation
"can be so certain and so lasting to you as that softened and

CARRARA:
1845.
Marble
theatre.

marble-merchant.*   "There is a beautiful little
"theatre there, built of marble; and they had it
"illuminated that night, in my honour.   There
"was really a very fair opera: but it is curious
"that the chorus has been always, time out of
"mind, made up of labourers in the quarries, who

"manly sorrow which springs up from the memory of the
"Dead.   I read your heart as easily as if I held it in my
"hand, this moment.   And I know—I *know*, my dear friend
"—that before the ground is green above him, you will be con-
"tent that what was capable of death in him, should lie there
". . . I am glad to think it was so easy, and full of peace.
"What can we hope for more, when our own time comes !—
"The day when he visited us in our old house is as fresh to
"me as if it had been yesterday.   I remember him as well
"as I remember you . . I have many things to say, but
"cannot say them now.   Your attached and loving friend
"for life, and far, I hope, beyond it. C. D." (8th of January,
"1845.)

Yorkshire
Italian.

* "A Yorkshireman, who talks Yorkshire Italian with
"the drollest and pleasantest effect ; a jolly, hospitable ex-
"cellent fellow; as odd yet kindly a mixture of shrewdness
"and simplicity as I have ever seen.   He is the only Eng-
"lishman in these parts who has been able to erect an Eng-
"lish household out of Italian servants, but he has done it to
"admiration.   It would be a capital country-house at home ;
"and for staying in 'first-rate.'   (I find myself inadvertently
"quoting *Tom Thumb*.)   Mr. Walton is a man of an ex-
"traordinarily kind heart, and has a compassionate regard
"for Fletcher to whom his house is open as a home,
"which is half affecting and half ludicrous.   He paid the
"other day a hundred pounds for him, which he knows he
"will never see a penny of again." C. D. to J. F. (25th of
January, 1845.)

"don't know a note of music, and sing entirely "by ear. It was crammed to excess, and I had a "great reception; a deputation waiting upon us "in the box, and the orchestra turning out in a "body afterwards and serenading us àt Mr. Wal- "ton's." Between this and Rome they had a some- what wild journey;* and before Radicofani was reached, there were disturbing rumours of bandits and even uncomfortable whispers as to their night's lodging-place. "I really began to think "we might have an adventure; and as I had "brought (like an ass) a bag of Napoleons with "me from Genoa, I called up all the theatrical "ways of letting off pistols that I could call to "mind, and was the more disposed to fire them "from not having any." It ended in no worse adventure, however, than a somewhat exciting dialogue with an old professional beggar at Ra- dicofani itself, in which he was obliged to confess that he came off second-best . It transpired at a little town hanging on a hill side, of which the inhabitants, being all of them beggars, had the habit of swooping down, like so many birds of prey, upon any carriage that approached it.

A wild Journey.

Birds of prey.

---

* "Do you think," he wrote from Ronciglione on the 29th January, "in your state room, when the fog makes "your white blinds yellow, and the wind howls in the brick "and mortar gulf behind that square perspective, with a "middle distance of two ladder-tops and a back-ground of "Drury-lane sky—when the wind howls, I say, as if its "eldest brother, born in Lincoln's-inn-fields, had gone to sea

"Houseless "Dick."

RADICOFANI:
1845.
A beggar and
his staff. "Can you imagine" (he named a first-rate bore,
for whose name I shall substitute) "M. F. G. in a
"very frowsy brown cloak concealing his whole
"figure, and with very white hair and a very white
"beard, darting out of this place with a long staff
"in his hand, and begging? There he was, whether
"you can or not; out of breath with the rapidity
"of his dive, and staying with his staff all the
"Radicofani boys, that he might fight it out with
"me alone. It was very wet, and so was I: for I
"had kept, according to custom, my box-seat. It
"was blowing so hard that I could scarcely stand;
"and there was a custom-house on the spot, be-
"sides. Over and above all this, I had no small
"money; and the brave C never has, when I want
"it for a beggar. When I had excused myself
"several times, he suddenly drew himself up and
"said, with a wizard look (fancy the aggravation
"of M. F. G. as a wizard!) 'Do you know what
"'you are doing, my lord? Do you mean to go
Warning to
my lord. "'on, to-day?' 'Yes,' I said, 'I do.' 'My lord,' he
"said, 'do you know that your vetturino is un-
"'acquainted with this part of the country; that
"'there is a wind raging on the mountain, which
"'will sweep you away; that the courier, the coach,
"'and all the passengers, were blown from the
"'road last year; and that the danger is great and
My lord loses
temper: "'almost certain?' 'No,' I said, 'I don't.' 'My lord,
"'you don't understand me, I think?' 'Yes I do,

"and was making a fortune on the Atlantic—at such times
"do you ever think of houseless Dick?"

RADICOFANI: 1845.

"'d—— you!' nettled by this (you feel it? I con-
"fess it). 'Speak to my servant. It's his business.
"'Not mine'—for he really was too like M. F. G.
"to be borne. If you could have seen him!—
"'Santa Maria, these English lords! It's not their
"business, if they're killed! They leave it to their
"'servants!' He drew off the boys; whispered them
"to keep away from the heretic; and ran up the
"hill again, almost as fast as he had come down.
"He stopped at a little distance as we moved on;
"and pointing to Roche with his long staff cried
"loudly after me, 'It's *his* business if you're killed,
"'is it, my lord? Ha! ha! ha! whose business is it,
"'when the English lords are born! Ha ha ha!' and has the worst of it.
"The boys taking it up in a shrill yell, I left the
"joke and them at this point. But I must confess
"that I thought he had the best of it. And he
"had so far reason for what he urged, that when
"we got on the mountain pass the wind became
"terrific, so that we were obliged to take Kate
"out of the carriage lest she should be blown
"over, carriage and all, and had ourselves to hang
"on to it, on the windy side, to prevent its going '
"Heaven knows where!"

The first impression of Rome was disappoint- At Rome.
ing. It was the evening of the 30th of January,
and the cloudy sky, dull cold rain, and muddy
footways, he was prepared for; but he was not
prepared for the long streets of common-place
shops and houses like Paris or any other capital,
the busy people, the equipages, the ordinary
walkers up and down. "It was no more my Rome, First thoughts.

"degraded and fallen and lying asleep in the sun
"among a heap of ruins, than Lincoln's-inn-fields
"is. So I really went to bed in a very indifferent
"humour." That all this yielded to later and
worthier impressions I need hardly say; and he
had never in his life, he told me afterwards, been
so moved or overcome by any sight as by that of
"the Coliseum, except perhaps by the first con-

"templation of the Falls of Niagara." He went
to Naples for the interval before the holy week;
and his first letter from it was to say that he had
found the wonderful aspects of Rome before he
left, and that for loneliness and grandeur of ruin
nothing could transcend the southern side of the
Campagna. But farther and farther south the
weather had become worse; and for a week before his letter (the 11th of February), the only
bright sky he had seen was just as the sun was

coming up across the sea at Terracina. "Of
"which place, a beautiful one, you can get a very
"good idea by imagining something as totally un-
"like the scenery in *Fra Diavolo* as possible." He

thought the bay less striking at Naples than at
Genoa, the shape of the latter being more perfect
in its beauty, and the smaller size enabling you
to see it all at once, and feel it more like an exquisite picture. The city he conceived the greatest dislike to.* "The condition of the common

* He makes no mention in his book of the pauper burial-
place at Naples, to which the reference made in his letters is
striking enough for preservation. "In Naples, the burying

"people here is abject and shocking. I am afraid
"the conventional idea of the picturesque is asso-
"ciated with such misery and degradation that a
"new picturesque will have to be established as
"the world goes onward. Except Fondi, there is

"place of the poor people is a great paved yard with three
"hundred and sixty-five pits in it: every one covered by a
"square stone which is fastened down. One of these pits is
"opened every night in the year; the bodies of the pauper
"dead are collected in the city; brought out in a cart (like
"that I told you of at Rome); and flung in, uncoffined.
"Some lime is then cast down into the pit; and it is sealed
"up until a year is past, and its turn again comes round.
"Every night there is a pit opened; and every night that
"same pit is sealed up again, for a twelvemonth. The cart
"has a red lamp attached, and at about ten o'clock at night
"you see it glaring through the streets of Naples: stopping
"at the doors of hospitals and prisons, and such places, to
"increase its freight: and then rattling off again. Attached
"to the new cemetery (a very pretty one, and well kept:
"immeasurably better in all respects than Père-la-Chaise)
"there is another similar yard, but not so large." . . . In
connection with the same subject he adds: "About Naples,
"the dead are borne along the street, uncovered, on an open
"bier; which is sometimes hoisted on a sort of palanquin,
"covered with a cloth of scarlet and gold. This exposure
"of the deceased is not peculiar to that part of Italy; for
"about midway between Rome and Genoa we encountered
"a funeral procession attendant on the body of a woman,
"which was presented in its usual dress, to my eyes (looking
"from my elevated seat on the box of a travelling carriage)
"as if she were alive, and resting on her bed. An attendant
"priest was chanting lustily—and as badly as the priests in-
"variably do. Their noise is horrible . . ."

NAPLES:
1845.

"nothing on earth that I have seen so dirty as
"Naples,   I don't know what to liken the streets
"to where the mass of the lazzaroni live.   You re-
"collect that favourite pigstye of mine near Broad-
"stairs? They are more like streets of such apart-
"ments heaped up story on story, and tumbled
"house on house, than anything else I can think
"of, at this moment." In a later letter he was
even less tolerant.   "What would I give that you

Lazzaroni.

"should see the lazzaroni as they really are—mere
"squalid, abject, miserable animals for vermin to
"batten on; slouching, slinking, ug ly, shabby, sca-
"venging scarecrows! And oh the raffish counts
"and more than doubtful countesses, the noodles
"and the blacklegs, the good society! And oh the
"miles of miserable streets and wretched occu-
"pants,* to which Saffron-hill or the Borough-mint
"is a kind of small gentility, which are found to

False pic-
turesque.

"be so picturesque by English lords and ladies;
"to whom the wretchedness left behind at home
"is lowest of the low, and vilest of the vile, and
"commonest of all common things.   Well! well!
"I have often thought that one of the best chances
"of immortality for a writer is in the Death of
"his language, when he immediately becomes

Unkindness
to brutes.

* "Thackeray praises the people of Italy for being kind
"to brutes. There is probably no country in the world
"where they are treated with such frightful cruelty. It is
"universal." (Naples, 2nd Feb. 1845.) Emphatic confirma-
tion of this remark has been lately given by the Naples
correspondent of the *Times*, writing under date of February
1872.

"good company; and I often think here,—What Rome, 1845.
"*would* you say to these people, milady and mi- What makes good company.
"lord, if they spoke out of the homely dictionary
"of your own 'lower orders.'" He was again at
Rome on Sunday the second of March.

Sad news from me as to a common and very
dear friend awaited him there; but it is a subject
on which I may not dwell farther than to say Sad English news.
that there arose from it much to redeem even
such a sorrow, and that this I could not indicate
better than by these wise and tender words from
Dickens. "No philosophy will bear these dreadful
"things, or make a moment's head against them,
"but the practical one of doing all the good we
"can, in thought and deed. While we can, God
"help us! ourselves stray from ourselves so easily;
"and there are all around us such frightful
"calamities besetting the world in which we live;
"nothing else will carry us through it. . . . What
"a comfort to reflect on what you tell me. Bul- True friends in calamity.
"wer Lytton's conduct is that of a generous
"and noble-minded man, as I have ever thought
"him. Our dear good Procter too! And
"Thackeray—how earnest they have all been! I
"am very glad to find you making special men-
"tion of Charles Lever. I am glad over every
"name you write. It says something for our
"pursuit, in the midst of all its miserable disputes
"and jealousies, that the common impulse of its
"followers, in such an instance as this, is surely
"and certainly of the noblest."

After the ceremonies of the holy week, of

which the descriptions sent to me were reproduced in his book, he went to Florence,* which lived always afterwards in his memory with Venice, and with Genoa.   He thought these the three great Italian cities.   "There are some places "here,**—oh Heaven how fine! I wish you could

* The reader will perhaps think with me that what he noticed, on the roads in Tuscany more than in any others, of wayside crosses and religious memorials, may be worth preserving. . . . "You know that in the streets and corners "of roads, there are all sorts of crosses and similar memo"rials to be seen in Italy. The most curious are, I think, "in Tuscany. There is very seldom a figure on the cross, "though there is sometimes a face; but they are remarkable "for being garnished with little models in wood of every "possible object that can be connected with the Saviour's

Wayside memorials.

"death. The cock that crowed when Peter had denied his "master thrice, is generally perched on the tip-top; and an "ornithological phenomenon he always is. Under him is the "inscription. Then, hung on to the cross-beam, are the "spear, the reed with the sponge of vinegar and water at the "end, the coat without seam for which the soldiers cast lots, "the dice-box with which they threw for it, the hammer that "drove in the nails, the pincers that pulled them out, the "ladder which was set against the cross, the crown of thorns, "the instrument of flagellation, the lantern with which Mary "went to the tomb—I suppose; I can think of no other— "and the sword with which Peter smote the high priest's "servant. A perfect toyshop of little objects; repeated at "every four or five miles all along the highway."

Visit to Landor's villa.

** Of his visit to Fiesole I have spoken in my LIFE OF LANDOR. "Ten years after Landor had lost this home, an "Englishman travelling in Italy, his friend and mine, visited

"see the tower of the palazzo Vecchio as it lies
"before me at this moment, on the opposite bank
"of the Arno! But I will tell you more about it,
"and about all Florence, from my shady arm-
"chair up among the Peschiere oranges. I shall
"not be sorry to sit down in it again. . . . Poor
"Hood, poor Hood! I still look for his death,

"the neighbourhood for his sake, drove out from Florence to
"Fiesole, and asked his coachman which was the villa in
"which the Landor family lived. 'He was a dull dog, and
"'pointed to Boccaccio's. I didn't believe him. He was
"'so deuced ready that I knew he lied. I went up to the
"'convent, which is on a height, and was leaning over a
"'dwarf wall basking in the noble view over a vast range of
"'hill and valley, when a little peasant girl came up and
"'began to point out the localities. *Ecco la villa Landora!*
"'was one of the first half-dozen sentences she spoke. My
"'heart swelled as Landor's would have done when I looked
"'down upon it, nestling among its olive-trees and vines,
"'and with its upper windows (there are five above the
"'door) open to the setting sun. Over the centre of these
"'there is another story, set upon the housetop like a tower;
"'and all Italy, except its sea, is melted down into the
"'glowing landscape it commands. I plucked a leaf of ivy
"'from the convent-garden as I looked; and here it is. For Ivy leaf from
"'Landor. With my love.' So wrote Mr. Dickens to me Fiesole.
"from Florence on the 2nd of April 1845; and when I turned
"over Landor's papers in the same month after an interval
"of exactly twenty years, the ivy-leaf was found carefully
"enclosed, with the letter in which I had sent it." Dickens
had asked him before leaving what he would most wish to
have in remembrance of Italy. "An ivy-leaf from Fiesole,"
said Landor.

"and he still lingers on.   And Sydney Smith's
"brother gone after poor dear Sydney himself!
"Maltby will wither when he reads it; and poor
"old Rogers will contradict some young man at
"dinner, every day for three weeks."

Before he left Florence (on the 4th of April)
I heard of a "very pleasant and very merry day"
at Lord Holland's; and I ought to have mentioned how much he was gratified, at Naples, by
the attentions of the English Minister there, Mr.
Temple, Lord Palmerston's brother, whom he
described as a man supremely agreeable, with
everything about him in perfect taste, and with
that truest gentleman-manner which has its root
in kindness and generosity of nature.   He was
back at home in the Peschiere on Wednesday the
ninth of April.   Here he continued to write to
me every week, for as long as he remained, of
whatever he had seen: with no definite purpose
as yet, but the pleasure of interchanging with
myself the impressions and emotions undergone
by him. "Seriously," he wrote to me on the 13th
of April, "it is a great pleasure to me to find
"that you are really pleased with these shadows
"in the water, and think them worth the looking
"at. Writing at such odd places, and in such odd
"seasons, I have been half savage with myself,
"very often, for not doing better. But d'Orsay,
"from whom I had a charming letter three days
"since, seems to think as you do of what he has
"read in those shown to him, and says they re-
"mind him vividly of the; real aspect of these

"scenes. . . . Well, if we should determine, after
"we have sat in council, that the experiences
"they relate are to be used, we will call B. and
"E. to their share and voice in the matter."
Shortly before he left, the subject was again referred to (7th of June). "I am in as great doubt To publish or
"as you about the letters I have written you with not?
"these Italian experiences. I cannot for the life
"of me devise any plan of using them to my own
"satisfaction, and yet think entirely with you
"that in some form I ought to use them." Circumstances not in his contemplation at this time
settled the form they ultimately took.

Two more months were to finish his Italian
holiday, and I do not think he enjoyed any part
of it so much as its close. He had formed a
real friendship for Genoa, was greatly attached
to the social circle he had drawn round him
there, and liked rest after his travel all the more Weekly
for the little excitement of living its activities letters.
over again, week by week, in these letters to me.
And so, from his "shady arm-chair up among the
Peschiere oranges," I had at regular intervals
what he called his rambling talk; went over with
him again all the roads he had taken; and of the
more important scenes and cities, such as Venice,
Rome, and Naples, received such rich filling-in
to the first outlines sent, as fairly justified the
title of *Pictures* finally chosen for them. The
weather all the time too had been without a flaw.
"Since our return," he wrote on the 27th April,
"we have had charming spring days. The garden

"is one grove of roses; we have left off fires; and "we breakfast and dine again in the great hall, "with the windows open. To-day we have rain, "but rain was rather wanted I believe, so it gives "offence to nobody. As far as I have had an "opportunity of judging yet, the spring is the "most delightful time in this country. But for "all that I am looking with eagerness to the
"tenth of June, impatient to renew our happy "old walks and old talks in dear old home."

Of incidents during these remaining weeks there were few, but such as he mentioned had in them points of humour or character still worth remembering.* Two men were hanged in the city; and two ladies of quality, he told me, agreed to keep up for a time a prayer for the souls of these two miserable creatures so incessant that Heaven should never for a moment be left alone:

---

* One message sent me, though all to whom it refers have now passed away, I please myself by thinking may still, where he might most have desired it, be the occasion of pleasure. ". . Give my love to Colden, and tell him if he "leaves London before I return I will ever more address him "and speak of him as *Colonel* Colden. Kate sends *her* love
"to him also, and we both entreat him to say all the affec- "tionate things he can spare for third parties—using so many "himself—when he writes to Mrs. Colden: whom you ought "to know, for she, as I have often told you, is BRILLIANT. "I would go five hundred miles to see her for five minutes. "I am deeply grieved by poor Felton's loss. His letter is "manly, and of a most rare kind in the dignified composure "and silence of his sorrow." (See Vol. II. p. 150).

to which end "they relieved each other" after Genoa: 1845. Morbid sympathies.
such wise, that, for the whole of the stated time,
one of them was always on her knees in the
cathedral church of San Lorenzo. From which
he inferred that "a morbid sympathy for criminals
"is not wholly peculiar to England, though it
"affects more people in that country perhaps than
"in any other."

Of Italian usages to the dead some notices Deaths among English residents.
from his letters have been given, and he had an
example before he left of the way in which they
affected English residents. A gentleman of his
friend Fletcher's acquaintance living four miles
from Genoa had the misfortune to lose his wife;
and no attendance on the dead beyond the city
gate, nor even any decent conveyance, being
practicable, the mourner, to whom Fletcher had
promised nevertheless the sad satisfaction of an
English funeral, which he had meanwhile taken A funeral.
enormous secret pains to arrange with a small
Genoese upholsterer, was waited upon, on the
appointed morning, by a very bright yellow hack-
ney-coach-and-pair driven by a coachman in yet
brighter scarlet knee-breeches and waistcoat, who Scarlet breeches out of place.
wanted to put the husband and the body inside
together. "They were obliged to leave one of the
"coach-doors open for the accommodation even
"of the coffin; the widower walked beside the
"carriage to the Protestant cemetery; and Fletcher
"followed on a big grey horse." *

* "It matters little now," says Dickens, after describing
this incident in one of his minor writings, "for coaches of

Scarlet breeches reappear, not less character-
istically, in what his next letter told of a couple
of English travellers who took possession at this
time (24th of May) of a portion of the ground
floor of the Peschiere. They had with them a
meek English footman who immediately confided

Complaint of a meek footman.

to Dickens's servants, among other personal griev-
ances, the fact that he was made to do everything,

"all colours are alike to poor Kindheart, and he rests far
"north of the little cemetery with the cypress trees,. by the
"city walls where the Mediterranean is so beautiful." What
was said on a former page (ante, 196) may here be completed by a couple of stories told to Dickens by Mr. Walton,
suggestive strongly of the comment that it required indeed a
kind heart and many attractive qualities (which undoubtedly
Fletcher possessed) to render tolerable such eccentricities.
Dickens made one of these stories wonderfully amusing. It
related the introduction by Fletcher of an unknown English-

Angus
Fletcher,
Vol. II. p. 73.

man to the marble-merchant's house; the stay there of the
Englishman, unasked, for ten days; and finally the walking
off of the Englishman in a shirt, pair of stockings, neckcloth,
pocket-handkerchief, and other etceteras belonging to Mr.
Walton, which never reappeared after that hour. On another
occasion, Fletcher confessed to Mr. Walton his having given
a bill to a man in Carrara for £30; and the marble-merchant
having asked, "And pray, Fletcher, have you arranged to
"meet it when it falls due?" Fletcher at once replied,
"Yes," and to the marble-merchant's farther enquiry "how?"
added, in his politest manner, "I have arranged to blow my
"brains out the day before!" The poor fellow did afterwards almost as much self-violence without intending it, dying
of fever caught in night-wanderings through Liverpool half-
clothed amid storms of rain.

even cooking, in crimson breeches; which in a Gɛɴoᴀ: 1845.
hot climate, he protested, was "a grinding of him
down." "He is a poor soft country fellow; and
"his master locks him up at night, in a basement
"room with iron bars to the window. Between
"which our servants poke wine in, at midnight.
"His master and mistress buy old boxes at the Ilɪ ᴇm-ployerᴍ.
"curiosity shops, and pass their lives in lining
"'em with bits of parti-coloured velvet. A droll
"existence, is it not? We are lucky to have had
"the palace to ourselves until now, but it is so
"large that we never see or hear these people;
"and I should not have known even, if they had
"not called upon us, that another portion of the
"ground floor had been taken by some friends of
"old Lady Holland—whom I seem to see again, A romem-branco of Lady Holland.
"crying about dear Sydney Smith, behind that
"green screen as we last saw her together." *

Then came a little incident also characteristic.
An English ship of war, the Phantom, appeared
in the harbour; and from her commander, Sir
Henry Nicholson, Dickens received, among attentions very pleasant to him, an invitation to lunch
on board and bring his wife, for whom, at a time
appointed, a boat was to be sent to the Ponte
Reale (the royal bridge). But no boat being Nautical Incident.
there at the time, Dickens sent off his servant in
another boat to the ship to say he feared some
mistake. "While we were walking up and down

* Sydney died on the 22nd of February ('45), in his
77th year.

GENOA:
1845.

"a neighbouring piazza in his absence, a brilliant
"fellow in a dark blue shirt with a white hem to
"it all round the collar, regular corkscrew curls,
"and a face as brown as a berry, comes up to
"me and says 'Beg your pardon sir—Mr. Dickens?'
"'Yes.' 'Beg your pardon sir, but I'm one of the
"'ship's company of the Phantom sir, cox'en of
"'the cap'en's gig sir, she's a lying off the pint
"'sir—been there half an hour.' 'Well but my
"'good fellow,' I said, 'you're at the wrong place!'
"'Beg your pardon sir, I was afeerd it was the
"'wrong place sir, but I've asked them Genoese
"'here sir, twenty times, if it was Port Real; and
"'they knows no more than a dead jackass!'—
"Isn't it a good thing to have made a regular
"Portsmouth name of it?"

A touch of
Portsmouth.

That was in his letter of the 1st June, which
began by telling me it had been twice begun
and twice flung into the basket, so great was his
indisposition to write as the time for departure
came; and which ended thus. "The fireflies at
"night now, are miraculously splendid; making
"another firmament among the rocks on the sea-
"shore, and the vines inland. They get into the
"bedrooms, and fly about, all night, like beautiful
"little lamps.* . . . I have surrendered much I

Fireflies at
night.

* A remark on this, made in my reply, elicited what
follows in a letter during his travel home: "Odd enough that
"remark of yours. I had been wondering at Rome that
"Juvenal (which I have been always lugging out of a bag,
"on all occasions) never used the fireflies for an illustration.
"But even now, they are only partially seen; and no where I

Fireflies only
in modern
Italy.

"had fixed my heart upon, as you know, admit-
"ting you have had reason for not coming to us
"here: but I stand by the hope that you and Mac
"will come and meet us at Brussels; it being so
"very easy. A day or two there, and at Antwerp,
"would be very happy for us; and we could still
"dine in Lincoln's-inn-fields on the day of arrival."
I had been unable to join him in Genoa, urgently
as he had wished it: but what is said here was
done, and Jerrold was added to the party.

His last letter from Genoa was written on the
7th of June, not from the Peschiere, but from a
neighbouring palace, "Brignole Rosso," into which
he had fled from the miseries of moving. "They
"are all at sixes and sevens up at the Peschiere,
"as you may suppose; and Roche is in a condi-
"tion of tremendous excitement, engaged in set-
"tling the inventory with the house-agent, who
"has just told me he is the devil himself. I had
"been appealed to, and had contented myself
"with this expression of opinion. 'Signor Noli,
"'you are an old impostor!' 'Illustrissimo,' said
"Signor Noli in reply, 'your servant is the devil

"believe in such enormous numbers as on the Mediterranean
"coast-road, between Genoa and Spezzia. I will ascertain
"for curiosity's sake, whether there are any at this time in
"Rome, or between it and the country-house of Mæcenas—
"on the ground of Horace's journey. I know there is a
"place on the French side of Genoa, where they begin at a
"particular boundary-line, and are never seen beyond it. . . .
"All wild to see you at Brussels! What a meeting we will
"have, please God!"

"'himself: sent on earth to torture me.' I look "occasionally towards the Peschiere (it is visible "from this room), expecting to see one of them "flying out of a window. Another great cause of "commotion is, that they have been paving the "lane by which the house is approached, ever "since we returned from Rome. We have not "been able to get the carriage up since that time, "in consequence; and unless they finish to-night, "it can't be packed in the garden, but the things "will have to be brought down in baskets, piece- "meal, and packed in the street. To avoid this "inconvenient necessity, the Brave made proposals "of bribery to the paviours last night, and in- "duced them to pledge themselves that the car- "riage should come up at seven this evening. "The manner of doing that sort of paving work "here, is to take a pick or two with an axe, and "then lie down to sleep for an hour. When I "came out, the Brave had issued forth to examine "the ground; and was standing alone in the sun "among a heap of prostrate figures: with a Great "Despair depicted in his face, which it would be "hard to surpass. It was like a picture—'After "'the Battle'—Napoleon by the Brave: Bodies by "the Paviours."

He came home by the Great St. Gothard, and was quite carried away by what he saw of Switzerland. The country was so divine that he should have wondered indeed if its sons and daughters had ever been other than a patriotic people. Yet, infinitely above the country he had

left as he ranked it in its natural splendours,
there was something more enchanting than these
that he lost in leaving Italy; and he expressed
this delightfully in the letter from Lucerne (14th
of June (which closes the narrative of his Italian
life.

"We came over the St. Gothard, which has
"been open only eight days. The road is cut
"through the snow, and the carriage winds along
"a narrow path between two massive snow walls,
"twenty feet high or more. Vast plains of snow
"range up the mountain-sides above the road,
"itself seven thousand feet above the sea; and
"tremendous waterfalls, hewing out arches for
"themselves in the vast drifts, go thundering down
"from precipices into deep chasms, here and
"there and everywhere: the blue water tearing
"through the white snow with an awful beauty
"that is most sublime. The pass itself, the
"mere pass over the top, is not so fine, I
"think, as the Simplon; and there is no plain
"upon the summit, for the moment it is reached
"the descent begins. So that the loneliness and
"wildness of the Simplon are not equalled *there*.
"But being much higher, the ascent and the
"descent range over a much greater space of
"country; and on both sides there are places of
"terrible grandeur, unsurpassable, I should ima-
"gine, in the world. The Devil's Bridge, terrific!
"The whole descent between Andermatt (where
"we slept on Friday night) and Altdorf, William
"Tell's town, which we passed through yesterday

"afternoon, is the highest sublimation of all you
"can imagine in the way of Swiss scenery.   Oh
"God! what a beautiful country it is!   How
"poor and shrunken, beside it, is Italy in its
"brightest aspect!

"I look upon the coming down from the Great
"St. Gothard with a carriage and four horses and
"only one postilion, as the most dangerous thing
"that a carriage and horses can do. We had two
"great wooden logs for drags, and snapped them
"both like matches. The road is like a geometrical
"staircase, with horrible depths beneath it; and at
"every turn it is a toss-up, or seems to be, whether
"the leaders shall go round or over.   The lives
"of the whole party may depend upon a strap in
"the harness; and if we broke our rotten harness
"once yesterday, we broke it at least a dozen
"times.   The difficulty of keeping the horses to-
"gether in the continual and steep circle, is im-
"mense.   They slip and slide, and get their legs
"over the traces, and are dragged up against the
"rocks; carriage, horses, harness, all a confused
"heap. The Brave, and I, and the postilion, were
"constantly at work, in extricating the whole con-
"cern from a tangle, like a skein of thread.   We
"broke two thick iron chains, and crushed the
"box of a wheel, as it was; and the carriage is
"now undergoing repair, under the window, on
"the margin of the lake: where a woman in short
"petticoats, a stomacher, and two immensely long
"tails of black hair hanging down her back very
"nearly to her heels, is looking on—apparently

"dressed for a melodrama, but in reality a waitress LUCERNE!
1845.
"at this establishment.

"If the Swiss villages looked beautiful to me
"in winter, their summer aspect is most charming: Swiss
villages.
"most fascinating: most delicious. Shut in by
"high mountains capped with perpetual snow;
"and dotting a rich carpet of the softest turf,
"overshadowed by great trees; they seem so many
"little havens of refuge from the troubles and
"miseries of great towns. The cleanliness of the
"little baby-houses of inns is wonderful to those
"who come from Italy. But the beautiful Italian What is left
behind the
Alps.
"manners, the sweet language, the quick recogni-
"tion of a pleasant look or cheerful word; the
"captivating expression of a desire to oblige in
"everything; are left behind the Alps. Remember-
"ing them, I sigh for the dirt again: the brick
"floors, bare walls, unplaistered ceilings, and
"broken windows."

We met at Brussels; Maclise, Jerrold, myself,
and the travellers; passed a delightful week in
Flanders together; and were in England at the
close of June.

CHAPTER XXXIII.

AGAIN IN ENGLAND.

1845—1846.

His first letter after again taking possession of Devonshire-terrace revived a subject on which opinions had been from time to time interchanged during his absence, and to which there was allusion in the agreement executed before his departure. The desire was still as strong with him as when he started *Master Humphrey's Clock* to establish a periodical, that, while relieving his own pen by enabling him to receive frequent help from other writers, might yet retain always the popularity of his name. "I really think I have an idea, and "not a bad one, for the periodical. I have turned "it over, the last two days, very much in my "mind: and think it positively good. I incline "still to weekly; price three halfpence, if possible; "partly original, partly select; notices of books, "notices of theatres, notices of all good things, "notices of all bad ones; *Carol* philosophy, cheer- "ful views, sharp anatomization of humbug, jolly "good temper; papers always in season, pat to "the time of year; and a vein of glowing, hearty,

London: 1845.

"generous, mirthful, beaming reference in every-
"thing to Home, and Fireside. And I would call
"it, sir,—

THE CRICKET.

A cheerful creature that chirrups on the Hearth.

Natural History.

Proposed weekly paper.

"Now, don't decide hastily till you've heard
"what I would do. I would come out, sir, with
"a prospectus on the subject of the Cricket that
"should put everybody in a good temper, and
"make such a dash at people's fenders and arm-
"chairs as hasn't been made for many a long day.
"I could approach them in a different mode under
"this name, and in a more winning and immediate
"way, than under any other. I would at once sit
"down upon their very hobs; and take a personal
"and confidential position with them which should
"separate me, instantly, from all other periodicals
"periodically published, and supply a distinct and
"sufficient reason for my coming into existence.
"And I would chirp, chirp, chirp away in every
"number until I chirped it up to——well, you
"shall say how many hundred thousand! . . .
"Seriously, I feel a capacity in this name and
"notion which appears to give us a tangible start-
"ing-point, and a real, defined, strong, genial drift
"and purpose. I seem to feel that it is an aim
"and name which people would readily and plea-

Prospectus for it.

Home confidence.

LONDON:
1845.

"santly connect with *me;* and that, for a good
"course and a clear one, instead of making circles
"pigeon-like at starting, here we should be safe.
"I think the general recognition would be likely
"to leap at it; and of the helpful associations that
"could be clustered round the idea at starting,
"and the pleasant tone of which the working of
"it is susceptible, I have not the smallest doubt.
". . . But you shall determine. What do you think?

Chances
for and
against it.

"And what do you say? The chances are, that it
"will either strike you instantly, or not strike you
"at all. Which is it, my dear fellow? You know
"I am not bigoted to the first suggestions of my
"own fancy; but you know also exactly how I
"should use such a lever, and how much power I
"should find in it. Which is it? What do you
"say?—I have not myself said half enough. In-
"deed I have said next to nothing; but like the
"parrot in the negro-story, I 'think a dam deal.'"

Too de-
pendent on
himself.

My objection, incident more or less to every
such scheme, was the risk of losing its general
advantage by making it too specially dependent
on individual characteristics; but there was much
in favour of the present notion, and its plan had
been modified so far, in the discussions that followed, as to involve less absolute personal iden-
tification with Dickens,—when discussion, project,

Swept away
by larger
venture.

everything was swept away by a larger scheme,
in its extent and its danger more suitable to the
wild and hazardous enterprises of that prodigious
year (1845) of excitement and disaster. In this
more tremendous adventure, already hinted at on

a previous page, we all became involved; and the
chirp of the Cricket, delayed in consequence until
Christmas, was heard then in circumstances quite
other than those that were first intended. The
change he thus announced to me about half way
through the summer, in the same letter which
told me the success of d'Orsay's kind exertion to
procure a fresh engagement for his courier Roche.*
"What do you think of a notion that has occurred
"to me in connection with our abandoned little
"weekly? It would be a delicate and beautiful
"fancy for a Christmas book, making the Cricket
"a little household god—silent in the wrong and
"sorrow of the tale, and loud again when all went

---

* Count d'Orsay's note about Roche, replying to Dickens's
recommendation of him at his return; has touches of the
pleasantry, wit, and kindliness that gave such a wonderful
fascination to its writer. "Gore House, 6 July, 1845.
"MON CHER DICKENS, Nous sommes enchantés de votre
"retour. Voici, thank God, Devonshire Place ressuscité.
"Venez luncheoner demain à 1 heure, et amenez notre brave
"ami Forster. J'attends la perle fine des couriers. Vous
"l'immortalisez par ce certificat—la difficulté sera de trouver
"un maître digne de lui. J'essayerai de tout mon cœur. La
"Reine devroit le prendre pour aller en Saxe-Gotha, car je
"suis convaincu qu'il est assez intelligent pour pouvoir dé-
"couvrir ce Royaume. Gore House vous envoye un cargo
"d'amitiés des plus sincères. Donnez de ma part 100,000
"kind regards à Madame Dickens. Toujours votre affectionné,
"Cᵉ D'ORSAY. J'ai vu le courier, c'est le tableau de l'hon-
"nêteté, et de la bonne humeur. Don't forget to be here at
"one to-morrow, with Forster."

"well and happy." The reader will not need to be told that thus originated the story of the *Cricket on the Hearth*, a Fairy Tale of Home, which had a great popularity in the Christmas days of 1845. Its sale at the outset doubled that of both its predecessors.

But as yet the larger adventure has not made itself known, and the interval was occupied with the private play of which the notion had been started between us at his visit in December, and which cannot now be better introduced than by
a passage of autobiography. This belongs to his early life, but I overlooked it when engaged on that portion of the memoir; and the accident gives it now a more appropriate place. For, though the facts related belong to the interval described in the chapter on his school-days and start in life, when he had to pass nearly two years as a reporter for one of the offices in Doctors' Commons, the influences and character it illustrates had their strongest expression at this later time. I had asked him, after his return to Genoa, whether he continued to think that we should have the play; and this was his reply. It will startle and interest More of the
story of his
early years. the reader, and I must confess that it took myself by surprise; for I did not thus early know the story of his boyish years, and I thought it strange that he could have concealed from me so much.

"ARE we to have that play??? Have I spoken "of it, ever since I came home from London, as "a settled thing! I do not know if I have ever

"told you seriously, but I have often thought, London:
1846.
"that I should certainly have been as successful
"on the boards as I have been between them.
"I assure you, when I was on the stage at Mont- Page 280 of
Vol. II.
"real (not having played for years) I was as
"much astonished at the reality and ease, to
"myself, of what I did as if I had been another
"man. See how oddly things come about! When
"I was about twenty, and knew three or four
"successive years of Mathews's At Homes from
"sitting in the pit to hear them, I wrote to Bart-
"ley who was stage manager at Covent-garden, Wish to try
the stage.
"and told him how young I was, and exactly
"what I thought I could do; and that I believed
"I had a strong perception of character and od-
"dity, and a natural power of reproducing in my
"own person what I observed in others. There
"must have been something in the letter that
"struck the authorities, for Bartley wrote to me, Applies to
Covent-
garden
manager.
"almost immediately, to say that they were busy
"getting up the *Hunchback* (so they were!) but
"that they would communicate with me again, in
"a fortnight. Punctual to the time, another letter
"came: with an appointment to do anything of
"Mathews's I pleased, before him and Charles
"Kemble, on a certain day at the theatre. My
"sister Fanny was in the secret, and was to go Sister Fanny
in the secret.
"with me to play the songs. I was laid up, when
"the day came, with a terrible bad cold and an
"inflammation of the face; the beginning, by the
"bye, of that annoyance in one ear to which I
"am subject at this day. I wrote to say so, and

"added that I would resume my application next
"season. I made a great splash in the gallery
"soon afterwards; the *Chronicle* opened to me; I
"had a distinction in the little world of the news-
"paper, which made me like it; began to write;
"didn't want money; had never thought of the
"stage, but as a means of getting it; gradually
"left off turning my thoughts that way; and never

"resumed the idea. I never told you this, did I?
"See how near I may have been, to another sort
"of life.

"This was at the time when I was at Doctors'
"Commons as a shorthand writer for the proctors.
"And I recollect I wrote the letter from a little
"office I had there, where the answer came also.
"It wasn't a very good living (though not a *very*
"bad one), and was wearily uncertain; which
"made me think of the Theatre in quite a busi-

"ness-like way. I went to some theatre every
"night, with a very few exceptions, for at least
"three years: really studying the bills first, and
"going to where there was the best acting: and
"always to see Mathews whenever he played. I
"practised immensely (even such things as walk-
"ing in and out, and sitting down in a chair):
"often four, five, six hours a day: shut up in my
"own room, or walking about in the fields. I

"prescribed to myself, too, a sort of Hamiltonian
"system for learning parts; and learnt a great
"number. I haven't even lost the habit now, for
"I knew my Canadian parts immediately, though
"they were new to me. I must have done a good

"deal: for, just as Macready found me out, they
"used to challenge me at Braham's: and Yates,
"who was knowing enough in those things, wasn't
"to be parried at all. It was just the same, that
"day at Keeley's, when they were getting up the
"*Chuzzlewit* last June.

"If you think Macready would be interested
"in this Strange news from the South, tell it him.
"Fancy Bartley or Charles Kemble *now!* And how
"little they suspect me!" In the later letter from
Lucerne written as he was travelling home, he
adds: "*Did* I ever tell you the details of my
"theatrical idea, before? Strange, that I should
"have quite forgotten it. I had an odd fancy, when
"I was reading the unfortunate little farce at
"Covent-garden, that Bartley looked as if some
"struggling recollection and connection were stir-
"ring up within him—but it may only have been
"his doubts of that humorous composition." The
last allusion is to the farce of the *Lamplighter*
which he read in the Covent-garden green-room,
and to which former allusion was made in speaking of his wish to give help to Macready's mana-
gerial enterprise.

What Might have Been is a history of too
little profit to be worth anybody's writing, and
here there is no call even to regret how great an
actor was in Dickens lost. He took to a higher
calling, but it included the lower. There was no
character created by him into which life and
reality were not thrown with such vividness, that
the thing written did not seem to his readers the

London:
1845.

Strange news
for Macready.

Then and
now.

Page 239 of
Vol. I.

The lower in
the higher
calling.

thing actually done, whether the form of disguise
put on by the enchanter was Mrs. Gamp, Tom
Pinch, Mr. Squeers, or Fagin the Jew. He had
the power of projecting himself into shapes and
suggestions of his fancy which is one of the
marvels of creative imagination, and what he
desired to express he became. The assumptions of
the theatre have the same method at a lower
pitch, depending greatly on personal accident;
but the accident as much as the genius favoured
Dickens, and another man's conception underwent in his acting the process which in writing
he applied to his own. Into both he flung himself with the passionate fullness of his nature; and
though the theatre had limits for him that may
be named hereafter, and he was always greater
in quickness of assumption than in steadiness of
delineation, there was no limit to his delight
and enjoyment in the adventures of our theatrical
holiday.

In less than three weeks after his return we
had selected our play, cast our parts, and all but
engaged our theatre; as I find by a note from
my friend of the 22nd of July, in which the good
natured laugh can give now no offence, since all
who might have objected to it have long gone
from us. Fanny Kelly, the friend of Charles Lamb,
and a genuine successor to the old school of
actresses in which the Mrs. Orgers and Miss
Popes were bred, was not more delightful on the
stage than impracticable .when off, and the little
theatre in Dean-street which the Duke of Devon-

shire's munificence had enabled her to build, and Lonpon:
1815.
which with any ordinary good sense might hand- Fanny Kelly
somely have realized both its uses, as a private and her
theatro.
school for young actresses and a place of public
amusement, was made useless for both by her
mere whims and fancies. "Heavens! Such a
"scene as I have had with Miss Kelly here, this
"morning! She wanted us put off until the theatre
"should be cleaned and brushed up a bit, and
"she would and she would not, for she is eager
"to have us and alarmed when she thinks of us.
"By the foot of Pharaoh, it was a great scene! C. D. and
Fanny Kelly.
"Especially when she choked, and had the glass
"of water brought. She exaggerates the import-
"ance of our occupation, dreads the least prejudice
"against the establishment in the minds of any of
"our company, says the place already has quite
"ruined her, and with tears in her eyes protests
"that any jokes at her additional expense in
"print would drive her mad.. By the body of
"Cæsar, the scene was incredible! It's like a pre-
"posterous dream." Something of our play is disclosed by the oaths à la Bobadil, and of our
actors by "the jokes" poor Miss Kelly was afraid
of. We had chosen EVERY MAN IN HIS HUMOUR, Every Man in
his Humour.
with special regard to the singleness and indi-
viduality of the "humours" portrayed in it; and
our company included the leaders of a journal
then in its earliest years, but already not more
renowned as the most successful joker of jokes
yet known in England, than famous for that ex-
clusive use of its laughter and satire for objects

LONDON:
1845.

the highest or most harmless which makes it still so enjoyable a companion to mirth-loving right-minded men. Maclise took earnest part with us, and was to have acted, but fell away on the eve

The company of actors.

of the rehearsals; and Stanfield, who went so far as to rehearse Downright twice, then took fright and also ran away:* but Jerrold, who played Master Stephen, brought with him Lemon, who took Brainworm; Leech, to whom Master Matthew

Parts cast.

was given; A'Beckett, who had condescended to the small part of William; and Mr. Leigh, who had Oliver Cob. I played Kitely, and Bobadil fell to Dickens, who took upon him the redoubtable Captain long before he stood in his dress at the footlights; humouring the completeness of

Enjoying a character.

his assumption by talking and writing Bobadil, till the dullest of our party were touched and stirred to something of his own heartiness of enjoyment. One or two hints of these have been given, and I will only add to them his refusal of

Troubles of management.

* "Look here! Enclosed are two packets—a large one "and a small one. The small one, read first. It contains "Stanny's renunciation as an actor!!! After receiving it, at "dinner time to-day" (22nd of August), "I gave my brains "a shake, and thought of George Cruikshank. After much "shaking, I made up the big packet, wherein I have put the "case in the artfullest manner. R—r—r—r—ead it! as a "certain Captain whom you know observes." The great artist was not for that time procurable, having engagements away from London, and Mr. Dudley Costello was substituted; Stanfield taking off the edge of his desertion as an actor by doing valuable work in management and scenery.

my wish that he should go and see some special
performance of the *Gamester*. "Man of the House.
"*Gamester!* By the foot of Pharaoh, I will *not* see
"the *Gamester*. Man shall not force, nor horses
"drag, this poor gentleman-like carcass into the
"presence of the *Gamester*. I have said it. . . .
"The player Mac hath bidden me to eat and
"likewise drink with him, thyself, and short-
"necked Fox to-night. An' I go not, I am a hog,
"and not a soldier. But an' thou goest not—
"Beware citizen! Look to it. . . . Thine as thou
"meritest. BOBADIL (Captain). Unto Master
"Kitely. These."

LONDON:
1845.

Bobadil to
Kitely.

The play was played on the 21st of September with a success that out-ran the wildest ex-
pectation; and turned our little enterprise into
one of the small sensations of the day. The applause of the theatre found so loud an echo in
the press, that for the time nothing else was
talked about in private circles; and after a week
or two we had to yield (we did not find it difficult) to a pressure of demand for more public
performance in a larger theatre, by which a useful charity received important help, and its committee showed their gratitude by an entertainment to us at the Clarendon, a month or two
later, when Lord Lansdowne took the chair.
There was also another performance by us at the
same theatre, before the close of the year, of a
play by Beaumont and Fletcher. I may not
farther indicate the enjoyments that attended the
success, and gave always to the first of our series

First per-
formance.

Second per-
formance.

"Elder
"Brother."

London:
1845.
of performances a preeminently pleasant place in memory.

Of the thing itself, however, it is necessary to be said that a modicum of merit goes a long way in all such matters, and it would not be safe now to assume that ours was much above the average of amateur attempts in general.

Of the acting. Lemon certainly had most of the stuff, conventional as well as otherwise, of a regular actor in ·him, but this was not of a high kind; and though Dickens had the title to be called a born comedian, the turn for it being in his very nature, his strength was rather in the vividness and variety of his assumptions, than in the completeness, finish, or ideality he could give to any part of

C. D. as performer. them. It is expressed exactly by what he says of his youthful preference for the representations of the elder Mathews. At the same time this was in itself so thoroughly genuine and enjoyable, and had in it such quickness and keenness of insight, that of its kind it was unrivalled; and it enabled him to present in Bobadil, after a richly coloured picture of bombastical extravagance and comic exaltation in the earlier scenes, a contrast in the later of tragical humility and abasement, that had a wonderful effect. But greatly as his acting contributed to the success of the night, this was nothing to the

C. D. as manager. service he had rendered as manager. It would be difficult to describe it. He was the life and soul of the entire affair. I never seemed till then to have known his business capabilities. He took everything on himself, and did the whole of it without an effort. He was stage-director, very often stage-carpenter, scene-arranger, property-man, prompter, and band-master. Without offending any one he kept every one in order. For all he had useful suggestions, and the dullest of clays under his potter's hand were transformed into little bits of porcelain. He adjusted scenes, assisted carpenters, invented costumes, devised playbills, wrote out calls, and enforced as well as exhibited in his proper person everything of which he urged the necessity on others. Such a chaos of dirt, confusion, and noise, as the little theatre was the day we entered it, and such a cosmos as he made it of cleanliness, order, and silence, before the rehearsals were over! There were only two things left as we found them, bits of humanity both, understood from the first as among the fixtures of the place: a Man in a Straw Hat, tall, and very fitful in his exits and entrances, of whom we never could pierce the mystery, whether he was on guard or in possession, or what he was; and a solitary little girl, who flitted about so silently among our actors and actresses that she might have been deaf and dumb but for sudden small shrieks and starts elicited by the wonders going on, which obtained for her the name of Fireworks. There is such humorous allusion to both in a letter of Dickens's of a year's later date, on the occasion of the straw-hatted mystery revealing itself as a gentleman in training

Everything changed in Dean Street:

except two human mysteries.

LONDON:
1815.
——————
22 Nov. '16,
from Paris.

The myste-
ries ex-
plained.

Training for
the stage.

Pantomimic.

for the tragic stage, that it may pleasantly close for the present our private theatricals.

"OUR STRAW-HATTED FRIEND from Miss Kelly's! "Oh my stars! To think of him, all that time— "Macbeth in disguise; Richard the Third grown "straight; Hamlet as he appeared on his sea-voyage "to England. What an artful villain he must be, "never to have made any sign of the melodrama "that was in him! What a wicked-minded and "remorseless Iago to have seen you doing Kitely "night after night! raging to murder you and "seize the part! Oh fancy Miss Kelly 'getting "'him up' in Macbeth. Good Heaven! what a "mass of absurdity must be shut up sometimes "within the walls of that small theatre in Dean- "street! FIREWORKS will come out shortly, depend "upon it, in the dumb line; and will relate her "history in profoundly unintelligible motions that "will be translated into long and complicated "descriptions by a grey-headed father, and a red- "wigged country-man, his son. You remember "the dumb dodge of relating an escape from "captivity? Clasping the left wrist with the right "hand, and the right wrist with the left hand— "alternately (to express chains)—and then going "round and round the stage very fast, and com- "ing hand over hand down an imaginary cord: "at the end of which there is one stroke on the "drum, and a kneeling to the chandelier? If "Fireworks can't do that—and won't somewhere— "I'm a Dutchman."

Graver things now claim a notice which need not be proportioned to their gravity, because, though they had an immediate effect on Dickens's fortunes, they do not otherwise form part of his story. But first let me say, he was at Broadstairs for three weeks in the autumn;* we had the

---

* Characteristic glimpse of this Broadstairs holiday is afforded by a letter of the 19th of August 1845. "Perhaps "it is a fair specimen of the odd adventures which befall the "inimitable, that the cab in which the children and the "luggage were (I and my womankind being in the other) got "its shafts broken in the city, last Friday morning, through "the horse stumbling on the greasy pavement; *and was drawn* "*to the wharf (about a mile) by a stout man*, amid such fright- "ful howlings and derisive yellings on the part of an in- "furiated populace, as I never heard before. Conceive the "man in the broken shafts with his back towards the cab; "all the children looking out of the windows; and the muddy "portmanteaus and so forth (which were all tumbled down "when the horse fell) tottering and nodding on the box! The "best of it was, that *our* cabman, being an intimate friend "of the damaged cabman, insisted on keeping him company; "and proceeded at a solemn walk, in front of the procession; "thereby securing to me a liberal share of the popular "curiosity and congratulation. . . . Everything here at "Broadstairs is the same as of old. I have walked 20 miles "a day since I came down, and I went to a circus at Rams- "gate on Saturday night, where *Mazeppa* was played in three "long acts without an H in it: as if for a wager. Evven, and "edds, and orrors, and ands, were as plentiful as black- "berries; but the letter H was neither whispered in Evven, "nor muttered in Ell, nor permitted to dwell in any form on "the confines of the sawdust." With this I will couple an-

At Broad- stairs.

Ramsgate entertain- ments.

private play on his return; and a month later, on the 28th of October, a sixth child and fourth son, named Alfred Tennyson after his godfathers d'Orsay and Tennyson, was born in Devonshire-terrace. A death in the family followed, the older and more gifted of his ravens having indulged the same illicit taste for putty and paint

which had been fatal to his predecessor. Voracity killed him, as it killed Scott's. He died unexpectedly before the kitchen-fire. "He kept his "eye to the last upon the meat as it roasted, and "suddenly turned over on his back with a sepul-

"chral cry of *Cuckoo!*" The letter which told me this (31st of October) announced to me also that he was at a dead lock in his Christmas story: "Sick, bothered and depressed. Visions of "Brighton come upon me; and I have a great "mind to go there to finish my second part, or

"to Hampstead. I have a desperate thought of "Jack Straw's. I never was in such bad writing "cue as I am this week, in all my life." The reason was not far to seek. In the preparation for the proposed new Daily Paper to which reference has been made, he was now actively assisting, and had all but consented to the publication of his name.

other theatrical experience of this holiday, when he saw a Giant played by a village comedian with a quite Gargantuesque felicity, and singled out for my admiration his fine manner of sitting down to a hot supper (of children), with the self-lauding exalting remark, by way of grace, "How pleasant is "a quiet conscience and an approving mind!"

I entertained at this time, for more than one
powerful reason, the greatest misgiving of his
intended share in the adventure. It was not
fully revealed until later on what difficult terms,
physical as well as mental, Dickens held the
tenure of his imaginative life; but already I knew
enough to doubt the wisdom of what he was at
present undertaking. In all intellectual labour,
his will prevailed so strongly when he fixed it on
any object of desire, that what else its attainment
might exact was never duly measured; and this
led to frequent strain and unconscious waste of
what no man could less afford to spare. To the
world gladdened by his work, its production
might always have seemed quite as easy as its
enjoyment; but it may be doubted if ever any
man's mental effort cost him more. His habits
were robust, but not his health; that secret had
been disclosed to me before he went to America;
and to the last he refused steadily to admit the
enormous price he had paid for his triumphs and
successes. The morning after his last note I
heard again. "I have been so very unwell this
"morning, with giddiness, and headache, and
"botheration of one sort or other, that I didn't
"get up till noon: and, shunning Fleet-street"
(the office of the proposed new paper), "am now
"going for a country walk, in the course of which
"you will find me, if you feel disposed to come
"away in the carriage that goes to you with this.
"It is to call for a pull of the first part of the
"*Cricket*, and will bring you, if you like, by way

London:
1845.
My misgiving
as to daily
paper.

Habits more
robust than
health.

Disturbing
engagements.

LONDON:
1845.
Old ways
interrupted.

"of Hampstead to me, and subsequently to din-
"ner.   There is much I should like to discuss, if
"you can manage it.   It's the loss of my walks,
"I suppose; but I am as giddy as if I were
"drunk, and can hardly see."   I gave far from
sufficient importance at the time to the frequency
of complaints of this kind, or to the recurrence,
at almost regular periods after the year following
the present, of those spasms in the side of which

Page 72 of
Vol. L

he has recorded an instance in the recollections
of his childhood, and of which he had an attack
in Genoa; but though not conscious of it to its
full extent, this consideration was among those
that influenced me in a determination to endeavour to turn him from what could not but be
regarded as full of peril.   His health, however,
had no real prominence in my letter; and it is
strange now to observe that it appears as an

My appeal
against the
enterprise.

argument in his reply.   I had simply put before
him, in the strongest form, all the considerations
drawn from his genius and fame that should
deter him from the labour and responsibility of a
daily paper, not less than from the party and
political involvements incident to it; and here
was the material part of the answer made.   "Many

Reply to my
appeal.

"thanks for your affectionate letter, which is full
"of generous truth.   These considerations weigh
"with me, *heavily:* but I think I descry in these
"times, greater stimulants to such an effort;
"greater chance of some fair recognition of it;
"greater means of persevering in it, or retiring
"from it unscratched by any weapon one should

LONDON: 1845.

"care for; than at any other period. And most
"of all I have, sometimes, that possibility of fail-
"ing health or fading popularity before me, which
"beckons me to such a venture when it comes
"within my reach. At the worst, I have written
"to little purpose, if I cannot *write myself right*
"in people's minds, in such a case as this."

And so it went on: but it does not fall within The issue.
my plan to describe more than the issue, which
was to be accounted so far at least fortunate that
it established a journal which has advocated
steadily improvements in the condition of all
classes, rich as well as poor, and has been able,
during late momentous occurrences, to give wider
scope in its influence by its enterprise and
liberality. To that result, the great writer whose
name gave its earliest attraction to the *Daily
News* was not enabled to contribute much; but
from him it certainly received the first impress of
the opinions it has since consistently maintained.
Its prospectus is before me in his handwriting, Prospectus
but it bears upon itself sufficiently the character written by
him.
of his hand and mind. The paper would be
kept free, it said, from personal influence or party
bias; and would be devoted to the advocacy of
all rational and honest means by which wrong
might be redressed, just rights maintained, and
the happiness and welfare of society promoted.

The day for the appearance of its first number was that which was to follow Peel's speech
for the repeal of the corn laws; but, brief as my
allusions to the subject are, the remark should be

LONDON:
1845.

Interruption. made that even before this day came there were interruptions to the work of preparation, at one time very grave, which threw such "changes of "vexation" on Dickens's personal relations to the venture as went far to destroy both his faith and

Renewal. his pleasure in it. No opinion need be offered as to where most of the blame lay, and it would be useless now to apportion the share that might possibly have belonged to himself; but, owing to this cause, his editorial work began with such diminished ardour that its brief continuance could not but be looked for. A little note written "before going home" at six o'clock in the morn-

The begin-
ning and the
end. ing of Wednesday the 21st of January 1846, to tell me they had "been at press three quarters of "an hour, and were out before the *Times*," marks the beginning; and a note written in the night of Monday the 9th of February, "tired to death and "quite worn out," to say that he had just re-signed his editorial functions, describes the end. I had not been unprepared. A week before (Friday 30th of January) he had written: "I want "a long talk with you. I was obliged to come "down here in a hurry to give out a travelling "letter I meant to have given out last night, and

Forming now
resolve. "could not call upon you. Will you dine with "us to-morrow at six sharp? I have been re-"volving plans in my mind this morning for quit-"ting the paper and going abroad again to write "a new book in shilling numbers. Shall we go "to Rochester to-morrow week (my birthday) if "the weather be, as it surely must be, better?"

To Rochester accordingly we had gone, he and London:
Mrs. Dickens and her sister, with Maclise and ~~Back to old~~
Jerrold and myself; going over the old Castle, scones.
Watts's Charity, and Chatham fortifications on
the Saturday, passing Sunday in Cobham church
and Cobham park; having our quarters both days
at the Bull inn made famous in *Pickwick;* and
thus, by indulgence of the desire which was always strangely urgent in him, associating his new
resolve in life with those earliest scenes of his Craving for
youthful time.   On one point our feeling had early associa-
been in thorough agreement.   If long continuance tions.
with the paper was not likely, the earliest possible
departure from it was desirable.   But as the letters descriptive of his Italian travel (turned afterwards into *Pictures from Italy*) had begun with
its first number, his name could not at once be
withdrawn; and, for the time during which they Editorship
were still to appear, he consented to contribute ceased:
other occasional letters on important social ques- continued.
tions.   Public executions and Ragged schools
were among the subjects chosen by him, and all
were handled with conspicuous ability.   But the
interval they covered was a short one.

　　To the supreme control which he had quitted, I become
I succeeded, retaining it very reluctantly for the editor.
greater part of that weary, anxious, laborious
year; but in little more than four months from
the day the paper started, the whole of Dickens's
connection with the *Daily News*, even that of
contributing letters with his signature, had ceased.
As he said in the preface to the republished *Pic-*

lures, it was a mistake to have disturbed the old relations between himself and his readers, in so departing from his old pursuits. It had however been "a brief mistake;" the departure had been only "for a moment;" and now those pursuits were "joyfully" to be resumed in Switzerland. Upon the latter point we had much discussion; but he was bent on again removing himself from London, and his glimpse of the Swiss mountains on his coming from Italy had given him a passion to visit them again. "I don't think," he wrote to me, "I *could* shut out the paper suf-

New book to
be written in
Switzerland.

"ficiently, here, to write well. No . . . I will "write my book in Lausanne and in Genoa, and "forget everything else if I can; and by living in "Switzerland for the summer, and in Italy or "France for the winter, I shall be saving money "while I write." So therefore it was finally determined.

There is not much that calls for mention before he left. The first conceiving of a new book was always a restless time, and other subjects beside the characters that were growing in his mind would persistently intrude themselves into his night-wanderings. With some surprise I heard from him afterwards, for example, of a communication opened with a leading member of the

Government to ascertain what chances there might be for his appointment, upon due qualification, to the paid magistracy of London: the reply not giving him encouragement to entertain the notion farther. It was of course but an out-

break of momentary discontent; and if the answer had been as hopeful as for others' sake ra-
ther than his own one could have wished it to
be, the result would have been the same. Just
upon the eve of his departure, I may add, he
took much interest in the establishment of the
General Theatrical Fund, of which he remained
a trustee until his death. It had originated in
the fact that the Funds of the two large theatres,
themselves then disused for theatrical perform-
ances, were no longer available for the ordinary
members of the profession; and on the occasion
of his presiding at its first dinner in April he
said, very happily, that now the statue of Shakespeare outside the door of Drury-lane, as empha-
tically as his bust inside the church of Stratford-
on-Avon, *pointed out his grave*. I am tempted
also to mention as felicitous a word which I
heard fall from him at one of the many private
dinners that were got up in those days of parting
to give him friendliest farewell. "Nothing is ever
"so good as it is thought," said Lord Melbourne.
"And nothing so bad," interposed Dickens.

The last incidents were that he again obtained
Roche for his travelling servant, and that he let
his Devonshire-terrace house to Sir James Duke
for twelve months, the entire proposed term of
his absence. On the 30th of May they all dined
with me, and on the following day left England.

CHAPTER XXXIV.

A HOME IN SWITZERLAND.

1846.

HALTING only at Ostend, Verviers, Coblentz, and Mannheim, they reached Strasburg on the seventh of June: the beauty of the weather * showing them the Rhine at its best. At Mayence there had come aboard their boat a German, who soon after accosted Mrs. Dickens on deck in excellent English: "Your countryman Mr. Dickens "is travelling this way just now, our papers say. "Do you know him, or have you passed him any-
"where?" Explanations ensuing, it turned out, by one of the odd chances my friend thought himself always singled out for, that he had with him a letter of introduction to the brother of this gentleman; who then spoke to him of the popularity of his books in Germany, and of the many persons he had seen reading them in the steamboats as he came along. Dickens remarking at

* "We have hardly seen a cloud in the sky since you and "I parted at Ramsgate, and the heat has been extra-'ordinary."

this how great his own vexation was not to be ON THE RHINE: 1846.
able himself to speak a word of German, "Oh
"dear! that needn't trouble you," rejoined the German readers of Dickens.
other; "for even in so small a town as ours,
"where we are mostly primitive people and have
"few travellers, I could make a party of at least
"forty people who understand and speak English
"as well as I do, and of at least as many more
"who could manage to read you in the original."
His town was Worms, which Dickens afterwards
saw, "... a fine old place, though greatly shrunken
"and decayed in respect of its population; with City of Worms.
"a picturesque old cathedral standing on the
"brink of the Rhine, and some brave old churches
"shut up, and so hemmed in and overgrown with
"vineyards that they look as if they were turning
"into leaves and grapes."

He had no other adventure on the Rhine.
But, on the same steamer, a not unfamiliar bit of
character greeted him in the well-known linea-
ments, moral and physical, of two travelling Eng- Travelling Englishmen.
lishmen who had got an immense barouche on
board with them, and had no plan whatever of
going anywhere in it. One of them wanted to
have this barouche wheeled ashore at every little
town and village they came to. The other was
bent upon "seeing it out," as he said—meaning,
Dickens supposed, the river; though neither of
them seemed to have the slightest interest in it.
"The locomotive one would have gone ashore
"without the carriage, and would have been de-
"lighted to get rid of it; but they had a joint

"courier, and neither of them would part with "*him* for a moment; so they went growling and "grumbling on together, and seemed to have no "satisfaction but in asking for impossible viands "on board the boat, and having a grim delight "in the steward's excuses."

From Strasburg they went by rail on the 8th to Bâle, from which they started for Lausanne next day, in three coaches, two horses to each, taking three days for the journey: its only enlivening incident being an uproar between the landlord of an inn on the road, and one of the voituriers who had libelled Boniface's establishment by complaining of the food. "After various de-

"fiances on both sides, the landlord said 'Scélé-"'rat! Mécréant! Je vous boaxerai!' to which the "voiturier replied, 'Aha! Comment dites-vous? "'Voulez-vous boaxer? Eh? Voulez-vous? Ah! "'Boaxez-moi donc! Boaxez-moi!'—at the same "time accompanying these retorts with gestures "of violent significance, which explained that this "new verb-active was founded on the well-known "English verb to boax, or box. If they used it "once, they used it at least a hundred times, and "goaded each other to madness with it always."

The travellers reached the hotel Gibbon at Lausanne on the evening of Thursday the 11th of June; having been tempted as they came along to rest somewhat short of it, by a delightful glimpse of Neuchâtel. "On consideration how-"ever I thought it best to come on here, in case "I should find, when I begin to write, that I want

"streets sometimes. In which case, Geneva (which
"I hope would answer the purpose) is only four
"and twenty miles away."

He at once began house-hunting, and had
two days' hard work of it. He found the greater
part of those let to the English like small villas
in the Regent's-park, with verandahs, glass-doors
opening on lawns, and alcoves overlooking the
lake and mountains. One he was tempted by,
higher up the hill, "poised above the town like a
"ship on a high wave;" but the possible fury of
its winter winds deterred him. Greater still was
the temptation to him of "L'Elysée," more a
mansion than a villa; with splendid grounds overlooking the lake, and in its corridors and stair-
cases as well as furniture like an old-fashioned
country house in England; which he could have
got for twelve months for £160. "But when I
"came to consider its vastness, I was rather dis-
"mayed at the prospect of windy nights in the
"autumn, with nobody staying in the house to
"make it gay." And so he again fell back upon
the very first place he had seen, Rosemont, quite
a doll's house; with two pretty little salons, a
dining-room, hall, and kitchen, on the ground
floor; and with just enough bedrooms upstairs to
leave the family one to spare. "It is beautifully
"situated on the hill that rises from the lake,
"within ten minutes' walk of this hotel, and
"furnished, though scantily as all here are, better
"than others except Elysée, on account of its
"having being built and fitted up (the little salons

"in the Parisian way) by the landlady and her
"husband for themselves. They live now in a
"smaller house like a porter's lodge, just within
"the gate. A portion of the grounds is farmed
"by a farmer, and *he* lives close by; so that,
"while it is secluded, it is not at all lonely." The
rent was to be ten pounds a month for half a
year, with reduction to eight for the second half,
if he should stay so long; and the rooms and
furniture were to be described to me, so that according to custom I should be quite at home
there, as soon as, also according to a custom
well-known, his own ingenious re-arrangements
and improvements in the chairs and tables should
be completed. "I shall merely observe at present
"therefore, that my little study is upstairs, and
"looks out, from two French windows opening

"into a balcony, on the lake and mountains; and
"that there are roses enough to smother the whole
"establishment of the *Daily News* in. Likewise,
"there is a pavilion in the garden, which has but
"two rooms in it; in one of which, I think you
"shall do your work when you come. As to

"bowers for reading and smoking, there are as
"many scattered about the grounds, as there are
"in Chalk-farm tea-gardens. But the Rosemont
"bowers are really beautiful. Will you come to
"the bowers . . ?"

Very pleasant were the earliest impressions of
Switzerland with which this first letter closed.
"The country is delightful in the extreme—as
"leafy, green, and shady, as England; full of deep

LAUSANNE:
1846.

"glens, and branchy places (rather a Leigh Hunt-
"ish expression), and bright with all sorts of
"flowers in profusion.* It abounds in singing
"birds besides—very pleasant after Italy; and the
"moonlight on the lake is noble. Prodigious
"mountains rise up from its opposite shore (it is
"eight or nine miles across, at this point), and
"the Simplon, the St. Gothard, Mont Blanc, and
"all the Alpine wonders are piled there, in tre- Green lanes and Alpine wonders.
"mendous grandeur. The cultivation is uncom-
"monly rich and profuse. There are all manner
"of walks, vineyards, green lanes, corn-fields, and
"pastures full of hay. The general neatness is
"as remarkable as in England. There are no
"priests or monks in the streets, and the people
"appear to be industrious and thriving. French
"(and very intelligible and pleasant French) seems
"to be the universal language. I never saw so
"many booksellers' shops crammed within the Booksellers' shops.
"same space, as in the steep up-and-down streets
"of Lausanne."

Of the little town he spoke in his next letter
as having its natural dulness increased by that
fact of its streets going up and down hill abruptly and steeply, like the streets in a dream;
and the consequent difficulty of getting about it.
"There are some suppressed churches in it, now Town described.

---

* "The green woods and green shades about here," he
says in another letter, "are more like Cobham in Kent,
"than anything we dream of at the foot of the Alpine
"passes."

"used as packers' warehouses: with cranes and
"pulleys growing out of steeple-towers; little doors
"for lowering goods through, fitted into blocked-
"up oriel windows; and cart-horses stabled in
"crypts. These also help to give it a deserted
"and disused appearance. On the other hand,

A free place. "as it is a perfectly free place subject to no pro-
"hibitions or restrictions of any kind, there are
"all sorts of new French books and publications
"in it, and all sorts of fresh intelligence from the
"world beyond the Jura mountains. It contains
"only one Roman Catholic church, which is
"mainly for the use of the Savoyards and Pied-
"montese who come trading over the Alps. As
"for the country, it cannot be praised too highly,
"or reported too beautiful. There are no great
"waterfalls, or walks through mountain-gorges,
"*close* at hand, as in some other parts of Switzer-
"land; but there is a charming variety of en-
"chanting scenery. There is the shore of the
"lake, where you may dip your feet, as you walk,
"in the deep blue water, if you choose. There
"are the hills to climb up, leading to the great
"heights above the town; or to stagger down,

Varieties of
nature. "leading to the lake. There is every possible
"variety of deep green lanes, vineyard, cornfield,
"pasture-land, and wood. There are excellent
"country roads that might be in Kent or Devon-
"shire: and, closing up every view and vista, is
"an eternally changing range of prodigious moun-
"tains—sometimes red, sometimes grey, some-
"times purple, sometimes black; sometimes white

"with snow; sometimes close at hand; and some-
"times very ghosts in the clouds and mist."

In the heart of these things he was now to
live and work for at least six months; and, as the
love of nature was as much a passion with him
in his intervals of leisure, as the craving for
crowds and streets when he was busy with the
creatures of his fancy, no man was better quali-
fied to enjoy what was thus open to him from
his little farm.

The view from each side of it was different
in character, and from one there was visible the
liveliest aspect of Lausanne itself, close at hand,
and seeming, as he said, to be always coming
down the hill with its steeples and towers, not
able to stop itself. "From a fine long broad
"balcony on which the windows of my little
"study on the first floor (where I am now writ-
"ing) open, the lake is seen to wonderful ad-
"vantage,—losing itself by degrees in the solemn
"gorge of mountains leading to the Simplon pass.
"Under the balcony is a stone colonnade, on
"which the six French windows of the drawing-
"room open; and quantities of plants are clustered
"about the pillars and seats, very prettily. One
"of these drawing-rooms is furnished (like a
"French hotel) with red velvet, and the other
"with green; in both, plenty of mirrors and nice
"white muslin curtains; and for the larger one
"in cold weather there is a carpet, the floors
"being bare now, but inlaid in squares with dif-
"ferent-coloured woods." His description did not

close until, in every nook and corner inhabited by the several members of the family, I was made to feel myself at home; but only the final sentence need be added. "Walking out into the

"balcony as I write, I am suddenly reminded, by "the sight of the Castle of Chillon glittering in "the sunlight on the lake, that I omitted to men-"tion that object in my catalogue of the Rose-"mont beauties. Please to put it in, like George "Robins, in a line by itself."

Regular evening walks of nine or ten miles were named in the same letter (22nd of June) as having been begun;* and thoughts of his books were already stirring in him. "An odd shadowy "undefined idea is at work within me, that I "could connect a great battle-field somehow with "my little Christmas story. Shapeless visions of "the repose and peace pervading it in after-time; "with the corn and grass growing over the slain, "and people singing at the plough; are so per- "petually floating before me, that I cannot but "think there may turn out to be something good "in them when I see them more plainly . . . . I "want to get Four Numbers of the monthly book "done here, and the Christmas book. If all goes "well, and nothing changes, and I can accomplish "this by the end of November, I shall run over "to you in England for a few days with a light "heart, and leave Roche to move the caravan to "Paris in the meanwhile. It will be just the very "point in the story when the life and crowd of

* To these the heat interposed occasional difficulties. "Setting off last night" (5th of July) "at six o'clock, in ac- "cordance with my usual custom, for a long walk, I was "really quite floored when I got to the top of a long steep "hill leading out of the town—the same by which we en- "tered it. I believe the great heats, however, seldom last "more than a week at a time; there are always very long "twilights, and very delicious evenings; and now that there "is moonlight, the nights are wonderful. The peacefulness "and grandeur of the Mountains and the Lake are in- "describable. There comes a rush of sweet smells with "the morning air too, which is quite peculiar to the "country."

"that extraordinary place will come vividly to my "assistance in writing." Such was his design; and, though difficulties not now seen started up which he had a hard fight to get through, he managed to accomplish it. His letter ended with a promise to tell me, when next he wrote, of the small colony of English who seemed ready to give him even more than the usual welcome. Two visits had thus early been paid him by Mr. Haldimand, formerly a member of the English parliament, an accomplished man, who, with his

Mr. Haldi-
mand and
Mrs. Marcet.

sister Mrs. Marcet (the well-known authoress), had long made Lausanne his home. He had a very fine seat just below Rosemont, and his character and station had made him quite the little sovereign of the place. "He has founded and endowed "all sorts of hospitals and institutions here, and "he gives a dinner to-morrow to introduce our "neighbours, whoever they are."

Other English
neighbours.

He found them to be happily the kind of people who rendered entirely pleasant those frank and cordial hospitalities which the charm of his personal intercourse made every one so eager to offer him. The dinner at Mr. Haldimand's was followed by dinners from the guests he met there; from an English lady* married to a Swiss,

Spiritual
tyranny.

* "One of her brothers by the bye, now dead, had large "property in Ireland—all Nenagh, and the country about; "and Cerjat told me, as we were talking about one thing "and another, that when he went over there for some months "to arrange the widow's affairs, he procured a copy of the

Mr. and Mrs. Cerjat, clever and agreeable both, far beyond the common; from her sister wedded to an Englishman, Mr. and Mrs. Goff; and from Mr. and Mrs. Watson of Rockingham-castle in Northamptonshire, who had taken the Elysée on Dickens giving it up, and with whom, as with Mr. Haldimand, his relations continued to be very intimate long after he left Lausanne. In his drive to Mr. Cerjat's dinner a whimsical difficulty presented itself. He had set up, for use of his wife and children, an odd little one-horse-carriage; made to hold three persons sideways, so that they should avoid the wind always blowing up or down the valley; and he found it attended with one of the drollest consequences conceivable. "It can't be easily turned; and as you face to the "side, all sorts of evolutions are necessary to "bring you 'broad-side to' before the door of the "house where you are going. The country houses "here are very like those upon the Thames be-"tween Richmond and Kingston (this, particularly), "with grounds all round. At Mr. Cerjat's we "were obliged to be carried, like the child's riddle, "round the house and round the house, without "touching the house; and we were presented in "the most alarming manner, three of a row, first "to all the people in the kitchen, then to the "governess who was dressing in her bedroom,

Sidenotes: LAUSANNE: 1846. / Mr. and Mrs. Watson. / Unaccommodating carriage. / On the way to dinner.

"curse which had been read at the altar by the parish priest "of Nenagh, against any of the flock who didn't subscribe to "the O'Connell tribute."

"then to the drawing-room where the company
"were waiting for us, then to the dining-room
"where they were spreading the table, and finally
"to the hall where we were got out—scraping the
"windows of each apartment as we glared slowly
"into it."

A dinner party of his own followed of course;
and a sad occurrence, of which he and his guests
were unconscious, signalised the evening (15th of
July). "While we were sitting at dinner, one of
"the prettiest girls in Lausanne was drowned in
"the lake—in the most peaceful water, reflecting
"the steep mountains, and crimson with the set-
"ting sun. She was bathing in one of the nooks
"set apart for women, and seems somehow to
"have entangled her feet in the skirts of her
"dress. She was an accomplished swimmer, as
"many of the girls are here, and drifted, sud-
"denly, out of only five feet water. Three or
"four friends who were with her, *ran away*,
"screaming. Our children's governess was on
"the lake in a boat with M. Verdeil (my prison-
"doctor) and his family. They ran inshore im-
"mediately; the body was quickly got out; and
"M. Verdeil, with three or four other doctors,
"laboured for some hours to restore animation;
"but she only sighed once. After all that time,
"she was obliged to be borne, stiff and stark, to
"her father's house. She was his only child, and
"but 17 years old. He has been nearly dead
"since, and all Lausanne has been full of the
"story. I was down by the lake, near the place,

"last night; and a boatman *acted* to me the whole Lausanne:
1846.
"scene: depositing himself finally on a heap of Boatman's
narrative.
"stones, to represent the body."

With M. Verdeil, physician to the prison and
vice-president of the council of health, introduced
by Mr. Haldimand, there had already been much
communication; and I could give nothing more
characteristic of Dickens than his reference to
this, and other similar matters in which his
interest was strongly moved during his first weeks
at Lausanne.*

"Some years ago, when they set about reform-
"ing the prison at Lausanne, they turned their Prison
"attention, in a correspondence of republican systems.

---

* In a note may be preserved another passage from the
same letter. "I have been queer and had trembling legs for the
"last week. But it has been almost impossible to sleep at
"night. There is a breeze to-day (25th of July) and I hope
"another storm is coming up . . . There is a theatre here; The theatre.
"and whenever a troop of players pass through the town,
"they halt for a night and act. On the day of our tre-
"mendous dinner party of eight, there was an infant phe-
"nomenon ; whom I should otherwise have seen. Last night
"there was a Vaudeville company; and Charley, Roche, and
"Anne went. The Brave reports the performances to have
"resembled Greenwich Fair . . . There are some Prome-
"nade Concerts in the open air in progress now; but as they
"are just above one part of our garden we don't go: merely
"sitting outside the door instead, and hearing it all where
"we are . . . Mont Blanc has been very plain lately. One
"heap of snow. A Frenchman got to the top, the other
"day."

Lausanne:
1846.
"feeling, to America; and taking the Philadelphian "system for granted, adopted it. Terrible fits, "new phases of mental affection, and horrible "madness, among the prisoners, were very soon "the result; and attained to such an alarming "height, that M. Verdeil, in his public capacity, "began to report against the system, and went on "reporting and working against it until he formed "a party who were determined not to have it,

Solitude and
silence.
"and caused it to be abolished—except in cases "where the imprisonment does not exceed ten "months in the whole. It is remarkable that in "his notes of the different cases, there is *every* "*effect* I mentioned as having observed myself "at Philadelphia; even down to those contained

Page 189 of
Vol. II.
"in the description of the man who had been "there thirteen years, and who *picked his hands* "so much as he talked. He has only recently, "he says, read the *American Notes;* but he is so "much struck by the perfect coincidence that he "intends to republish some extracts from his own "notes, side by side with these passages of mine "translated into French. I went with him over "the prison the other day. It is wonderfully well "arranged for a continental jail, and in perfect "order. The sentences however, or some of them,

Terrible
sentence.
"are very terrible. I saw one man sent there for "murder under circumstances of mitigation—for "30 years. Upon the silent social system all the "time! They weave, and plait straw, and make "shoes, small articles of turnery and carpentry, "and little common wooden clocks. But the

"sentences are too long for that monotonous and
"hopeless life; and, though they are well-fed and
"cared for, they generally break down utterly
"after two or three years. ~ "One delusion seems
"to become common to three-fourths of them
"after a certain time of imprisonment. Under
"the impression that there is something destruc-
"tive put into their food 'pour les guérir de
"'crime' (says M. Verdeil), they refuse to eat!"

It was at the Blind Institution, however, of
which Mr. Haldimand was the president and
great benefactor, that Dickens's attention was
most deeply arrested; and there were two cases
in especial of which the detail may be read with
as much interest now as when my friend's letters
were written, and as to which his own suggestions open up still rather startling trains of
thought. The first, which in its attraction for
him he found equal even to Laura Bridgman's,
was that of a young man of 18: "born deaf and
"dumb, and stricken blind by an accident when
"he was about five years old. The Director of
"the institution is a young German, of great
"ability, and most uncommonly prepossessing
"appearance. He propounded to the scientific
"bodies of Geneva, a year ago (when this young
"man was under education in the asylum), the
"possibility of teaching him to speak—in other
"words, to play with his tongue upon his teeth
"and palate as if on an instrument, and connect
"particular performances with particular words
"conveyed to him in the finger-language. They

Lausanne:
1846.

Deaf, dumb,
and blind
patient.

Interesting
case.

Punishment
for falsehood.

"unanimously agreed that it was quite impos-
"sible. The German set to work, and the
"young man now speaks very plainly and dis-
"tinctly: without the least modulation, of course,
"but with comparatively little hesitation; ex-
"pressing the words aloud as they are struck, so
"to speak, upon his hands; and showing the most
"intense and wonderful delight in doing it. This
"is commonly acquired, as you know, by the deaf
"and dumb who learn by sight; but it has never
"before been achieved in the case of a deaf,
"dumb, and blind subject. He is an extremely
"lively, intelligent, good-humoured fellow; an
"excellent carpenter; a first-rate turner; and runs
"about the building with a certainty and con-
"fidence which none of the merely blind pupils
"acquire. He has a great many ideas, and an
"instinctive dread of death. He knows of God,
"as of Thought enthroned somewhere; and once
"told, on nature's prompting (the devil's of
"course), a lie. He was sitting at dinner, and
"the Director asked him whether he had had
"anything to drink; to which he instantly replied
"'No,' in order that he might get some more,
"though he had been served in his turn. It was
"explained to him that this was a wrong thing,
"and wouldn't do, and that he was to be locked
"up in a room for it: which was done. Soon
"after this, he had a dream of being bitten in the
"shoulder by some strange animal. As it left a
"great impression on his mind, he told M. the
"Director that he had told another lie in the

"night. In proof of it he related his dream, and LAUSANNE: 1846.
"added, 'It must be a lie you know, because
"'there is no strange animal here, and I never
"'was bitten." Being informed that this sort of Falsehood without punishment.
"lie was a harmless one, and was called a dream,
"he asked whether dead people ever dreamed*
"while they were lying in the ground. He is
"one of the most curious and interesting studies
"possible."

The second case had come in on the very Blind Institution and inmates.
day that Dickens visited the place. "When I was
"there" (8th of July) "there had come in, that
"morning, a girl of ten years old, born deaf and
"dumb and blind, and so perfectly untaught that
"she has not learnt to have the least control
"even over the performance of the common
"natural functions .. And yet she *laughs some-*
"*times* (good God! conceive what at!)—and is Idiot girl.
"dreadfully sensitive from head to foot, and very
"much alarmed, for some hours before the com-
"ing on of a thunder storm. Mr. Haldimand
"has been long trying to induce her parents to
"send her to the asylum. At last they have con-
"sented; and when I saw her, some of the little
"blind girls were trying to make friends with her,
"and to lead her gently about. She was dressed
"in just a loose robe from the necessity of chang-
"ing her frequently, but had been in a bath, and

---

    *   ". . . Ay, there's the rub;
"For in that sleep of death what dreams may come,
"When we have shuffled off this mortal coil. . ."

LAUSANNE:
1816.

Blind Institu-
tion and in-
mates.
"had had her nails cut (which were previously
"very long and dirty), and was not at all ill-look-
"ing—quite the reverse; with a remarkably good
"and pretty little mouth, but a low and undeve-
"loped head of course. It was pointed out to
"me, as very singular, that the moment she is
"left alone, or freed from anybody's touch (which
Crouching
attitudes.
"is the same thing to her), she instantly crouches
"down with her hands up to her ears, in exactly
"the position of a child before its birth; and so
"remains. I thought this such a strange coinci-
"dence with the utter want of 'advancement in
"her moral being, that it made a great impression
"on me; and conning it over and over, I began
"to think that this is surely the invariable action
"of savages too, and that I have seen it over and
"over again described in books of voyages and
"travels. Not having any of these with me, I
"turned to *Robinson Crusoe;* and I find De Foe
"says, describing the savages who came on the
"island after Will Atkins began to change for
"the better and commanded under the grave
Suggestive.
"Spaniard for the common defence, 'their posture
"'was generally sitting upon the ground, with
"'their knees up towards their mouth, and the
"'head put between the two hands, leaning down
"'upon the knees'—exactly the same attitude!,"
In his next week's letter he reported further: "I
"have not been to the Blind asylum again yet,
"but they tell me that the deaf and dumb and
"blind child's *face* is improving obviously, and
"that she takes great delight in the first effort

"made by the Director to connect himself with LAUSANNE: 1846.
"an occupation of her time. He gives her, every Blind Institu-
"day, two smooth round pebbles to roll over and tion and in-mates.
"over between her two hands. She appears to
"have an idea that it is to lead to something;
"distinctly recognizes the hand that gives them
"to her, as a friendly and protecting one; and
"sits for hours quite busy."

To one part of his very thoughtful suggestion
I objected, and would have attributed to a mere
desire for warmth, in her as in the savage, what
he supposed to be part of an undeveloped or
embryo state explaining also the absence of sen-
tient and moral being. To this he replied (25th
of July): "I do not think that there is reason for Habits in
"supposing that the savage attitude originates in idiot life and savage.
"the desire of warmth, because all naked savages
"inhabit hot climates; and their instinctive atti-
"tude, if it had reference to heat or cold, would
"probably be the coolest possible; like their
"delight in water, and swimming. I do not think
"there is any race of savage men, however low
"in grade, inhabiting cold climates, who do not
"kill beasts and wear their skins. The girl de-
"cidedly improves in face, and, if one can yet
"use the word as applied to her, in manner too.
"No communication by the speech of touch has
"yet been established with her, but the time has
"not been long enough." In a later letter he
tells me (24th of August): "The deaf, dumb, and Girl im-
"blind girl is decidedly improved, and very much proves.
"improved, in this short time. No communication

"is yet established with her, but that is not to
"be expected. They have got her out of that
"strange, crouching position; dressed her neatly;
"and accustomed her to have a pleasure in
"society. She laughs frequently, and also claps
"her hands and jumps; having, God knows how,
"some inward satisfaction. I never saw a more
"tremendous thing in its way, in my life, than
"when they stood her, t'other day, in the centre
"of a group of blind children who sang a chorus
"to the piano; and brought her hand, and kept

"it, in contact with the instrument. A shudder
"pervaded her whole being, her breath quickened,
"her colour deepened,—and I can compare it to
"nothing but returning animation in a person
"nearly dead. It was really awful to see how
"the sensation of the music fluttered and stirred
"the locked-up soul within her." The same
letter spoke again of the youth: "The male sub-
"ject is well and jolly as possible. He is very
"fond of smoking. I have arranged to supply
"him with cigars during our stay here; so he and

"I are in amazing sympathy. I don't know
"whether he thinks I grow them, or make them,
"or produce them by winking, or what. But it
"gives him a notion that the world in general
"belongs to me." . . . Before his kind friend left
Lausanne the poor fellow had been taught to say,
"Monsieur Dickens m'a donné les cigares," and
at their leavetaking his gratitude was expressed
by incessant repetition of these words for a full
half-hour.

Certainly by no man was gratitude more per- Lausanne:
1846.
sistently earned, than by Dickens, from all to
whom nature or the world had been churlish or
unfair. Not to those only made desolate by
poverty or the temptations incident to it, but to
those whom natural defects or infirmities had
placed at a disadvantage with their kind, he gave
his first consideration; helping them personally Attending to
the neglected.
where he could, sympathising and sorrowing with
them always, but above all applying himself to
the investigation of such alleviation or cure as
philosophy or science might be able to apply to
their condition. This was a desire so eager as
properly to be called one of the passions of his
life, visible in him to the last hour of it.

Only a couple of weeks, themselves not idle Beginning
work.
ones, had passed over him at Rosemont when he
made a dash at the beginning of his real work;
from which indeed he had only been detained
so long by the non-arrival of a box dispatched
from London before his own departure, contain-.
ing not his proper writing materials only, but
certain quaint little bronze figures that thus early
stood upon his desk, and were as much needed
for the easy flow of his writing as blue ink or
quill pens. "I have not been idle" (28th of June)
"since I have been here, though at first I was
"'kept out' of the big box as you know. I had
"a good deal to write for Lord John about the Ante, p. 57.
"Ragged schools. "I set to work and did that.
"A good deal for Miss Coutts, in reference to
"her charitable projects. I set to work and did

LAUSANNE:
1846. "*that.* Half of the children's New Testament* to
"write, or pretty nearly. I set to work and did
"*that.* Next I cleared off the greater part of such
"correspondence as I had rashly pledged myself
"to; and then . . . . .

"BEGAN DOMBEY!

First slip of
new novel. "I performed this feat yesterday—only wrote the
"first slip—but there it is, and it is a plunge
"straight over head and ears into the story. . .
"Besides all this, I have really gone with great
"vigour at the French, where I find myself greatly
"assisted by the Italian; and am subject to two
"descriptions of mental fits in reference to the
"Christmas book: one, of the suddenest and
"wildest enthusiasm; one, of solitary and anxious
"consideration. . . . By the way, as I was un-
"packing the big box I took hold of a book, and said
Sortes
Shandyanæ. "to 'Them,'—'Now, whatever passage my thumb
"'rests on, I shall take as having reference to my
"'work.' It was TRISTRAM SHANDY, and opened
"at these words, 'What a work it is likely to turn
"'out! Let us begin it!'"

Children's
Life of Christ. * This was an abstract, in plain language for the use of
his children, of the narrative in the Four Gospels. Allusion
was made, shortly after his death, to the existence of such a
manuscript, with expression of a wish that it might be published; but nothing would have shocked himself so much as
any suggestion of that kind. The little piece was of a
peculiarly private character, written for his children, and ex-
clusively and strictly for their use only.

The same letter told me that he still inclined
strongly to "the field of battle notion" for his
Christmas volume, but was not as yet advanced
in it; being curious first to see whether its
capacity seemed to strike me at all. My only
objection was to his adventure of opening two
stories at once, of which he did not yet see the
full danger; but for the moment the Christmas
fancy was laid aside, and not resumed, except in
passing allusions, until after the close of August,
when the first two numbers of *Dombey* were done.
The interval supplied fresh illustration of his life
in his new home, not without much interest; and
as I have shown what a pleasant social circle,
"wonderfully friendly and hospitable"* to the
last, already had grouped itself round him in
Lausanne, and how full of "matter to be heard
"and learn'd" he found such institutions as its
prison and blind school, the picture will receive
attractive touches if I borrow from his letters
written during this outset of *Dombey*, some farther
notices as well of the general progress of his
work, as of what was specially interesting or

---

* So he described it. "I do not think," he adds, "we
"could have fallen on better society. It is a small circle
"certainly, but quite large enough. The Watsons improve
"very much on acquaintance. Everybody is very well in-
"formed; and we are all as social and friendly as people can
"be, and very merry. We play whist with great dignity
"and gravity sometimes, interrupted only by the occasional
"facetiousness of the inimitable."

amusing to him at the time, and of how the country and the people impressed him. In all of these his character will be found strongly marked.

CHAPTER XXXV.

SWISS PEOPLE AND SCENERY.

1846.

ı WHAT at once had struck him as the wonder- LAUSANNE: 1846.
ful feature in the mountain scenery was its ever-
changing and yet unchanging aspect. It was
never twice like the same thing to him. Shifting
and altering, advancing and retreating, fifty times
a day, it was unalterable only in its grandeur.
The lake itself too had every kind of varying
beauty for him.   By moonlight it was inde-
scribably solemn; and before the coming on of a
storm had a strange property in it of being disturbed, while yet the sky remained clear and the
evening bright, which he found to be mysterious
and impressive in an especial degree. Such a
storm had come among his earliest and most
grateful experiences; a degree of heat worse even
than in Italy* having disabled him at the outset

---

* "When it is very hot, it is hotter than in Italy. The
"over-hanging roofs of the houses, and the quantity of wood
"employed in their construction (where they use tile and
"brick in Italy), render them perfect forcing-houses. The

for all exertion until the lightning, thunder, and
rain arrived. The letter telling me this (5th July)
described the fruit as so abundant in the little
farm, that the trees of the orchard in front of his
house were bending beneath it; spoke of a field
of wheat sloping down to the side window of his
dining-room as already cut and carried; and said
that the roses, which the hurricane of rain had
swept away, were come back lovelier and in
greater numbers than ever.

Of the ordinary Swiss people he formed from
the first a high opinion which everything during
his stay among them confirmed. He thought it
the greatest injustice to call them "the Americans
"of the Continent." In his first letters he said of
the peasantry all about Lausanne that they were
as pleasant a people as need be. He never
passed, on any of the roads, man, woman, or
child, without a salutation; and anything churlish
or disagreeable he never noticed in them. "They
"have not," he continued, "the sweetness and

"walls and floors, hot to the hand all the night through, in-
"terfere with sleep; and thunder is almost always booming
"and rumbling among the mountains." Besides this, though
there were no mosquitoes as in Genoa, there was at first a
plague of flies, more distressing even than at Albaro.
"They cover everything eatable, fall into everything drink-
"able, stagger into the wet ink of newly-written words and
"make tracks on the writing paper, clog their legs in the
"lather on your chin while you are shaving in the morning,
"and drive you frantic at any time when there is daylight if
"you fall asleep."

"grace of the Italians, or the agreeable manners
"of the better specimens of French peasantry,
"but they are admirably educated (the schools of
"this canton are extraordinarily good, in every
"little village), and always prepared to give a
"civil and pleasant answer. There is no greater
"mistake. I was talking to my landlord* about
"it the other day, and he said he could not con-
"ceive how it had ever arisen, but that when he
"returned from his eighteen years' service in the
"English navy he shunned the people, and had
"no interest in them until they gradually forced
"their real character upon his observation. We Native
"have a cook and a coachman here, taken at cook and coachman.
"hazard from the people of the town; and I never
"saw more obliging servants, or people who did
"their work so truly *with a will*. And in point
"of cleanliness, order, and punctuality to the mo-
"ment, they are unrivalled. . . ."

The first great gathering of the Swiss pea-

* His preceding letter had sketched his landlord for Child's fête.
me . . . "There was an annual child's fête at the Signal the
"other night: given by the town. It was beautiful to see
"perhaps a hundred couple of children dancing in an im-
"mense ring in a green wood. Our three eldest were
"among them, presided over by my landlord, who was 18
"years in the English navy, and is the Sous Prefet of the
"town—a very good fellow indeed; quite an Englishman.
"Our landlady, nearly twice his age, used to keep the Inn
"(a famous one) at Zürich; and having made £50,000 be-
"stowed it on a young husband. She might have done
"worse."

santry which he saw was in the third week after his arrival, when a country fête was held at a place called The Signal; a deep green wood, on the sides and summit of a very high hill overlooking the town and all the country round; and he gave me very pleasant account of it. "There "were various booths for eating and drinking, "and the selling of trinkets and sweetmeats; and "in one place there was a great circle cleared, in "which the common people waltzed and polka'd, "without cessation, to the music of a band. "There was a great roundabout for children (oh "my stars what a family were proprietors of it!

"A sunburnt father and mother, a humpbacked "boy, a great poodle-dog possessed of all sorts "of accomplishments, and a young murderer of "seventeen who turned the machinery); and there "were some games of chance and skill established "under trees. It was very pretty. In some of "the drinking booths there were parties of Ger- "man peasants, twenty together perhaps, singing "national drinking-songs, and making a most ex- "hilarating and musical chorus by rattling their "cups and glasses on the table and drinking them "against each other, to a regular tune. You "know it as a stage dodge, but the real thing is "splendid. Farther down the hill, other peasants

"were rifle-shooting for prizes, at targets set on "the other side of a deep ravine, from two to "three hundred yards off. It was quite fearful to "see the astonishing accuracy of their aim, and "how, every time a rifle awakened the ten thou-

"sand echoes of the green glen, some men
"crouching behind a little wall immediately in
"front of the targets, sprung up with large num-
"bers in their hands denoting where the ball had
"struck the bull's eye—and then in a moment
"disappeared again. Standing in a ring near
"these shooters was another party of Germans
"singing hunting-songs, in parts, most melodi-
"ously. And down in the distance was Lausanne, Summer-
"with all sorts of haunted-looking old towers evening
"rising up before the smooth water of the lake, picture.
"and an evening sky all red, and gold, and
"bright green. When it closed in quite dark, all
"the booths were lighted up; and the twinkling
"of the lamps among the forest of trees was
"beautiful. . . ." To this pretty picture, a letter
of a little later date, describing a marriage on
the farm, added farther comical illustration of Marriage on
the rifle-firing propensities of the Swiss, and had the farm.
otherwise also whimsical touches of character.
"One of the farmer's people—a sister, I think—
"was married from here the other day. It is
"wonderful to see how naturally the smallest
"girls are interested in marriages. Katey and
"Mamey were as excited as if they were eighteen.
"The fondness of the Swiss for gunpowder on Gunpowder
"interesting occasions, is one of the drollest festivities.
"things. For three days before, the farmer him-
"self, in the midst of his various agricultural
"duties, plunged out of a little door near my
"windows, about once in every hour, and fired
"off a rifle. I thought he was shooting rats who

"were spoiling the vines; but he was merely re-
"lieving his mind, it seemed, on the subject
"of the approaching nuptials. All night after-
"wards, he and a small circle of friends kept
"perpetually letting off guns under the casement
"of the bridal chamber. A Bride is always drest
"here, in black silk; but this bride wore merino
"of that colour, observing to her mother when
"she bought it (the old lady is 82, and works on

Bride and
mother.

"the farm), 'You know, mother, I am sure to
"'want mourning for you, soon; and the same
"'gown will do.'" *

Meanwhile, day by day, he was steadily moving on with his first number; feeling sometimes

Progress in
work.

the want of streets in an "extraordinary nervous-
"ness it would be hardly possible to describe,"
that would come upon him after he had been
writing all day; but at all other times finding the
repose of the place very favourable to industry.
"I am writing slowly at first, of course" (5th of
July), "but I hope I shall have finished the first
"number in the course of a fortnight at farthest.

First chapter
of Dombey.

"I have done the first chapter, and begun another.
"I say nothing of the merits thus far, or of the

Page 228 of
Vol. I.

* The close of this letter sent family remembrances in
characteristic form. "Kate, Georgy, Mamey, Katey,
"Charley, Walley, Chickenstalker, and Sampson Brass,
"commend themselves unto your Honour's loving remem-
"brance." The last but one, who continued long to bear
the name, was Frank; the last, who very soon will be found
to have another, was Alfred.

"idea beyond what is known to you; because I
"prefer that you should come as fresh as may be ———
"upon them. I shall certainly have a great sur-
"prise for people at the end of the fourth num-
"ber;* and I think there is a new and peculiar
"sort of interest, involving the necessity of a little
"bit of delicate treatment whereof I will expound
"my idea to you by and by. When I have done
"this number, I may take a run to Chamounix
"perhaps . . . My thoughts have necessarily been
"called away from the Christmas book. The first
"*Dombey* done, I think I should fly off to that,
"whenever the idea presented itself vividly before
"me. I still cherish the Battle fancy, though it is
"nothing but a fancy as yet." A week later he
told me that he hoped to finish the first number
by that day week or thereabouts, when he should
then run and look for his Christmas book in the
glaciers at Chamounix. His progress to this point
had been pleasing him. "I think *Dombey* very
"strong—with great capacity in its leading idea;
"plenty of character that is likely to tell; and some
"rollicking facetiousness, to say nothing of pathos
"I hope you will soon judge of it for yourself,
"however; and I know you will say what you
"think. I have been very constantly at work." Six
days later I heard that he had still eight slips to
write, and for a week had put off Chamounix.

But though the fourth chapter yet was in-

* The life of Paul was nevertheless prolonged to the fifth
number.

complete, he could repress no longer the desire
to write to me of what he was doing (18th of
July). "I think the general idea of *Dombey* is
"interesting and new, and has great material in
"it But I don't like to discuss it with you till
"you have read number one, for fear I should
"spoil its effect. When done—about Wednesday
"or Thursday, please God—I will send it in two
"days' posts, seven letters each day. If you have
"it set at once (I am afraid you couldn't read it,
"otherwise than in print) I know you will impress
"on B. & E. the necessity of the closest secrecy.
"The very name getting out, would be ruinous. The
"points for illustration, and the enormous care
"required, make me excessively anxious. The
"man for Dombey, if Browne could see him, the
"class man to a T, is Sir A— E—,of D—'s. Great
"pains will be necessary with Miss Tox. The
"Toodle family should not be too much cari-
"catured, because of Polly. I should like Browne
"to think of Susan Nipper, who will not be wanted
"in the first number. After the second number,
"they will all be nine or ten years older, but this
"will not involve much change in the characters,
"except in the children and Miss Nipper. What
"a brilliant thing to be telling you all these names
"so familiarly, when you know nothing about 'em!
"I quite enjoy it By the bye, I hope you may
"like the introduction of Solomon Gills.* I think

' * The mathematical-instrument-maker, whom Mr. Taine
describes as a marine store dealer.

"he lives in a good sort of house. . . . One word
"more.   What do you think, as a name for the
"Christmas book, of THE BATTLE OF LIFE?   It is
"not a name I have conned at all, but has just
"occurred to me in connection with that foggy
"idea. If I can see my way, I think I will take it
"next, and clear it off. If you knew how it hangs
"about me, I am sure you would say so too.   It
"would be an immense relief to have it done, and
"nothing standing in the way of *Dombey.*" '

Within the time left for it the opening number
was done, but two little incidents preceded still
the trip to Chamounix. The first was a visit from
Hallam to Mr. Haldimand. "Heavens! how Hallam
"did talk yesterday! I don't think I ever saw him
"so tremendous. Very good-natured and pleasant,
"in his way, but Good Heavens! how he did talk.
"That famous day you and I remember was no-
"thing to it. His son was with him, and his daughter
"(who has an impediment in her speech, as if
"nature were determined to balance that faculty
"in the family), and his niece, a pretty woman,
"the wife of a clergyman and a friend of Thack-
"eray's.   It strikes me that she must be 'the
"'little woman' he proposed to take us to drink
"tea with, once, in Golden-square. Don't you re-
"member? His great favourite? She is quite a
"charming person anyhow." I hope to be pardoned
for preserving an opinion which more familiar
later acquaintance confirmed, and which can
hardly now give anything but pleasure to the lady
of whom it is expressed. To the second incident

18 *

he alludes more briefly. "As Haldimand and Mrs.
"Marcet and the Cerjats had devised a small
"mountain expedition for us for to-morrow, I didn't
"like to allow Chamounix to stand in the way.
"So we go with them first, and start on our own
"account on Tuesday. We are extremely plea-
"sant with these people." The close of the same
letter (25th of July), mentioning two pieces of
local news, gives intimation of the dangers incident 'to all Swiss travelling, and of such special
precautions as were necessary for the holiday
among the mountains he was now about to take.

"My first news is that a crocodile is said to have
"escaped from the Zoological gardens at Geneva,
"and to be now 'zigzag-zigging' about the lake.
"But I can't make out whether this is a great fact,
"or whether it is a pious fraud to prevent too
"much bathing and liability to accidents. The
"other piece of news is more serious. An Eng-
"lish family whose name I don't know, consisting
"of a father, mother, and daughter, arrived at the
"hotel Gibbon here last Monday, and started off
"on some mountain expedition in one of the car-
"riages of the country. It was a mere track, the
"road, and ought to have been travelled only by
"mules, but the Englishman persisted (as Eng-

"lishmen do) in going on in the carriage; and in
"answer to all the representations of the driver
"that no carriage had ever gone up there, said he
"needn't be afraid he wasn't going to be paid for
"it, and so forth. Accordingly, the coachman got
"down and walked by the horses' heads. It was

"fiery hot; and, after much tugging and rearing,
"the horses began to back, and went down bodi-
"ly, carriage and all, into a deep ravine. The
"mother was killed on the spot; and the father
"and daughter are lying at some house hard by,
"not expected to recover."

His next letter (written on the second of
August) described his own first real experience of
mountain-travel. "I begin my letter to-night, but
"only begin, for we returned from Chamounix in
"time for dinner just now, and are pretty con-
"siderably done up. We went by a mountain pass
"not often crossed by ladies, called the Col de
"Balme, where your imagination may picture
"Kate and Georgy on mules *for ten hours at a
"stretch*, riding up and down the most frightful
"precipices. We returned by the pass of the Tête
"Noire, which Talfourd knows, and which is of
"a different character, but astonishingly fine too.
"Mont Blanc, and the Valley of Chamounix, and
"the Mer de Glace, and all the wonders of that
"most wonderful place, are above and beyond
"one's wildest expectations. I cannot imagine
"anything in nature more stupendous or sublime.
"If I were to write about it now, I should quite
"rave—such prodigious impressions are rampant
"within me. . . . You may suppose that the mule-
"travelling is pretty primitive. Each person takes
"a carpet-bag strapped on the mule behind him-
"self or herself: and that is all the baggage that
"can be carried. A guide, a thorough-bred moun-
"taineer, walks all the way, leading the lady's

Lausanne:
1846.
mule; I say the lady's par excellence, in compliment to Kate; and all the rest struggle on as they
"please.   The cavalcade stops at a lone hut for
"an hour and a half in the middle of the day,
"and lunches brilliantly on whatever it can get.

Col de Balme. "Going by that Col de Balme pass, you climb up
"and up and up for five hours and more, and
"look—from a mere unguarded ledge of path on
"the side of the precipice—into such awful valleys,
"that at last you are firm in the belief that you have
"got above everything in the world, and that there
"can be nothing earthly overhead.   Just as you
"arrive at this conclusion, a different' (and oh
"Heaven! what a free and wonderful) air comes
"blowing on your face; you cross a ridge of snow;
"and lying before you (wholly unseen till then),
"towering up into the distant sky, is the vast range
Mont Blanc
range.
"of Mont Blanc, with attendant mountains dimi-
"nished by its majestic side into mere dwarfs
"tapering up into innumerable rude Gothic pin-
"nacles; deserts of ice and snow; forests of firs
"on mountain sides, of no account at all in the
"enormous scene; villages down in the hollow,
"that you can shut out with a finger; waterfalls,
"avalanches, pyramids and towers of ice, torrents,
"bridges; mountain upon mountain until the very
"sky is blocked away, and you must look up,
"overhead, to see it.   Good God, what a country
"Switzerland is, and what a concentration of it is
"to be beheld from that one spot!   And (think
Effect upon
C. D.
"of this in Whitefriars and in Lincoln's-inn!) at
"noon on the second day from here, the first day

"being but half a one by the bye and full of un-
"common beauty, you lie down on that ridge and
see it all! . . . I think I must go back again
"(whether you come or not!) and see it again
"before the bad weather arrives. We have had
"sunlight, moonlight, a perfectly transparent at-
"mosphere with not a cloud, and the grand pla-
"teau on the very summit of Mont Blanc so clear
"by day and night that it was difficult to believe
"in intervening chasms and precipices, and almost
"impossible to resist the idea that one might sally
"forth and climb up easily. I went into all sorts
"of places; armed with a great pole with a spike
"at the end of it, like a leaping-pole, and with
"pointed irons buckled on to my shoes; and am
"all but knocked up. I was very anxious to make
"the expedition to what is called 'The Garden:'
"a green spot covered with wild flowers, lying
"across the Mer de Glace, and among the most
"awful mountains: but I could find no Englishman
"at the hotels who was similarly disposed, and
"the Brave *wouldn't go*. No sir! He gave in
"point blank (having been horribly blown in a
"climbing excursion the day before), and couldn't
"stand it. He is too heavy for such work, un-
"questionably.* In all other respects, I think he
"has exceeded himself on this journey: and if you
"could have seen him riding a very small mule,
"up a road exactly like the broken stairs of Ro-

* Poor fellow! he had latent disease of the heart, which
developed itself rapidly on Dickens's return to England.

"chester-castle; with a brandy bottle slung over
"his shoulder, a small pie in his hat, a roast
"fowl looking out of his pocket, and a mountain
"staff of six feet long carried cross-wise on the

"saddle before him; you'd have said so. He was
"(next to me) the admiration of Chamounix, but
"he utterly quenched me on the road."

On the road as they returned there had been
a small adventure, the day before this letter was
written. Dickens was jingling slowly up the

Tête Noire pass (his mule having thirty-seven
bells on its head), riding at the moment quite
alone, when—' an Englishman came bolting out
"of a little châlet in a most inaccessible and ex-
"traordinary place, and said with great glee
"'There has been an accident here sir!' I had
"been thinking of anything else you please; and,
"having no reason to suppose him an English-
"man except his language, which went for no-
"thing in the confusion, stammered out a reply
"in French and stared at him, in a very damp
"shirt and trowsers, as he stared at me in a
"similar costume. On his repeating the announce-
"ment, I began to have a glimmering of common
"sense; and so arrived at a knowledge of the
"fact that a German lady had been thrown from
"her mule and had broken her leg, at a short

"distance off, and had found her way in great
"pain to that cottage, where the Englishman, a
"Prussian, and a Frenchman, had presently come
"up; and the Frenchman, by extraordinary good
"fortune, was a surgeon! They were all from

"Chamounix, and the three latter were walking
"in company. It was quite charming to see how
"attentive they were. The lady was from Lau-
"sanne; where she had come from Frankfort to
"make excursions with her two boys, who are at
"the college here, during the vacation. She had
"no other attendants, and the boys were crying
"and very frightened. The Englishman was in
"the full glee of having just cut up one white
"dress, two chemises, and three pocket hand-
"kerchiefs, for bandages; the Frenchman had set
"the leg, skilfully; the Prussian had scoured a
"neighbouring wood for some men to carry her
"forward; and they were all at it, behind the
"hut, making a sort of hand-barrow on which to
"bear her. When it was constructed, she was
"strapped upon it; had her poor head covered
"over with a handkerchief, and was carried away;
"and we all went on in company: Kate and
"Georgy consoling and tending the sufferer, who
"was very cheerful, but had lost her husband
"only a year." With the same delightful observation, and missing no touch of kindly character that might give each actor his place in the
little scene, the sequel is described; but it does
not need to add more. It was hoped that by
means of relays of men at Martigny the poor
lady might have been carried on some twenty
miles, in the cooler evening, to the head of the
lake, and so have been got into the steamer; but
she was too exhausted to be borne beyond the

(margin notes: Lausanne: 1846. English, French, and Prussian help. Result of adventure.)

inn, and there she had to remain until joined by
relatives from Frankfort.

A few days' rest after his return were interposed, before he began his second number; and
until the latter has been completed, and the
Christmas story taken in hand, I do not admit
the reader to his full confidences about his writing.
But there were other subjects that amused and
engaged him up to that date, as well when he
was idle as when again he was at work; to which
expression so full of character is given in his
letters that they properly find mention here.

Between the second and the ninth of August
he went down one evening to the lake, five
minutes after sunset, when the sky was covered
with sullen black clouds reflected in the deep

water, and saw the Castle of Chillon. He thought
it the best deserving and least exaggerated in
repute, of all the places he had seen. "The in-
"supportable solitude and dreariness of the white
"walls and towers, the sluggish moat and draw-
"bridge, and the lonely ramparts, I never saw the
"like of. But there is a court-yard inside; sur-
"rounded by prisons, oubliettes, and old chambers
"of torture; so terrifically sad, that death itself is
"not more sorrowful. And oh! a wicked old
"Grand Duke's bedchamber upstairs in the tower,
"with a secret staircase down into the chapel
"where the bats were wheeling about; and Bon-
"nivard's dungeon; and a horrible trap whence
"prisoners were cast out into the lake; and a

Lausanne 1846.

"stake all burnt and crackled up, that still stands
"in the torture-ante-chamber to the saloon of
"justice (!)—what tremendous places!   Good
"God, the greatest mystery in all the earth, to me,
"is how or why the world was tolerated by its
"Creator through the good old times, and wasn't
"dashed to fragments."

On the ninth of August he wrote to me that
there was to be a prodigious fête that day in
Lausanne, in honour of the first anniversary of
the proclamation of the New Constitution: *
"beginning at sunrise with the firing of great
"guns, and twice two thousand rounds of rifles
"by two thousand men; proceeding at eleven
"o'clock with a great service, and some speechi-
"fying, in the church; and ending to-night with
"a great ball in the public promenade, and a
"general illumination of the town."   The authorities had invited him to a place of honour in the
ceremony; and though he did not go ("having
"been up till three o'clock in the morning, and
"being fast asleep at the appointed time"), the

Fête in honour of New Constitution.

Political celebration.

Domestic excitements.

* Out of the excitements consequent on the public
festivities arose some domestic inconveniences.   I will give
one of them.   "Fanchette the cook, distracted by the forth-
"coming fête, madly refused to buy a duck yesterday as
"ordered by the Brave, and a battle of life ensued between
"those two powers.   The Brave is of opinion that 'datter
"'woman have went mad.'   But she seems calm to-day;
"and I suppose won't poison the family . . ."

reply that sent his thanks expressed also his
sympathy.   He was the readier with this from
having discovered, in the "old" or "gentlemanly"
party of the place ("including of course the
"sprinkling of English who are always tory,
"hang 'em!"), so wonderfully sore a feeling
about the revolution thus celebrated, that to
avoid its fête the majority had gone off by
steamer the day before, and those who remained
were prophesying assaults on the unilluminated
houses, and other excesses.   Dickens had no
faith in such predictions.   "The people are as
"perfectly good tempered and quiet always, as
"people can be.   I don't know what the last
"Government may have been, but they seem to
"me to do very well with this, and to be ration-
"ally and cheaply provided for.   If you believed
"what the discontented assert, you wouldn't be-
"lieve in one solitary man or woman with a grain
"of goodness or civility.   I find nothing *but* ci-
"vility; and I walk about in all sorts of out-of-the-
"way places, where they live rough lives enough,
"in solitary cottages."   The issue was told in
two postscripts to his letter, and showed him to
be so far right.   "P.S. 6 o'clock afternoon.   The
"fête going on, in great force.   Not one of 'the
"'old party' to be seen.   I went down with one
"to the ground before dinner, and nothing would
"induce him to go within the barrier with me.
"Yet what they call a revolution was nothing
"but a change of government.   Thirty-six thou-

"sand people, in this small canton, petitioned
"against the Jesuits—God knows with good
"reason. The Government chose to call them
"'a mob.' So, to prove that they were not, they
"turned the Government out. I honour them for
"it. They are a genuine people, these Swiss.
"There is better metal in them than in all the
"stars and stripes of all the fustian banners of
"the so-called, and falsely called, U-nited States.
"They are a thorn in the sides of European des-
"pots, and a good wholesome people to live near
"Jesuit-ridden Kings on the brighter side of the
"mountains." "P.P.S. August 10th. . . . The fête
"went off as quietly as I supposed it would; and
"they danced all night."

These views had forcible illustration in a Political good
subsequent letter, where he describes a similar sense.
revolution that occurred at Geneva before he left
the country; and nothing could better show his
practical good sense in a matter of this kind. The
description will be given shortly; and meanwhile
I subjoin a comment made by him, not less worthy
of attention, upon my reply to his account of the
anti-Jesuit celebration at Lausanne. "I don't
"know whether I have mentioned before, that in
"the valley of the Simplon hard by here, where
"(at the bridge of St. Maurice, over the Rhone)
"this Protestant canton ends and a Catholic canton Protestant
"begins, you might separate two perfectly distinct cantons.
"and different conditions of humanity by drawing
"a line with your stick in the dust on the ground.

"On the Protestant side, neatness; cheerfulness;
"industry; education; continual aspiration, at
"least, after better things.   On the Catholic side,
"dirt, disease, ignorance, squalor, and misery.   I
Timely word "have so constantly observed the like of this,
on Ireland. "since I first came abroad, that I have a sad mis-
"giving that the religion of Ireland lies as deep
"at the root of all its sorrows, even as English
"misgovernment and Tory villainy."   Almost the
counterpart of this remark is to be found in one
of the later writings of Macaulay.

END OF VOL. III.